What We Won't Do For Love

BY MZ. ROBINSON

Published by:
G Street Chronicles
P.O. Box 490082
College Park, GA 30349

www.gstreetchronicles.com
fans@gstreetchronicles.com

Cover design:
Marion Designs
www.mariondesigns.com

Typesetting & Ebook Conversion:
G&S Typesetting & Ebook Conversions
www.gstypesetting.com

ISBN: 9780615329819
LCCN: 2009938905

Join us on Facebook G Street Chronicles Fan Page

Dedication

This book is dedicated to my beautiful Mother, Shirley. Mommy, you have always been my best cheerleader and biggest fan. I love you and I thank you for always believing in me! I also have to say, thank you for never judging me and allowing me to be me. You are the best!

Smooches!

Acknowledgements

First, I give all the glory to my Lord and Savior Jesus Christ. Thank you for blessing me, I am nothing without you!

To my Father, Ray, I love you Daddy, thank you for always being there for me.

To my husband, Michael, I love you and I look forward to seeing where this journey leads us.

To my ride or die, laugh or cry, Banita Brooks, I love you sis.

To all the dreamers, writers, and publishers: PUSH (Pray Until Something Happens)

Prologue

Here I am alone on a Friday night. I'm tempted to pick up the phone and call Tony for a little one on one personal attention. Tony is my call whenever I want some brother. He knows there could never be anything between us but sex and he accepts it. I educated him on my "no strings policy", the first day we met and he's been "on call" for me every since.

I'm not like most women; I don't need a full-time man to validate who I am. I'm educated, independent, and sexy. The only time or place I have for a man is in my bed because no matter how independent and strong I may be, the fact still remains that I can't fuck myself so I dial the digits..

"Hello."

"Are you busy?" I ask, getting right to the point.

"What's up?" He responds, knowing exactly what I'm calling for, but playing his little game anyway.

"Answer the question," I said. "Are you busy?"

"Depends on what's up." You see this is how a brother messes up the groove, asking a lot of stupid questions.

"Are you busy or not?" I ask, impatiently.

Sighing, he said, "No, I'm chillin' over my home boy's house."

"Oh, well you're busy so I will let you go."

"What you doing tonight?" He asks, in a low, sexy voice, and I know he's on the hook.

"I don't know, there's no telling," I said. So what if I'm lying he doesn't know that. I could have something real important to do tonight.

"Can I come over?" He asks.

Yeah, that's what I'm talking about! I hesitate shortly then say, "What time you talking about?"

"Like in thirty minutes?" Tony responds.

"Give me an hour and a half—I have to run an errand." I have nothing to do but I want to at least take another quick shower. It's like a pre-sex ritual for me.

"That's fine," He said. "I need to run by the drug store anyhow. I'll see you in a few."

The good thing about Tony is he always wears a condom. I don't have to ask or anything, he takes the initiative and I am quite grateful. The last thing I want to do is to have to put him out my house because he refused to strap up. I want some but not that bad, if a man does not want to wear protection I can do without. There are enough women in this world with unwanted babies and incurable diseases because they got caught up in the moment. I'm not trying to be anybody's Baby Mama nor am I trying to be another statistic. It's simple to me: no condom equals no sex!

After I hang up I take a quick shower, spray on my Very Sexy by Victoria Secret and slip into my black lace see thru nightgown. I think if you are going to do it; you might as well do it right. So I lit my vanilla aromatherapy candles and popped the Isley Brothers CD in the stereo. About thirty minutes later, Tony arrives dressed in jeans and a blue striped Polo shirt.

Tony is a light-skinned brother, about 5'9' with a low cut fade and a little on the slim side. The brother could definitely use a few home-cooked meals, but he won't get them here.

"I see you got the mood set," He said, stepping through the front door.

Giving him a small smirk, I shut the door behind him. The ambiance is for me, not for him. Tony is cool but he's not working with the biggest jewel there is, so I need all the help I can get to experience the Big O.

"Damn you look good!" He says, as he turns to face me with a big stupid grin.

Smiling, I make my way to the bedroom. I don't want conversation, just straight action. I want him to do what he came to do then hit the road so I can get me some rest. Following me down the hall, Tony began stripping down to his briefs. Slipping the straps of my nightgown off my shoulders, I let it slip down around my ankles. I had no panties to remove because I wasn't wearing any. Stretching out across my satin sheets, I closed my eyes before Tony can say anything, then I spread my legs wide. He knew what I wanted immediately and showed it when he ran his tongue up in between my thighs. This is definitely one thing he's good at. Grabbing his head, I pushed it farther in between my thighs until his lips were buried deep in between mine. Tony rotates his tongue inside of me slowly and smoothly, as he stirs my wetness with his tongue. He moves from my pussy to my clit and back down to my pussy, causing a wave of heat to surge through my northern region. Tony eats my pussy until he's out of breath and the insides of my thighs are sticky from my warm cream.

I opened my eyes and smiled, letting him know I'm content with his oral performance. I got mine and at that moment that was all that was important, that and the fact that he's sliding the condom over his erection right at this very moment. Tony enters me slow and easy. I don't know why, because although I keep my coochie tight, sex with him is like throwing a wrench in a toolbox. Nonetheless Tony is taking his time moving in and out of my warmth, until finally his leg starts to shake and he begins to moan my name.

"Ugggghhhhhhhh."

It's over. His job here is done.

The next morning I woke up feeling good and somewhat satisfied. Unlike a lot of women, I am content with a man only coming over for a booty call. What is the big deal? I get some of my needs taken care of and he gets to bust a nut. It's a win - win situation. I know there are some good men in the world whom are relationship worthy. I just don't know any personally. Besides knowing what I know about men, there is no possible way I'll give one the chance to break my heart. It's my personal philosophy that a man can't break your heart if you never let him in it.

My first and only heartbreak came on a cold frosty night in December, 1987. It was two a.m. and I was lying in my bed with my eyes wide open staring into the darkness.

"Where have you been all day?" I hear mama ask in a strong tone.

My parents were in the kitchen having another argument.

"Don't start Charlene," Daddy said.

I could hear the sound of dishes clanking. Daddy was re-heating the dinner Mama had made for us the night before.

"Don't start?" She asked, loudly, just like a dozen times before, but something told me that this argument was going to be different.

"You walk in this house at two a.m. and you have the audacity to tell me don't start?"

Ding. I hear the microwave timer go off.

"Let me tell you one fucking thing," She continued.

I propped myself up on my elbows. I couldn't believe my ears! I had never heard my mother curse before. She never so much as used the word Hell out of context.

"I'm not going to continue to put up with your bullshit, Charles," She said.

"I'm tired Charlene and I don't want to hear this shit." I could hear daddy open and close the microwave and pull open the silverware drawer.

"You're tired?" Mama was practically screaming, "No, Charles! *Im* tired! I'm tired of you coming in here all hours of the morning smelling of liquor and that bitch's cheap perfume!"

What bitch? I was tempted to run my nosey little ass in the kitchen and ask.

"You don't know what the fuck you're talking about, Charlene," Daddy said.

I could hear one of our rickety kitchen chairs squeak. Someone had sat down.

"I found the picture of Cheryl Ann in your wallet," She said.

That ugly old woman? I asked myself. Cheryl Ann was the neighborhood bootlegger. She had to be at least fifty and she didn't hold a candle to my mother. My mother was a walking mold of brown sugar, smooth sweet and thick. My mother had and still has to this very day what you call an hour glass figure. Cheryl Ann reminded me of the wicked witch from the Wizard of Oz. She had this long nose and at the tip was a hairy black mole. What my father wanted with her, I'll never know. Going from my mother to Cheryl Ann was without a doubt, like going from sugar to shit. Even at the tender age of 10 I knew I was fine because everyone told me I was the miniature version of my mother. The only thing she didn't have that I did was my honey brown eyes and curly jet-black hair. I had to give thanks to my father for those.

"Oh, so now you going through my things? Charlene, you trippin'. And you better settle down before you wake my baby," He said.

"Were you thinking about your baby when you were laying on top of that nasty ass bitch?"

My mother lowered her voice. There was brief silence then I heard the sound of glass shattering across the floor.

"Woman, what in the hell is your problem?" Daddy screamed.

"You are my problem!" She yelled, "You and your ugly ass whore!"

"Well I can fix that."

I heard the chair go across the floor again. Then there were footsteps coming up the hallway. I knew it was my father because they were loud. Daddy always walked hard. He was going into their bedroom. I knew when I heard their closet door swing open, he was packing his bags. I lay back in my bed and pulled my covers tightly up around my neck as a cascade of tears ran down my cheeks. I hadn't heard Mama say a word as our front door slammed closed behind him but I knew she was standing or sitting in that kitchen crying too.

I watched Mama cry what seemed to be at least a hundred times before and since that day. She did everything for my father except wipe his ass. How did he show his gratitude? By cheating with the ugliest woman in the neighborhood and then sending her divorce papers by mail. Don't get me wrong; I love my father deeply. To this day we still have a relationship. I just can't get over the fact that he chose ugly ass Cheryl Ann over his family.

I've also chosen not to get caught up based on the drama my best friend Shontay has had with her husband Kenny. She has been with Kenny for at least six years and she's caught him with numerous females in their car or at some ran down motel. The majority of his cheating came before their marriage but I'm prone to think once a cheater always a cheater. I hate to sound cliche but it's been said time and time again: You can't teach an old dog, new tricks. I agree, especially if that dog walks upright on two legs and thinks with his dick.

I promised myself after my daddy left that I would never let a man get close enough to bring me to tears. So when I was old enough to date I set a guideline that I wouldn't keep a man longer than a year. This wasn't a big issue back then because it was high school and most relationships didn't last longer than six months. When I got to college I had to change my game plan. I wasn't dealing with immature high school students anymore; I was dealing with immature high school graduates. So my policy changed from not keeping a man for longer than a year to not having a man at all.

From my freshman year at Spelman College up until now I've had nothing more than homey -lover friends and that's exactly how I like it. I'll go out with a man, and if we have sexual chemistry, we became sex partners. I think it's the perfect arrangement and most of the men I meet think so, too but occasionally, I'll meet a man who can't stick with my "no strings attached" policy.

I'll never forget Thomas. I met him my junior year at Spelman College and he was a senior at Morehouse. We went out a couple of times; had a one night rendezvous. He graduated and I never heard from him again. Two years later after I had moved back home to Alabama and was on my way to starting my own business, I got a phone call from Thomas. I was surprised that he knew how to locate me. I don't know why, considering I still had the same cell phone number I had in college. Anyway, Thomas explained that he was in town on business and that it would be good to see me again. I agreed, and the two of us met up for dinner that same night. Thomas was still the light skinned cutie I remembered. We talked and had a few drinks then ended up back at his hotel. For the entire week he was in town, we went out and had a good time, that ended back at the hotel for an even better time. The day he left for Denver, we promised to keep in touch. You know the whole "If you're ever in Denver, call me" and the "If you're ever in Huntsville, call me." People say it all the time but mostly because they have nothing else to say to you and they're just trying to be polite. Thomas didn't see it that way because the next thing I know he's in Huntsville every weekend and he's calling me. After a month, he finally asked me where our relationship was going.

"I didn't know we were in a relationship," I said.

"I just assumed after everything that's been happening, we were committed," He said, frowning.

"Thomas, I'm not looking for a man."

"Well, what am I?" He asked.

"A friend," I responded, and this is when things got a little ugly.

"A friend?" He asked, grimacing," I left my wife for you and now you're telling me I'm a friend."

The peculiar thing about this whole mess was that I didn't know his ass was married. There was no wedding ring or even any discoloration on his finger to indicate he had been wearing one. When I asked him about what he had been doing since college it would have been nice if he had told me he got married.

"Your wife," I said, cutting my eyes at him," I didn't know you were married."

"You didn't ask!"

He had a point but I was not about to be blamed for his mistakes. "Well you should have asked if I wanted a commitment before your dumb ass left your wife," I snapped.

The conversation got worse with every word. It finally ended with him yelling "Fuck you!" as I stormed out of his hotel room.

That was the last time I saw Thomas. After that, I changed my cell number for the first of five times. There would be four more brothers who couldn't adhere to the rules. Each of them gave me the: "I want to take this to the next level" speech. Each of them received the: "This is the only level I want us to go to" speech. Even though there were a couple of good prospects out of the four- I wasn't trying to pursue anything serious. I had my mind made up that even when a man asked to see you exclusively; he still has his share of on the side booty waiting in the rafters.

Chapter 1

I had a free day so I decided to go visit my mother and stepfather, Bill at their home. Mama met William Moore a year after she and my father had gotten their divorce. She was working as a receptionist for his software company, and he fell in love with her. He asked her out on numerous occasions and each time she turned him down. Then one day he invited her to go to lunch and she accepted. I guess he wore her down. Not long after that, the two of them got married. He moved us into a beautiful split-level home outside of Huntsville and gave us everything we ever wanted. Bill treated her like a queen and me like a princess. He was nowhere near as handsome as my father was, but he was very good to us and had proven himself to be one of the few good men still left on Earth. He did everything in his power to make my mother happy and for that I learned to love him.

Bill had never been married before but he had an older daughter, Opal, from a previous relationship. Opal lived in Boston where she attended college. After she graduated, she chose not to return to Alabama.

Mama was sitting on her porch, swinging on her antique wood swing when I drove up. I smiled as I admired how beautiful she still was even at the age of fifty. Her hair was cut short in a page style and only had a few strands of gray. People always said that if you put us side-by-side she could pass for my beautiful, older sister.

Kissing her cheek gently I sat down on the swing next to her.

"How are you?" She asked, smiling at me.

"Fine. And you?"

"I can't complain." She said.

"Where's Bill?" I had noticed his car wasn't parked in the driveway.

"He's in Boston," She said, "He went to see Opal."

Bill had been taking more and more trips to see Opal. I knew Opal was having problems but he still had responsibilities as a husband. He has a wife and a home of his own to look after. Before I could comment, our conversation was interrupted by a blue Ford F150 pulling up the driveway. The paint was shining as if it had just been driven off the dealership lot.

"Bill got a new truck?" I asked, smiling.

"That's not Bill," She said.

Looking at her strangely I stood to see who it was. My jaw dropped when I saw the tall, lean dark chocolate man striding towards my mother's front porch.

"Hey baby girl!"

Turning around I looked at her. She continued to swing back and forth in silence. Redirecting my attention to my father, I stood like a zombie as he wrapped his long arms around my shoulders.

"What are you doing here?" I asked, shocked.

He looked at my mother begging her for help with his eyes.

"We're about to go out for lunch," She said, finally coming to his rescue. "Are you hungry? You could join us."

I couldn't believe my ears. "Why?" I asked.

"Why what?" He asked.

"Why are the two of you going to lunch?" I asked.

"Because," Mama said, standing, "We're hungry."

She stepped inside and left me standing on the front porch with Daddy. There was silence until she returned with her purse swinging on her shoulder and keys in hand.

"Well, we better get going," He said, extending his arm so Mama could wrap hers around it.

Kissing my cheek softly, she asked," Are you coming?"

I was still trying to process the sudden turn of events. Shaking my head from side to side, I closed my eyes and chewed on my bottom lip.

"Charles I guess it's just me and you," She said, sliding her arm through his. "Oh, are you going to be here for awhile?" She asked me.

"I...I don't know." I stuttered. I was still trying to figure out what was going on.

"Well lock the front door before you leave," She told me. I stood and watched as Daddy assisted Mama in on the passenger side.

"Bye, Baby Girl." Daddy yelled at me as he climbed in the driver side.

I stood there and watched as the two of them backed out the driveway and preceded onto the main road.

My parents had been cordial to each other after their divorce but I don't ever remember them being friends. I hadn't heard them say more than "hello" to each other since their divorce, therefore, I could not figure out why the two of them were suddenly spending time together.

Only a short time had passed, and I was still sitting on the porch and waiting for my parents to return when a silver Mercedes CLS pulled into the driveway. I watched in silence as the car stopped and out stepped a tall caramel- brown, bald brother. He was wearing a royal blue Hugo Boss pin striped suit with matching gators. His shoulders were so broad; he looked like he could have been a player in the NFL. He moved like water as he approached me on the porch. As he moved closer, I observed his smooth hairless skin and nice full lips. Damn, the brother is fine!

"Excuse me," He said, in a smooth deep voice, "Can you tell me how to get to the city?"

"Yes. Go north until you see exit thirteen. Then make a right and merge left. From there you take the second exit and go two miles or you can go north and take exit thirteen and…" I was rambling through the directions like an auctioneer.

He was looking at me with big dark eyes and a beautiful white smile.

There was something about the way he looked at me. It was like he was looking through me.

When I had finished giving him three different sets of directions and acting like I was not used to talking to a good looking man, I was practically out of breath.

"Did you get that?" I asked, exhaling.

"Yeah," He laughed slightly, "I go north."

Shaking my head, I laughed at myself and said "Yeah."

"Thank you," he said, smiling at me again. "By the way, I'm Damon Whitmore," he said. He extended his hand to me. A big hand with nice long fingers and clean, well kept nails. I stared at it as I imagined it gliding all over my body and I got moist just thinking about it.

"I'm Octavia Ellis," I smiled, shaking his hand. "That's a beautiful name." He said. He was still holding my hand and I didn't mind one bit. "Thank you." I said, releasing his hand.

"Well, I'd better get going," He said, still smiling at me. "Thank you." "You know," I said quickly." I'm bad with directions, why don't you follow me into the city?"

"I don't want to inconvenience you."

"You're not. I live in the city," I told him. "I was just here visiting my family."

Smiling he stuck his hands in his pants pockets, "Are you sure you don't mind?" He asked.

"No. I don't." I said. I had every intention of waiting for my mother and father to return from lunch but it didn't seem like they would be back any time soon. Plus I was not going to miss the chance to spend a little more time with the oh- so fine Mr. Whitmore.

"Where are you going downtown?" I asked him, ensuring my Mother's front door was locked.

"The Hilton Hotel on thirty-fourth."

"Okay, I'll take you there."

Looking at me with those big almond eyes, he smiled, "Alright."

Returning his smile, I intentionally sauntered off the steps of the porch slowly. I put a little added swerve in my hips because I knew he was watching. Turning around casually I looked back at him. I knew it- he was staring at me with this huge grin on his face. Sometimes men are so predictable!

*****

"I would really like to see you again," Damon said. We were standing next to his car in the parking lot of the hotel. "I'd like that."

"I'm staying in room three-fifty," He said. Smiling, I nodded my head and continued to look at him.

"Listen, I heard there is this really great jazz restaurant here," He began.

"Amb…"

"Ambiance," I finished his sentence.

"Yeah," He said, giving me that look again." Do you have plans for tonight?"

I had made plans to kick it with my friend, Shontay, but I'm sure she would understand especially with this brother being so fine. "No, I'm free."

Smiling Damon loosened his necktie "Would you like to have dinner with me? I hear it's the bomb." "It is." I said confidently.

Ambiance was my baby. I devoted the last year of my life to establishing it. I had managed to make it like no other restaurant in town. Upstairs was a bar and lounge that featured a live DJ six days a week. On Sundays the bar was closed, however the lounge remained open for local poets to come in and freestyle. Downstairs was the restaurant, which specialized in everything from Soul to Caribbean cuisine. In the restaurant there was strictly jazz being played through the sound system. We even showcased local jazz artists live from time to time. There were plenty of other joints in the city to eat or party but my place was considered the most upscale.

"What time should I pick you up?" He asked.

"What about eight?" I answered. "But I'll come meet you." I had a policy that I always drove on the first date. That way if I didn't like the way the evening was going. I could leave him at anytime and go my separate way.

Damon looked completely surprised that I offered.

"I told you I'm bad with directions," I reminded him.

"It'll be easier this way." I wasn't about to tell him the truth.

"Okay," He agreed. "I'll see you at eight."

Chapter 2

It was eight fifteen when I arrived at the hotel to meet Damon. It was my intention to be on time but there was a thirty-minute wait at the salon and I had to get a manicure and pedicure.

"Wow," He said.

Smiling, Damon looked me from head to toe as we stood in the hotel lobby. I was wearing a pink low cut, short wrap around dress with pink heels that tied around my ankles. My hair was up in a bun with a few spiral curls framing my face.

I had chosen this dress because it not only hugged my breasts just right but it also accentuated my wide hips and nice, round ass.

"Wow, yourself. Sorry I'm a little late." I smiled, returning his head to toe glance. He was wearing black slacks and a baby blue, button down shirt. I almost started foaming at the mouth when I saw his well-toned biceps bulging from under his short sleeves. Everything about him was turning me on—even the scent of his cologne. I recognized it right away as Burberry and it was one of my favorite scents on a man.

"No problem. I just arrived in the lobby myself." He casually took my hand and we walked to the restaurant.

When we arrived at the Ambiance, my bouncer, Tarik was turning people way. At 6'8" with milk chocolate skin and bulging muscles, Tarik was definitely fine. If it wasn't for the fact that he worked for me, I would have gotten at him a long time ago but I'm a businesswoman, therefore I don't sex anyone on payroll. You never know when things might get messy. The last thing I need is a sexual harassment suit.

"I don't know what I was thinking, bringing you here on a Saturday," I said, as I led Damon by the hand to the front of the crowd.

I always brought men to my restaurant on weekdays or Sundays, because Saturday's were much too busy.

"I don't think we're going to be able to get in," He said, following behind me.

Smiling, I looked back at him, "Trust me. We will."

When we finally made it to the front door, I smiled at Tarik. Stepping aside, he winked his eye before letting us through the doorway.

"How did you do that?" Damon asked, looking back at Tarik.

"I have a little pull here," I laughed softly.

Inside, my head waitress, Amel sat us in the VIP section. The VIP section consisted of five booths in a nicely secluded area in the back of the restaurant.

"This is really nice," Damon said, moving his head to the sounds of Dizzy Gillespie.

"I love this atmosphere," He added.

"Me, too." I said.

"Do you come here often?"

"At least three to four times a week."

"That's explains the VIP status," He laughed, flipping through the menu. Amel returned with two large glasses of ice tea. Before she departed, she took both of our dinner orders.

"So exactly what is it you do?" I asked, taking a sip of my drink.

"I'm an investment banker."

That would explain his fine taste in clothing and the nice whip he was driving.

"So you're here on business?" I questioned. Nodding his head, he said, "Yes." "For how long?"

"At least six months," He answered. "Or as long as it takes."

"Whom do you work for?" I asked, trying to sound nonchalant.

He reached for his glass, and then asked, "Have you ever heard of Nomad Investments and Savings?"

I had. "They're one of the fastest growing investment corporations on the market right now."

Smiling, he said, "Yes, they are."

"Isn't their founder a brother?"

"Yes, he is."

"I read about him in Essence," I said unsuccessfully trying to recall the name.

"What's his name again?" I finally asked Damon who was sipping on his ice tea.

Swallowing, he put his glass down. "Damon," He answered.

"That's right," I said snapping my fingers. "Damon...Damon... Whit..."

He was looking at me with this sly grin. I just sat there staring at him for a moment. According to Essence, Nomad had grossed over ten million in the last two years.

"So, you're *that* Damon Whitmore?"

"Actually I'm Damon Whitmore Jr.," He answered. "My father is the founder and I'm President."

"Your father is quickly becoming the man in the market." "Yes, he is," Damon said, smiling.

I could tell he was proud of his father's accomplishments. Looking at him I knew he was also reaping the benefits.

"So what are you here doing for Nomad?" I asked.

"I'm here to open our southern region office," he began. "I'm also looking at some investment property."

"Really?"

"Yes. I have my own company, also."

Looking at him with raised eyebrows, I paused and waited for him to elaborate.

"Have you ever heard of Gold Mortgage?" He asked.

He better not say he owns Gold Mortgage. "Well, that's mine," he said.

Damn. There was nothing more attractive to me, than a man that could handle his business financially as well as sexually. Not because I was a woman who needed a man to pay her bills; anything I wanted or needed, I worked hard enough to buy myself, but I just appreciated a man that could hold his own.

"You invest in property," I began. "Then assist low income families with home ownership."

"That's right," He said smiling. He seemed impressed that I knew so much about his company. I believed in staying on the up and up when it came down to the latest business news.

"It's good to hear of a brother giving back," I said, sincerely.

"Yeah," he said, leaning forward. "I try. So tell me. What it is that you do?"

"I'm in the food industry," I said casually.

"Really, doing what?" He asked.

Normally I didn't tell men what I did on the first date out of fear that they would start seeing dollar signs. I figured with the type of money Damon was pulling in I could take a chance.

Throwing my hands in the air as if I had just performed a magic trick, I said "Tada."

Looking around as if he was waiting for something to fall out of midair Damon finally asked, "Here?"

Nodding, I said nothing.

"Manager?" He asked, slowly.

"More like owner." I laughed.

Sitting back he ran his hand across his head, "Wow, so you're smart, successful, and sexy."

Winking my eye at him affectionately, I said, "I was just about to say the same thing about you."

After we devoured our Cajun chicken and grilled shrimp, we went upstairs to the lounge. Upstairs, Scar, my DJ was playing "When we Make Love" by Ginuwine. Holding my hand, Damon led me to the center of the dance floor. Wrapping his arms around my waist he pulled me close. As our hips swayed in synchronized rhythm, Damon caressed the small of my back with his fingertips. Pressing my breast into the curves of his chest I ran my fingers along the back of his neck until I was cupping his smooth bald head.

I was moving to the music. At the same time I was thinking about how much I would love to wake up with his head between my legs. My kitty-cat was purring and she was calling his name.

After we bumped and grinded to song after song, Damon and I went back to his hotel suite. There was a part of me that wanted to go for it and attempt to get some on the first date, but I decided to wait and let it simmer a little. Sitting and facing each other on the sofa, we shared everything from childhood experiences to our parents, and previous relationships. I'm not the type to air my personal business so I did more listening than I did talking. Damon, on the other hand, was like no other man I had met when it came down to opening up. He talked about his parents Damon and Ilene and how they had been married for thirty years and currently lived in Stone Mountain, Georgia. He also told me about the women he had come into contact with and how the majority of them were either trifling or gold diggers. He claimed this was the reason he was still single, but I knew better. A man like Damon- fine, intelligent, and rich, should be able to fine a decent woman somewhere. I'm thinking if he's still on the market it's because he has a little of the four legged pet in him. Meaning he had to be a dog!

"I'm going to run down to the vending machine," He said, standing to stretch." Would you like something?"

"Water, if you don't mind," I said, letting out a small yawn.

Smiling he told me," I'll be right back."

Chapter 3

Rolling over onto my back I stretched my legs out under the sheets. Opening my eyes I blinked attempting to adjust to the sunlight shinning into the room. I debated on getting a little more rest until I realized I was not at home in my bed. Instead I was still in Damon's suite.

Sitting up I looked around the room. The door to the bedroom was closed and the other side of the bed was empty with the sheets still intact. I was still fully dressed minus my shoes. Slipping out of the bed I ran my fingers through my hair. *Damn!*

The bun I had it in the night before had been undone and my hair was now scattered all over my head. I had to tie my hair up every night to prevent a blowout the next morning. I could hear Damon moving in the next room so I decided to slip into the bathroom to make sure my face was clean.

When I entered the bathroom I found a large gift basket sitting on the sink counter. It had a big purple ribbon with my name attached. Ripping the clear wrap open, I smiled as I looked through the contents. There was soap and Noxzema as well as lotion and the basic toiletries. Also inside was a pair of flip-flops and a cute pink DKNY tank shirt with matching shorts. Digging down to the bottom I found scrunches a comb and a brush. He had definitely covered the basics and then some.

After I washed my face and brushed my teeth, I took a long hot shower and washed my hair. I brushed my hair and used one of the scrunches to pull it up in a ponytail. I had just finished getting dressed when Damon knocked on the bathroom door.

"Thank y..." My words were interrupted when I opened the door to see him wearing a white tank shirt and dark denim shorts. I could see every ounce of muscle on his arms, chest, and legs. It was a shame that one man should be so fine.

"Thank you." I finally finished.

"Thank you." He said, with his eyes fixated on my breast.

The shirt he bought me fit so snug that he could see every slope and curve including my stiff, dark brown nipples.

"For dinner," He added, raising his eyes to look in mine.

Laughing I slide by him through the doorway. "How did I get in bed?" I asked.

"I carried you."

The thought of it made me want to leap in his arms so he could do it again.

"Don't worry," he said, interrupting my thoughts. "Nothing happened."

"That's too bad," I teased, making my way to the living room.

There was a little round table with two chairs and two plates covered with fruit and pancakes.

"I ordered us breakfast," he said. Walking over he pulled out one of the chairs for me. "I hope you don't mind."

"Not at all, thank you." I said, as I sat down.

Sitting down across from me, Damon passed a small container of maple syrup.

"So what's on your agenda for today?" He asked.

"I'll probably go back and see my mom later on," I answered, pouring syrup over the stack of three pancakes on my plate. I still wanted an explanation for her sudden lunch date with my father.

"Besides that…nothing," I added.

Looking at his lips I watched as Damon sucked a ripe strawberry into his mouth.

After he had slowly and seductively chewed each bite, he finally said, "I was wondering if you might be able to give me a short tour around town."

"Sure," I said, still watching his lips.

His tongue flickered across the inner edge of his bottom lip and I wanted to throw myself across the table with my legs spread. "What time today?" I asked.

I redirected my attention to his eyes and found that soul-searching stare waiting for me. "Now," he smiled.

"Well, I need to get some more appropriate clothes, first. How about you go ahead and change and I will see you back here in about an hour or so?"

We ended up spending the entire day together. We went everywhere from the public library to City Hall. By lunchtime we had covered every inch of Huntsville. We stopped at Jamo's a local sandwich and juice bar for lunch before deciding to go back to my apartment.

"This is nice," Damon said, looking around my living room.

My apartment is small but cozy. It's not that I can't afford a house, but I figure with it just being me, the additional space is not necessary. The living room is decorated with light leather furniture and dark wood accents. On my walls are dark wood shelves holding framed portraits of my family.

"Is this your mother?" Damon asked, picking up one of the frames.

"Yes," I said, smiling.

"You look just like her except for the eyes."

Returning the frame to the shelf he picked up one that contained a portrait of me with my father. "Is this your father?"

Nodding, my head I plopped down on my sofa.

"You have his eyes," he said.

Smiling, I nodded my head in agreement.

"Your parent's did a good thing," He said, sitting down close to me on the sofa.

"What do you mean?"

Looking at me intently, he leaned forward. I could feel his breath on my lips.

"When they made you," He whispered.

That line had to be one of the oldest and corniest I had ever heard. But there was something about his lips that made it sound brand new.

Then with no warning at all it happened. That suckable and kissable mouth I had been longing for was pressed to mine. My body went into instant overdrive but there was something about the way Damon was kissing me that made me tell it to slow down. So I shifted to neutral and enjoyed the ride.

We sat there kissing like two twelve-year olds under the school bleachers, until my phone rang. Reluctantly, I pulled away and reached for it.

"Hello?"

"Hey baby." I thought mama would be calling since I wasn't there when she and daddy got back from lunch yesterday.

"Hey, Mama. How are you?"

"Fine. Are you coming by for dinner?" Mama asked.

Looking over at Damon I began to contemplate. I could stay here and continue what we started or I could interrogate my mother about yesterday's events. I chose to seek answers for my questions.

"Yes, ma'am," I told her. "I'll see you at four."

"Love you."

"Love you, too." I said, as I disconnected the call.

Looking at Damon I shrugged my shoulders. I gave him my "I'm sorry" look.

"It's okay," He said, smiling. "I understand."

Thinking for a moment I finally asked," Would you like to come with me?" I figured what's the big deal? I was enjoying his company and I was not ready for our date to end.

Without hesitation he said, "I'd like that."

Chapter 4

When Damon and I arrived at my mother's, my dad's truck was parked in the driveway.

"Nice truck," Damon said, putting his car in park.

"Yeah, it's my father's," I said, confused.

I wanted to scream out "What in the hell is he doing here?" But I decided against it. I didn't want Damon to think I had lost my mind.

"Your stepfather, Bill?" He asked.

"No, my father...Charles."

Damon's expression told me I had thoroughly confused him as well.

"Your father and Bill are friends?" He questioned.

I was so lost I didn't know what to say.

"It's a long story." Was all I could come up with.

"Well, let's go in," He said, looking at me with raised eyebrows.

I was glad for the moment that he didn't probe for further information. Mainly because I had no idea what in the hell was going on.

Inside my mother and father were sitting in the dining room, laughing and talking. For a moment seeing them together brought back memories of our old house and how they use to be before the divorce.

"Hey, baby." Daddy stood and embraced me.

"Hi, daddy," I cut my eyes over at my mother. "Hi, mama."

"Hi, baby," She smiled, looking like a teenager on prom night.

Standing, she walked over and gave me a kiss on the cheek.

"And who is this?" She cooed, smiling at Damon.

"Damon Whitmore," Damon said, quickly extending his hand to my father and then bending down to hug my mother.

"Nice to meet you," Daddy said smiling.

"Damon, I hope you're hungry," She said, turning to head towards her kitchen.

Rubbing his six-pack, Damon said, "Yes, Ma'am. I am."

"I'll be right back." I yelled, as I trailed behind Mama.

Mama had prepared greens, mac & cheese, corn bread and a baked ham. Mama knew how to throw down in the kitchen! She stood at the kitchen island slicing the ham. Standing at the corner, I stared at her waiting on an explanation. She didn't give me one as she continued to slice.

"Ma," I was whining. "What's going on?"

"What do you mean?" My mother has this way of playing innocent. "Daddy." I said, gritting my teeth.

"Your Daddy and I are friends," She said, as she continued to slice. "Why?" I asked, raising my eyebrows.

Putting the electric knife down on the cutting board, she paused as if to gather her words. I waited for her mind-blowing answer. Then she opened her mouth and said, "Because."

"Because?" I whined, annoyed by her answer. What type of answer was that? Because. She never let me get away with that piss poor excuse when I was growing up.

"Because what?" I asked her. "That's not an answer!"

Arranging the ham slices on the serving platter, she pointed to the bowls of greens and macaroni on the kitchen counter.

"Grab those for me, baby."

"Ma!"

Picking up the platter she headed for the swinging kitchen doors. "Ma!" I said again.

"Stop whining!" She chastised, as she walked through the doors.

I picked up both bowls and followed her into the dining room.

"Charlene, Damon is looking to purchase some property," My father said, reaching out to help her with the platter.

"Really, Damon?" She asked, sitting back down next to my father.

After placing the bowls down on the table, I took a seat next to Damon.

"Yes, ma'am," Damon answered.

"Yeah. And he's the president of Nomad Investments," Daddy said.

"Nomad? Wow!" Mama seemed genuinely impressed. Looking at me, she smiled and winked.

Giving her my "don't go there" look I listened as Daddy gave her the run down on his conversation with Damon.

After dinner, we all sat in my mother's family room watching repeats of the Cosby show and eating peach cobbler. Damon and my father seemed to get along perfectly. They found that they shared some of the same interests and hobbies. They even agreed to take a trip out on the lake to do some fishing. My mother seemed to enjoy having Damon over as well. More than once she commented, "Some young lady is going to be very lucky". It was hard but I fought the urge to tell her that Damon was not going to be around very long and that she was trippin'. Instead I just nodded my head and smiled. I had never brought a man around her before, so it was my fault she was getting the wrong impression. I made a mental note to clear up the misunderstanding the next time she and I were alone, right next to the one reminding me to get the 411 on her and my father.

That night, after Damon walked me to my front door, we stood in the doorway for what seemed like hours wrapped in each other arms and conjoined at the lips. It wasn't until he pulled away that we stopped. To my surprise, he declined when I asked him to come in. I'm not use to rejection but I will admit - I love it when a man shows me something new.

Chapter 5

Mondays at the Ambiance are hectic for me. I do payroll as well as go over inventory with the manager. I had my nose buried in a stack of papers when Shontay called.

"Hey, girl."

"What's up?" I asked, in between adding numbers.

"Nothing much," she said." Just checking on you."

I could tell by the tone of Shontay's voice that she was lying. Marking my place on my inventory log, I sat back in my leather chair.

"What's going on?" I asked.

She exhaled slowly, as if she was trying to find the words.

"Well?" I asked, impatiently.

"I think Kenny's having an affair."

"What makes you think that?" I said.

"I went online and checked his cell phone bill last night."

"And?" I was trying to be sympathetic, but I also had a lot of work to do and wanted her to get to the point.

"He's been making calls to a particular number everyday."

"So. It could be one of his friends."

"How many straight men do you know talk to each other five times a day?" She asked.

"Every day?" I asked, hoping she was exaggerating.

"Yes, every damn day."

"What made you check his call history?" I asked. I thought Shontay and Kenny had been doing well since they got married last year. She had stop following him when he left the house and from what she told me the fighting had ceased.

"He came home at four this morning," she informed me.

"What?"

"Yeah, he claimed he fell asleep over one of his co-worker's houses."

I didn't say it to my girl but it was obvious that Kenny was up to his old games. For all we knew he probably never quit.

"Did you call the number yet?" I asked.

"Nope," she responded.

"Why not?"

"I was waiting on three-way."

I knew the answer before Shontay said a word. Just like when she and Kenny were dating, I was the chosen flunky to call the other woman.

"Okay," I said. "But make it quick. I have got to finish my payroll."

"555-6972," Shontay recited the number to me.

The phone rang three times before a child answered.

"Helloooo." She sounded about two or three.

"Hello," I said.

"Hellllooooo," she said again.

She sounded so cute I almost forgot why we were calling.

"Hellllooooo," she continued.

"Helloooo," she said again. I was fighting the urge to erupt in laughter.

"Bring Daddy the phone." There was a distant male voice on the other end.

"Otay Dad-dy," She said, cheerfully.

"I told you it was probably one of his friends," I whispered.

"I know," Shontay replied.

"Hello."

Silence.

"Hello?" He repeated himself. I couldn't believe the voice I was hearing on the other end was Kenny.

"Hello?" Kenny repeated.

"Daddy?!" Shontay broke her silence.

"Tay?" Kenny asked, slowly.

"Did she just call you Daddy?" Shontay's voice was shaky.

"Baby, I can explain," Kenny said quickly.

"Is that your child?" Shontay screamed.

"I'll be home in ten minutes so we can talk."

"Answer the fucking question!" She yelled.

Kenny exhaled and then he softly answered, "Yes."

I was practically holding my breath. I couldn't believe what I was hearing.

"I want you out of my house!" She screamed. "Tonight!"

Without saying another word she hung up. I sat there listening to Kenny say "Hello" until I finally hung up too. I tried to gather my words together before I called Shontay back but there were no appropriate words for what had just happened. I finally took a deep breath and dialed her number. The phone rang several times until finally she picked up. She didn't say anything on the other end; she just held the phone and cried. I didn't say anything, I just listened. Besides, what can be said to your best friend when she's just found out her husband fathered another woman's child?

Chapter 6

The next day I finished my paperwork at the restaurant then stopped by Shontay's to see how she was doing. "So, what did he say?" I asked her.

We were sitting at her kitchen table munching on the two pieces of "Better than Sex" chocolate cheesecake I had brought from the Ambiance. To my surprise Shontay was unbelievably calm. Too calm, if you ask me.

"Her name is Kiya and she's two years old."

I waited, hoping she was going to continue but she didn't. She just continued to consume bite after bite. Placing my fork down on my plate, I contemplated on whether or not I should ask anything else.

"Soooo, who is her mother?" I asked slowly. I was too curious to be quiet.

"Alicia Green."

The name sounded familiar but I couldn't picture a face.

"Alicia Green. Sounds familiar," I said, thinking about where I had heard the name before.

Wiping her mouth on her crumbled napkin, Shontay placed her fork down.

"Oh, you know her," She said, slowly pushing away from the table.

"Who is she?"

"Room 262 in 1999."

"What?"

Four years prior, Shontay and I had caught Kenny and Alicia at the Charles Motel on Hwy 65. We hadn't been looking for Kenny but we just happened to be driving past the motel when we spotted Shontay's car. It was parked in front of room 262. Not only was he stupid enough to drive her car to the motel but he also parked directly in front of the room. The only thing worse than being a dog was being a dumb dog.

When we knocked on the door, Alicia opened it wearing nothing but a dingy bed sheet. She was about 5'4, 145 pounds, and dark-skinned with platinum blonde hair. Kenny was sitting in a chair, butt naked, with a half smoked blunt in between his fingertips. Before anyone could say anything, Shontay was standing in front of Kenny, laying blow after blow to his face. I gave Alicia credit- she was somewhat intelligent. When she saw the smack down Shontay put on Kenny; she quietly put her clothes on and made a quick dash for the door.

"Yeah," She continued. "He never stopped seeing her."

Staring at her, I tried to gather my words but once again I didn't know what to say.

"I'm sorry."

"Me too," she said, shaking her head." Me, too."

I always felt Kenny was still sleeping around and I was right. Normally, I love it when I'm right but today I really wish that I had been wrong.

That night, Damon called to see how my day had been and to ask if I wanted to join him for lunch on Friday. We agreed to meet each other around one p.m. at Sergio's, an Italian restaurant not far from his office. I wanted to invite him over to my place, but after a long week at work and trying to comfort Shontay, I was exhausted. I decided to wait until Friday and in the meantime I would just have to settle for wet dreams.

Chapter 7

Every first and third Wednesday of the month I had a standing appointment with Mona at the Hairtip. The Hairtip was a full service salon, where the stylist specialized in everything from weaves and braids to curls and perms. Mona owned the salon and specialized in all types of hair. She had two other stylists working under her, Kim, who mainly specialized in hair braiding and weaving, and Torey, who was the best at giving cuts. She also had a part-time nail tech, Jade, who worked three times a week. Mona was the only stylist I allowed to touch my hair. I had seen the other girl's work and they were good but they weren't Mona. Mona could make a hairless Chihuahua look good, so you can imagine what she can do with good hair like mine.

I walked into the salon at exactly 3pm and like clockwork Mona was waiting for me by the shampoo bowl. That's another reason I've been her client for the last seven years. Mona is always on time and I don't have to endure the bull of her overbooking her clients or taking a bunch of walk-ins when she has scheduled appointments. The other girl's in the shop would have their customers waiting sometimes thirty minutes to an hour because they didn't know how to manage their time.

I smiled at the other women in the room then proceeded towards Mona. I could feel someone's eyes on me and I knew it was Jade. I cut my eyes in her direction and gave her a fake smile.

That bitch is gay.

Jade was tall with lean hips, a Jennifer Lopez ass, and emerald green eyes. She claimed she had a long-term live in boyfriend but no one in the shop had ever seen him. I told Mona that's because her boyfriend was really a girl.

"Looking good," she said, in her thick Latino accent. Ignoring her comment I continued my stroll.

"Hey Ms. O." Mona laughed.

"Hey Mon." I smiled, before sitting down in the chair.

"Ms. Jade was checking you out again." Mona whispered, securing the plastic cape around my neck.

"She'd better chill out before I plant this size 9 in the crack of her ass." I whispered back.

"Don't do it girl, those shoes are too cute!" We both laughed.

"Not working today?" Mona asked.

I reclined in the chair, so that my neck was resting in the crease of the shampoo bowl.

"I took the day off," I said, looking up at her. How'd you know?"

"I've never seen you in jeans before." She was right. Normally I came in professionally dressed. Today I was simple but sexy in a pair of fitted Calvin Klein jeans, a blue off -the -shoulder fitted knit shirt, and a pair of open toe wedge heels.

"The benefits of being your own boss," she said. "One day I'm going to take a day off."

"And you should," I told her. "Just as long as it's not the first or third Wednesday."

"I already know," she laughed. Mona washed, then rinsed my hair, and gave me a soothing scalp massage before rubbing a scalp tingling, lilac scented conditioner in my hair. After sitting under the dryer for fifteen minutes, I returned to the shampoo chair so Mona could rinse the conditioner out. She towel dried my hair lightly, then we walked over to her styling station.

"I saw your girl and her man the other day."

"Who?"

"Shontay and Kenny." Mona turned on the hand dryer then began combing out my hair. "They were at the park with a pretty little girl that looks just like Kenny." I didn't want to put Shontay's business in the streets so I played dumb.

"Oh, really?"

"Um hum," Mona said, sucking her teeth. "So he finally told her."

"Told her what?" I asked.

"About his daughter," Mona replied, pausing with the comb in mid-air.

"How do you know he has a daughter?" I asked, staring at her reflection in the mirror.

"Hell, O, damn near everyone in Huntsville knows." Mona shook her head. "It's a damn shame Kenny's triflin' ass had your girl out here looking like boo boo the fool!"

"I thought he was keeping Kiya on the low?" I said, confused.

"He was, but Alicia wasn't." Mona laid the dryer on her station, and then began to section my hair. "You know Torey does Alicia's hair."

"Since when?" I questioned.

"Since about two years ago," Mona answered.

"Wait a minute," I said, looking up at her.

"Alicia's been getting her hair done here and she and Shontay have never crossed paths?"

"Nope."

"How is that possible?" I asked.

"Because I run a clean business," Mona said. "I know Alicia's ugly ass only started coming here for one reason."

"And when I found out that reason, I told Torey to keep her ass on the opposite day of Shontay or pack her shit and go."

"Damn."

I was speechless at how something can be right under your nose and you not realize it.

"Kenny is dirty, Octavia," Mona said, straightening my hair with flat irons. "He's about as dirty as they come. She paused a moment before adding, "You know he bought Alicia a ring."

"Mona he ain't bought Alicia's ass anything." I said, laughing.

Kenny was a dog but he was a cheap dog.

"He did, O!" Mona's eyes were wide. "One of my clients works at Friedman's in the mall and she said she seen him in there buying it." "Then I had her in here on the same day I knew Alicia was going to be here. Girl, she said it was the same ring Alicia had on her finger."

"Are you sure?" I asked.

"Yes, plus she says her and Kenny are going to get married someday."

"Now I know that's a lie." I stated, confidentially. "Kenny may be a dog and we both know he is a hoe, but he's not stupid. He's never going to leave Shontay." I said, shaking my head. "And even worse, she's never going to leave him."

"Well let's talk about you," Mona said, excitedly.

"What about me?" I said, slowly, wondering what was coming next.

"You know your Mama told me you got a man." *Ain't that some shit?*

"When you talk to my Mama?" I asked.

"She came in a few weeks ago to get a pedicure."

"She was looking hot, O," Jade said, as she jumped into the conversation. "Your Mama is sexy for an older woman."

"I know and like me she's strictly down for dick." I said, with attitude.

"So you say O, so you say." Jade giggled.

Note to self If I ever see that bitch out in public, beat her coochie licking ass! "Shut up, Jade!" Mona snapped.

"Anyway, Octavia, your Mama told me you have a new man." "We're just friends."

"Um hum," Mona said, sucking her teeth. "And you took him to meet your Mama."

"He just happened to be in the right place at the right time." I responded flatly.

"Well, Ms. Charlene says he is fine."

"And?" I waited, wanting to know what else she shared with my stylist.

"And she can't wait to have a son in law." Mona said, smiling.

"Well, she'll be waiting a long time," I said. I made another mental note to get on Mama for putting my business in the streets. "because I have no intentions of ever getting married."

"Me neither." Jade said, proudly.

"That's because same sex marriages are illegal in Alabama," Mona whispered to me. We both laughed.

Have you ever had the feeling that someone was watching you? That's exactly how I felt when I left Mona's shop. Naturally, there were the brothers standing around the barber shop next door eyeing me like a hot fudge sundae, but I continued to have that feeling even after I got into my car and pulled off.

Chapter 8

Damon called me on Friday to ask me to meet him at his office instead of at the restaurant. He said he had to wait on a late delivery from Fed Ex.

I arrived at exactly one 'o clock and found Damon waiting outside looking extremely delectable. He was wearing black dress slacks and a white oxford shirt.

"Hey beautiful," he said, smiling at me.

I parted my lips to return his greeting when he silenced me with a light kiss. His lips were on mine for only a few seconds but it was long enough to send a chill down my spine.

"There's been a change of plans," He said. Looking at him curiously I waited for an explanation.

Smiling he took me by the hand and led me through Nomad's front doors. Inside, the waiting area was completely furnished with sofas and coffee tables as well as two large wall mounted TVs. There were several cubicles sitting behind the waiting area, each equipped with a desk, two chairs and a desktop computer. Following Damon I saw that we approached a pair of glass French doors.

"This is my office," he said, pushing the doors open.

When I stepped thru the doorway the first thing I noticed was a huge velvet blanket spread out on the floor. On top of the blanket were two velvet body pillows, a wicker picnic basket and two glass champagne flutes.

Next to the flutes was a frosty ice filled bucket holding a bottle of Dom P. I stood there smiling until Damon led me by the hand over to the blanket.

"You are full of surprises." I said, as I stretched out on one of the pillows.

"You have no idea," he said, stretching out next to me.

Opening the basket, he removed two saran covered plates holding submarine sandwiches. After sitting the plates in front of us, Damon popped open the champagne and filled both glasses.

"I hope you like roast beef and champagne." He said, handing me one of the glasses.

"You're in luck," I said, taking the glass in my hand. "Both are my favorites." I was being honest. He had made an accurate guess.

After we ate our sandwiches he cleared our plates from the blankets.

"Are you ready for dessert?" He asked, seductively.

I was thinking, Hell yeah, if you're the dessert. Instead I asked, "What dessert?"

Reaching in the basket he pulled out two bowls. One full of plump, chocolate covered strawberries and the other filled with whip cream. Watching as Damon removed the lids from both bowls, I sipped on my second glass of Dom.

Dipping one of the strawberries in the whip cream, Damon leaned in close to me. Opening my mouth I allowed him to slowly feed the fruit to me.

"Was it sweet?" He asked.

"Yes," I said, softly.

"Are you sure?" He asked, seductively.

"I'm positive."

"Maybe I should find out for myself," He suggested.

I took that as a hint he wanted me to return his gesture, but as I reached for the strawberries he pulled me into his arms. Taking my face in his hands, Damon gently licked and sucked each of my lips.

"Very sweet," he whispered.

Pulling away, I took one of the berries into my hand and swirled it around the cream. Holding it to Damon's lips, I watched as he ate each piece never taking his eyes of me. After he had swallowed the last morsel, I lightly pressed my lips to his and licked and sucked each of his lips.

"Delicious," I said, looking in his eyes.

Pushing me down on the pillow, Damon positioned himself in between my legs. The skirt I was wearing slid up around my hips, revealing my freshly waxed legs. Kissing me passionately, he moved his tongue to enter my mouth and I allowed it to meet mine.

My heart began to pound fiercely as his lips moved to my neck then back up to my lips. The warmth and sweetness of his lips made me wet inside and I wanted him to take me right there on his office floor.

Pulling him up on me, I felt him growing in his pants. Wrapping my legs around his waist, I slowly began to grind my pelvis into his. I could feel him hard as a rock in between my thighs and the feel of him made me wetter and wetter.

Grabbing the back of my head, Damon kissed me harder. I could not stand it any longer and I wanted him inside of me right then. As I began to unbutton his shirt, Damon gently grabbed my hands. Pulling back slowly he moved his hands to my face. Stroking the curls framing my forehead, he took a deep breath then exhaled.

"We can't. Not like this," he said.

"What's the matter?" I asked.

"Nothing, it's just I don't want to rush this."

I was at a loss for words so I just laid there staring at him. This has got to be an all time first.

Pulling me up with him, Damon sat upright. Squeezing my hands gently he brushed his lips across mine. "I am a very patient man," he said "And although I would love to spend the rest of the afternoon getting to know every inch of your body right here."

Damn!

"I would much rather I got to know all about you first," He continued.

Damn! Damn!

Smiling, I agreed to slow it down a notch. I was highly disappointed that the two of us were not going to spend the rest of the day wearing out the velvet on his blanket. But at the same time it felt good having a man tell me no.

I hit Park Place Mall after I left Nomad, to do a little window-shopping. Instead, I ended up purchasing two new suits, three cocktail dresses and matching shoes to complete each ensemble. I was shopping out of pure frustration and trying my hardest to stop thinking about Damon pushing inside of me.

After I left the mall, I made a stop by Buzzing Baby Daycare to invite Shontay out for drinks. Shontay was the lead teacher for the one and two year old class. I found her wiping one of what I presume to be many runny noses inside her classroom.

"I have no idea how you do it," I said, watching her in disgust.

"Do what?" She asked.

"The crying, the screaming..."

Frowning, I watched as one of the little girls loudly blew her nose in a tissue Shontay was holding. "The snot." I finished.

Laughing she shook her head, "Its more than just that," She said. "With kids the good always outweighs the bad."

I watched as a pretty Hispanic girl turned her sippy cup upside down. I asked, "So is that a part of the good?"

"Ana Marie," Shontay called. "That is a no- no!"

"No no," Ana repeated, as she continued to watch juice trickle down to the floor.

Rushing to Ana's side, Shontay removed the cup from Ana's chubby little fingers. Ana let go of the cup and threw her little arms around Shontay's waist.

"Sorry," She said, sweetly.

"It's okay, Ana," Shontay said, squeezing her gently. "It's okay."

When the other children saw Shontay hugging Ana, they stopped what they were doing and joined Ana at her side. Bending down to their level, Shontay extended her arms to the group. The whole scene was so cute I had to smile. For a moment I understood what she meant by the "good".

That night, Shontay and I sat at the bar inside Club Hydro bobbing our heads to the sounds of Ludacris "Just Like That" blasting from the club sound system. We were sipping on a couple of panty droppers when two slim, light-skinned men approached us. As they got closer, I realized they were identical twins dressed in polo shirts, jeans, and tennis shoes. They were cute but not even close to being what I consider fine.

"What's up, ladies?" One of them asked.

Smiling, I continued to sip on my drink.

"What's up?" Shontay replied.

"Mind if we join the two of you?" He asked.

"Not at all," she said.

I assumed it was the alcohol talking because normally she would have told him "yes, I do mind" and sent him on his way. The one doing all the talking sat on the empty seat next to Shontay and the other one plopped down beside me.

"I'm Greg and this is my brother Brad," he smiled.

Greg was sitting next to Shontay and Brad was sitting to the right of me.

"I'm Shontay and this is my girl, Octavia," she said.

"That's a pretty name," Brad said to me.

Looking at him briefly I said, "Thanks."

"You wanna dance?" Greg asked Shontay.

"Sure."

Before I could blink Shontay had hopped off the stool and made a bee-line to the center of the dance floor. I was praying Brad didn't offer because I did not want to have to decline.

"So what do you do?" He asked.

Slurping down the last of my drink I placed the empty glass on the bar. "I 'm in the food industry." I answered. "So you're like a caterer or something?"

"Yep." I kept my answer short with the hope he would not ask me anything else.

"That's tight," he smiled. "Are you from here?"

"Yep."

"That's good."

"Yep."

"It's jumping in here tonight."

"Yep."

There was a long period of silence between the two of us. Finally he said, "I'll be back."

Smiling, I watched as he got up and walked away. I knew he wouldn't be back and I was glad. Shontay was still on the dance floor backing her ass up with Greg when I finished my third and final drink. Removing my cell phone from my purse to check the time I realized it was one a.m. and that I had three missed calls. Checking my call log, I smiled when I saw all three calls had been from Damon. Smells like a booty call to me. Grabbing my purse I headed for the ladies room. Once inside a stall I contemplated whether or not I should just wait and call him tomorrow. Looking at the time of his last call I decided to take a chance - it had only been an hour ago.

The phone rang twice and then he answered.

"Hello."

"Did I wake you?" I asked.

"No, you didn't," he answered. "What's all that noise in the background?"

"I'm at the Hydro with Shontay."

"The Hydro?"

"Yeah, it's a club," I informed him.

"Oh."

"You called me earlier?" I already knew the answer.

"Yeah," he hesitated.

"What was up?"

"I was calling to see if I could come see you."

"Oh, I had my phone on vibrate." I have no idea why I felt the need to explain myself but I did.

"What time are you leaving there?" He asked.

"I'm leaving now," I lied, hoping he would take a hint.

"Well, call me when you get home."

I didn't want to call him when I got home. What I wanted is for him to meet me there. "Would you still like to come by?" I finally asked.

"I don't know," he said, "It's a little late."

"It's just one a.m."I said. "But, if you don't want to…"

"It's not that I don't want to…" He began. There was a small pause, and then he finally said, "See you in an hour."

When I got home, I was still buzzing a little from the alcohol but I was grateful I hadn't gotten drunk. I wasn't sure what was going to happen once Damon arrived but I wanted to be ready for whatever. I quickly showered and I had to wash my hair because it reeked from the smoke in the club. Once my hair was dry, I brushed my teeth before slipping on the DKNY set he bought me.

It was exactly two a.m. when Damon knocked on my door. When I opened it I had to do a double take. He was wearing a white tank top and a pair of gray sweats. His broad linebacker shoulders and large biceps made my mouth water. Stepping back, I inhaled as he walked pass me through the door. The smell of his cologne filled my nostrils, enticing me even more. Securing the door, I turned to find him looking at me with that damn stare. His arms to his side and his legs spread shoulder length apart. He reminded me of a soldier- a well built, hand crafted soldier.

I remembered what he said about taking it slow, but there was no way I was going to let him come over to my place at two a.m., looking and smelling this good and just talk. "Come here," I said.

For a brief moment he stood there looking at me. Finally, he began to approach me his eyes locked with mine. When he was close enough that my breath could rustle the small fine hairs on his chest,

I slid my arms up around his neck. Pulling his lips to mine, I slid my tongue in his mouth. He responded by kissing me harder.

Picking me up, he wrapped my legs around his waist. Once he had carried me to my bedroom he laid me down on my queen size bed. Removing all his clothes, he stood in front of me naked. Looking at his beautiful body I took a deep breath. I let my eyes travel down to that place between his legs. I slowly exhaled as I stared at his thick, long, perfect "thank his Mama she made him" dick.

I pulled my clothes off so fast I was almost out of breath. Propping myself up on my elbows, I watched him. He slowly looked down at my breasts and then finally to my exposed hairless vagina.

Climbing on to the bed, Damon captivated my lips and tongue with his. Lying back against my silk comforter, I wrapped my fingers around his neck. Slowly he moved his lips down my neck to my breasts. Pushing them together so that my nipples stood out like two hot rockets, he licked over and around each of them. He suckled on my left nipple then on my right. He alternated from one to the other then he spread his mouth wide enough to suck them both at the same time. My body's temperature was rising and I could feel the juices gathering in between my legs. Still holding my breasts together with one hand he allowed the other to slip in between my legs until his finger was exploring inside of me. As his mouth continued to feast on my tight nipples, his finger moved in and out of my wetness. Kissing then licking down and around my belly button, he spread my legs wide. Rolling his tongue over my protruding clit he continued to work his finger just below. His licks slowly increased to hard, pleasurable sucks.

Grabbing his smooth head I moaned as my body began to tremble. Using both hands to spread my lips open, Damon dug his tongue inside of me and licked and ate me until my juices were pouring into his mouth. While I lay beneath him still shaking from my orgasm, he reached on to the floor into his pants pockets and removed a gold packaged condom. *Thank you!*

"Lay down," I told him, watching as he slid the protection on.

"No," He said. "You lay down."

Doing as he instructed I laid back and gave him complete control. When he entered me, I relaxed so he could fill me with every inch. As he began to rotate and grind inside of me, I started to thrust. "Slow down," He whispered, looking down at me. Slowing my pace, I let him lead me. His rhythm was nice and slow, like he was serenading my body with his. Wrapping my legs around his waist I pulled him down farther on me. He felt so good I wanted him in me as far and as deep as possible. Elevating my hips, I moaned as he dove deeper. Staring in his eyes, I rotated harder and harder until the pleasure inside of me became more than I could hold.

I let go allowing one orgasm immediately followed by another to course through my body. Droplets of sweat trickled down my forehead as I struggled to calm my breathing and stop my trembling. I came so hard I wanted to cry.

He was still inside me hitting every corner and wall. After my body relaxed, he began to increase his speed. Holding him with every muscle inside of me, I moved with him. As he began to climax, he grabbed the sheets on each side of me and thrust as deep as he could go. I squeezed him tightly until I felt him deflate. Once his orgasm was complete, he slowly withdrew. Lowering his lips to my face he kissed my forehead, my nose and then my lips.

"You are so beautiful," He said, admiring my nakedness.

I had been told this by plenty of men but there was something about the way Damon said it. Something about the way he looked at me when he said it.

Smiling, I ran my fingers along the mounds of his chest. "Thank you," I said. "You're not so bad yourself." I was not only referring to his body but to the dick down he just given me. The man had brought me to multiple orgasms and had managed not to work up a sweat!

Laughing he rolled onto his back, pulling me on top of him. Against my normal routine, I lay with my face pressed into his chest and his arms wrapped securely around me. We lay there for a moment then we got up and showered together. When we returned to my bed, he held me until we slowly fell asleep.

Chapter 10

The next morning I cooked the two of us steaks, rice with gravy, and biscuits. It's amazing how one night of good sex and multiple orgasms can turn a sister into Martha Stewart. After having breakfast with Damon, he left and I dressed and rode out to the country to visit my mother. I found her looking beautiful as always sitting on her porch swing with Bill.

"Good morning," I said to them as I stepped on the porch.

"Hey baby," She smiled, sweetly.

"Good morning," Bill said, standing.

After kissing my mother's cheek I gave Bill a hug.

"So, how's the business?" He asked, sitting back down.

Sitting in the wicker chair in front of them, I told him, "Business is good."

"Your mother tells me you have a new friend," He said, smiling at me. *I wonder if she told him about her new friend.*

"Oh, she did?" I asked, darting my attention to my mother. She was smiling innocently.

"Damon is a real catch," She said.

"So is Bill," I said, giving her a fake smile

She gave me a look that took me all the way back to my childhood. The look she gave right before she whooped my ass.

"You don't have to tell me," she said, patting Bill on his hand.

"Just wanted to make sure you were still aware," I said.

"Charlene doesn't let a day go by without telling me she loves me," Bill said, smiling at my mother.

"Besides," He added. "There is no place we would rather be than together."

I was beginning to doubt my mother's feelings on that but I kept my comments to myself.

"So how was Boston?" I asked, changing the subject. "And how is Opal?"

"She's doing a lot better," He told me. "She sends her love."

Opal had been locked up in a mental health facility for the past month. She had a nervous breakdown when her husband Rick walked off and left her for another woman. She came home from work one day and the only thing she found in her house was a stray cat and her clothes. He had taken everything, even the rugs. I wouldn't wish a breakdown on anyone, not even Opal. The two of us have never been close. Bill says it's because of our twelve-year age difference. My mother says it's because I got so much attention from Bill growing up. The truth is that Opal is a colossal bitch. That's it-plain and simple. Despite how I feel about her, I hated to hear she was having problems.

"That's good," I said, sincerely.

"She's getting out next week," He added. "I'm going to go stay with her for awhile."

"Oh, really?" I asked.

"Yep, it was actually Charlene's suggestion," He said." She didn't want Opal to come home alone."

Looking at my mother suspiciously, I questioned, "Why don't you let Opal come down here for awhile?"

"I thought about that," He said "But Opal hates Alabama."

"Besides," Mama said, "She'll feel more comfortable in her own home."

How can the woman be comfortable reminiscing as she stares at her bare floors and a mangy cat? Mama was up to no damn good and I knew it. Eyeing her, I shook my head in disapproval.

"So, Mom what will you being doing while Bill is gone?"

"A little bit of this-a little bit of that," She said, nonchalantly.

"I'm sure you'll find some way to get along without me," He said.

I was thinking I'm sure she will, too.

"Besides," He continued, "She'll have you to look after her." Smiling at the innocence of my stepfather, I laughed. "Oh, I'll be sure to do that", I said.

"So how is Ms. Charlene doing?" Shontay asked.

We were sitting in my living room watching Four Brothers on DVD. "I think she's having an affair."

Pressing pause on the remote, Shontay turned to face me. "With whom?" She asked.

"Daddy." I said, flatly.

"Charles?" Shontay asked.

"That's the only Daddy I have."

"No way," She said, her mouth wide open.

"Yep."

"What makes you think that?" Shontay questioned.

"He was at the house the other weekend." I responded.

"Where was Bill?"

"In Boston, visiting Opal."

"Again?"

"Yep," I told her. "Plus, he is going back next week."

"Without your mother?"

"Yep," I answered. "And guess what?"

"What?"

"It was her suggestion."

Raising her eyebrows, Shontay thought for a moment. "So, you think," She began, "She is sending Bill away so she can get her freak on with Charles?"

"Yep."

"Well," She said, smiling. "Charles is fine." Frowning, I cut my eyes at her.

Shrugging her shoulders, Shontay said, "You're probably over-reacting."

Pressing play on the remote, I restarted the movie. "I guess we will find out soon enough," I told her. Looking at her, I asked, "What's up with you and Kenny?"

"I just need some time to think about everything. I don't know yet." Nodding my head I said, "I understand". I really didn't. What was there to think about? Kenny is a cheater, liar, and the father of another woman's child. The end!

*****

The morning Bill left for Boston he called me to tell me he loved me and to remind me to keep an eye on my mother. I returned his love and reassured him I would make sure she was okay. I told Bill I would check on her but I had a suspicion that Mama was going to do just fine, with Bill not around.

Chapter 11

When I first opened my restaurant, I vowed I would never handle wedding receptions. Brides-to-be can be a pain and no one was going to tell me how to run my business. I didn't care if it was on her "special day". I quickly changed my mind when John Santiago offered to pay me a two-thousand dollar room rental fee plus one hundred dollars a head for catering to use my lounge for his daughter's reception. With a guest list of a hundred and fifty I figured it was well worth it. The only downfall was I had to look at the bride's ugly paper decorations for two hours.

The bride Erica had chosen huge yellow and blue wedding bells with matching yellow and blue streamers. The only thing worse than the decorations was her wedding dress. Coordinating with the colors of the decorations, the dress was also yellow and blue. It was one of those old fashioned ballroom gowns - the kind Scarlet wore in Gone with the Wind. The sleeves looked like satin water balloons with rows of tiny yellow daisies. The skirt was accordion folded like a lampshade with a piece of yellow chiffon overlapping. In the back right in the center of her behind was a yellow and blue ribbon.

What really amazed me was that John paid over ten grand for the train wreck his daughter was wearing. If I were Erica, the person who created it would have to pay me for buying the thing.

I did enjoy looking at all the eye candy that attended. Especially a sexy, dark-skinned brother with braids. He kept his eyes on me during the entire event. It wasn't until I was outside in the parking lot opening my car that he approached me. He was sagging in a denim Sean John outfit and a pair of wheat colored Timberland boots. "What's up, sexy?" He asked. Smiling I said, "Hello." "Yo, what's your name?" "Octavia."

"What's up baby, I'm Beau Malone," He said, licking his lips. "Are you a friend of Erica's?"

Looking at him I thought he resembled DMX only without the sexy baldhead.

"Something like that," I said.

"So, you gotta man?"

"Why?"

"Cause I wanna know."

Lowering my eyes, I asked, "Do you have a woman?"

He let out a small laugh and said," No." The laugh gave me the impression he was lying. Running his hand over the hair on his chin he asked," So can I get your number?"

"No," I said.

"Why not?" He asked, holding himself. I looked down at his crotch and saw he was definitely working with something. "I'm tryin' to get to know you better," he said.

"Is that right?" I asked.

"Yeah," he said. Licking his lips he scanned my body with his eyes. "It's whatever."

I knew what he had in mind, but still there is something sexy about a thug. "Give me *your* number," I said.

Patting his pockets, he finally pulled out a crumbled piece of paper and a pen. Scribbling his number down, he asked, "What about yours?"

Taking the paper I winked my eye. "I'll call you," I said.

Waiting for a minute, he finally said, "Yeah, you do that."

Closing the door of my Infiniti, I watched him through the

rearview mirror. He took out a set of keys from his pocket and unlocked a black Escalade sitting on what had to be at least 24" rims. Once inside, he cranked up the stereo and rolled out the parking lot.

Damon and I went to see Mr. and Mrs. Smith at Cinema 18. He had stopped by the theater earlier that day and bought our tickets. I was grateful he did, because that night the line for tickets was curved out to the parking lot. The extra time we had before the movie was spent in line at the concession booth. We waited for ten minutes behind a family of six who looked like they might have been Eddie Murphy's inspiration for the Klumps. Damon noticed the resemblance, too, because he whispered in my ear: "Is it just me or do they look like the people off the Nutty Professor?"

"Yes," I said." They eat like 'em too." Laughing at the same time we watched as they left the counter walking one behind the other. Each of them carrying double nachos, 2 jumbo buckets of popcorn, and super sip-per drinks.

After ordering us a bucket of popcorn and two cherry cokes, Damon and I headed toward Cinema A1 where the movie was playing. I almost dropped our popcorn when I saw my parents coming out of the theater across the hall. They were holding hands and giggling like they were high school sweethearts.

"Hi, Baby!" Mama yelled, approaching us. "Hi, Damon!"

"Hi, Damon,"Daddy said, following behind her." Hi, Baby."

Damon appeared to be equally thrilled to see the two of them.

"Hello, Mrs. Moore," He greeted them." How you doing, Mr. Ellis?"

"Fine," my parent's said in unison. They sounded like a pair of double mint twins.

"Going to see Mr. And Mrs. Smith?" Daddy asked, Damon.

"Yes, sir," Damon said.

"You'll love it," Mama said, smiling. "Brad Pitt was the bomb."

"He was okay," Daddy said," Personally I was focused on Angelina Jo-lie."

"Charles, Angelina is happily involved with Brad," Mama told him. "You don't stand a chance." I don't know about that one. He was obviously getting next to her and she had Bill. With my father's obvious pimp juice it wouldn't surprise me if Angelina were next.

"Maybe next time the four of us can come together," Damon said.

"I'd like that a lot," Daddy said, smiling.

"Me ,too," Mama said, smiling at me.

Giving her my-what-in the-hell-are-you-doing look, I said, "Well, we better get in there before the movie starts."

"Baby Girl has to catch everything, even the previews," Daddy told Damon. "Say, why don't you and I rent a boat and go down to the lake tomorrow?" He asked him.

"That's a great idea," Damon said. "We can catch some of those big catfish you told me about."

"Yeah," Daddy said, grinning. "It's been awhile since we had an ole' fashioned fish fry."

My father and his brother Leroy would go out to Guntersville Lake every summer to fish. They'd bring back a bucket full of fat catfish. The men would clean them and then fry them outside in my father's deep fryer, while my mother and her sister Rachel prepared homemade hushpuppies, slaw, baked beans, and green beans.

"Charlene, you think Roy and Rachel would be up for a small fish fry?"

"I'll call Rachel when we get home." Mama said, smiling. "But I'm sure they're up for it." Am I the only one that thinks this is a bad idea? In fact this is utter bullshit. How was my mother going to explain my father's presence to my Aunt Rachel? What was going to happen if this got back to Bill?

"Great," Damon said, smiling. "What time tomorrow?"

"Meet me at the house at six," Daddy told him. "A.M".

"I'll see you then," Damon said.

We said our good-byes then Damon and I went in to see Brad and Angelina kick some serious ass.

After the movie, Damon and I grabbed some Chinese takeout and then went back to his suite. We were stretched out on the bed watching Comic view on TV when he finally brought up my parents.

"I think it's nice that your mother and father are still close," He said. "Why is that?"

"Most people get divorced and can't stand to be in the same room together," He said. "So being friends is definitely out of the question."

"I guess everyone is different," I said, acting nonchalant. The truth was that I didn't want to talk about my parents with Damon. I was uncomfortable just thinking about what the two of them had going on. I was even more uncomfortable discussing it with Damon.

"You don't like it," He stated, waiting for me to explain my demeanor.

Sitting up against the headboard of the bed I focused on the commercial that had just come on the television. I had never been so intrigued by a tampon commercial!

"I don't like what?" I asked, playing dumb.

"The fact that they're so close," Damon said.

"I'm not bothered by it," I lied.

Rolling onto his side, Damon looked at me. Propping his head up with his hand he paused for a moment.

"What happened between the two of them?" He asked, "Why did they get divorced?"

I knew that if I gave him an answer it would only lead from one question to another. I was not ready nor did I have any intentions of opening up. Scooting down the bed until we were eye level I pushed Damon down against the pillows. Slipping my tongue in his mouth I kissed him hard.

He was trying to mumble something so I pulled back and looked him in the eyes.

"I don't want to talk," I said.

Slipping my hands down to his jeans, I popped open the button then slid down his zipper. Sliding his pants off his hips, I pushed them down his thighs. His boxers were standing up like a tent around a campfire. Smiling, I pulled them down until they were resting against his jeans around his ankles. Gently wrapping both of my hands around his dick I took the head in my mouth. I sucked slow and seductively while Damon held me by the back of my head. I then let go with my hands and took all of him in my mouth.

"Um," He moaned, pulling my hair.

I continued to suck until I saw his toes curl. Climbing off the bed, I pulled Damon's pants and boxers to the floor. As I removed my clothes he slipped his shirt off and threw it on the floor as well.

"Do you have a condom?" I asked him. "In the bureau the top drawer."

Once I retrieved the condom I climbed back on the bed. Kissing his lips I tore the package open then slide it over his erection. Planting both of my feet flat on the bed I slid down on him. We stared into each other's eyes as I rocked and rode him like a blue ribbon cowgirl. Afterwards we showered and then climbed back into his bed. We fell asleep and in the middle of the night he woke me for a second round.

Chapter 13

I was still trying to recover from the early morning workout Damon had given me, when I pulled up to my mother's home. Damon's Benz was parked in the driveway along with my father's truck and my Aunt Rachel's blue Taurus. I assumed they had jumped in the car with my Uncle Leroy. I walked into the kitchen to find my mother standing at the island shredding a large head of cabbage and talking to my Aunt Rachel. Aunt Rachel is my mother's only sibling and although she hates to admit it she is also the oldest. She refuses to grow old gracefully, so instead she keeps her hair dyed fiery red, which wouldn't be a bad thing, if she weren't a drop away from being midnight. She also refuses to tell her real age, but Mama told me she's fifty-eight. She was sitting at the kitchen table slowly peeling a small carrot.

"Hello," I said, kissing Mama's cheek.

"Hey, Baby," Mama said.

"Well, look at you," Aunt Rachel said, wiping her hands on a towel.

"Hi, Aunt Rachel," I said, smiling. "How are you?" Walking over to my Aunt, I placed a kiss on her cheek.

"I'm just fine," Aunt Rachel said. "So how is the restaurant?"

"Business is good," I said, walking back over to Mama. Taking the shredder from her hand, I took her place with preparing the cabbage. "Sit down Mama," I said.

"Thank you Baby," she said, before sitting down at the table. Within seconds, she was back to work helping my Aunt peel the carrots.

"Well that's good," Aunt Rachel said." So when are you getting married?"

I almost knocked the glass bowl of cabbage on the floor. "Where did that come from?" I asked.

"I told her about Damon," Mama said, smiling at me. "She wasn't here when the men left this morning."

"Yes, she did," Aunt Rachel said, smiling." He sounds wonderful."

"Yes," I told her. "But we are just friends."

"Well some of the best-friends make the best husbands," she told me. "And a woman your age could use a man."

What in the hell does she mean *my age?* "Aunt Rachel, I am only twenty-seven," I told her.

"I know," she said, putting down the carrot. "And it's about time you start thinking about having some babies." I hadn't been in the room for fifteen minutes and she was already getting on my biological clock.

"I mean your clock is ticking," She added. Why does she always go there about my biological clock?

"Darlene started her family early. Now she doesn't have to worry about it," she continued, referring to her daughter. Darlene was Aunt Rachel's' and Uncle Leroy's only daughter. At twenty-nine she had never been married but she had six kids. She had six bad ass kids and five possible baby daddies.

"Yes, but what man is she going to find to take care of all those kids?" Mama asked. "There are not a whole lot of men who will take a woman with that much baggage," She added. The look on my Aunt Rachel's face made me want to melt. She loved to tell other people about their business, but she couldn't stand it when you got into her family's shit.

"Darlene has a good man," Aunt Rachel said, sucking on her teeth. "His name is Ben."

"Let's just keep our fingers crossed that she doesn't end up pregnant." Mama said. "Again."

Never looking up from the task in her hand, she continued to peel the last carrot. My Aunt Rachel looked like she wanted to retaliate but she knew better. My mother could talk noise with the best of them. "Octavia is educated," Mama said. "And she is a successful business owner." My lovely mother was right.

"There was nothing wrong with her choosing to establish herself before she got her man," Mama continued. What man was she talking about?

"Now she has a good man. She has Damon," Mama said. She lost me right there. I was all for her singing my praises but I didn't want her to get this thing I have with Damon twisted.

"Mama, Damon and I are just friends," I said, jumping into the conversation.

"Friendships can lead to something else," she said.

"Your mother's right," Aunt Rachel said. She had obviously calmed down.

"That's how it started with me and your Uncle Leroy." "That's how it started with me and your father," Mama said.

"Are you talking about the first time or right now?" I blurted out.

Aunt Rachel's eyes lit up like fireworks. "What was that?" She asked.

"You haven't told her yet?" I eyed Mama suspiciously.

"Tell me what?" Aunt Rachel asked.

"Daddy went with Damon and Uncle Leroy this morning," I tattled.

Aunt Rachel's mouth popped open. "You told me they went with Bill!" She screamed, staring at her sister. Watching Mama rise from the table I waited for her response. Walking to the fridge she removed the other ingredients for the slaw. Sitting them on the kitchen table she eased back down on her chair. "I didn't tell you they went with Bill," She finally responded.

"You did when you called us last night!" Aunt Rachel insisted, folding her arms in front of her at the table.

"What I said," Mama said calmly, "was that my man wanted to go fishing with your man." Her man? So now Daddy was her man?

"Your man?" I asked. "I thought you said you were just friends."

"Yes," Mama said, looking up at me. "Just like you and Damon." I had the slightest feeling she was insinuating something.

"So you're sleeping with Charles again?" Aunt Rachel asked. I was not ready for that.

"Again?" I asked, "What do you mean again?"

"It's been a year since their last affair," Aunt Rachel informed me. My jaw dropped open then. Grabbing the bowl of shredded cabbage I took a seat between them at the table.

"You cheated on Bill with Daddy?" I asked.

Exhaling slightly Mama said," Yes, we shared a night in Vegas."

"I thought you went to Vegas with Bill." I said to her.

"I did," She answered.

"So how did you end up there with Daddy?"

"She called him and told him to come see her," Aunt Rachel said, smiling. I was surprised by the new information, but I was even more surprised that my Aunt knew before me. Mama never told her sister anything before she told me.

"Let me get this right," I said, sorting the info. "You called Daddy and told him to meet you in Vegas, even though you were already there with Bill?"

"Yep," Aunt Rachel answered. "And Charles hopped on a plane without hesitation."

"How did you get away from Bill long enough to hook-up with Dad?" I asked.

"Your father only stayed for one night," she answered. "I waited for Bill to fall asleep before I went to him."

"So the two of you have been seeing each other since then?" I asked.

"No, after that we didn't speak again until you saw him here the other weekend," she told me.

"Whose idea was that?" Aunt Rachel asked.

Ignoring the question my mother started mixing the ingredients.

"What about Bill?" I asked.

"Bill is a good man," Mama said. "But he's not my man."

"You've been married for fifteen years!" I yelled.

"It was a marriage of convenience," Aunt Rachel said, shaking her head.

I sat there looking at the two of them like they had lost their damn minds.

"Did you forget that Daddy dumped you for Cheryl-Ann?" I sounded like I was trying to plea bargain. It was obvious my mother was still hung up on my father. So it was up to me to bring her back to her senses.

"Ugly Cheryl-Ann?" Aunt Rachel asked. "You haven't told her the truth about that?"

Looking from my Aunt Rachel to Mama I asked, "What?"

"For goodness sakes Charlene, the girl is old enough to handle it," Aunt Rachel said.

"That's between Octavia and her father," Mama said, cutting her eyes at her.

"Well he needs to go ahead and clarify it with her then," Aunt Rachel said, sucking her teeth. "Clarify what?" I asked. "Ask your father," They said in unison.

"Maybe I will," I said agitated. I knew the chances of me asking him about his relationship with Cheryl Ann were slim to none. After all these years I still couldn't bring myself to address the subject.

"So does Bill know?" Aunt Rachel asked, changing the subject.

"I'm going to let him know once he returns home," Mama said, looking at me.

"Let him know about Daddy?" I asked.

"Yes, and to tell him that it is over," she said.

"Just like that?" I asked.

Looking at me with wide eyes, Mama said, "Just like that."

I sat in silence thinking about my conversation with the two women and wondering what else they were keeping from me.

*****

"Octavia I'm glad you finally got yourself a man," Uncle Leroy said, sucking on a toothpick. We were sitting around the dining room table after dinner.

Rubbing the thick patch of hair on his chin, he added, "I was worried about you for awhile."

"Damon and I are friends, Uncle Roy," I said, smiling at Damon. He was sitting beside me sipping on a glass of ice tea.

"Well I'm glad to see you got you a male friend," He said, letting out a small laugh. "For a minute I thought you might be one of those lezz-bians."

My mother and father looked at each other then started laughing. Damon almost choked on his tea. Covering his mouth with his hand he looked at me with raised eyebrows.

"Uncle Leroy, why would you think that?" I asked, loudly.

"Your Aunt Rachel suggested it," he said, looking over at my Aunt. She was sitting beside her husband with a look of innocence on her face.

"Aunt Rachel, why would you say that?" I asked her.

Waving her hand in the air, "I didn't," she said rolling her eyes at her husband. "I said I don't think you like men." Is that not the same thing?

"Trust me Uncle Roy, I am not gay," I said strongly. My uncle had no idea just how much I loved men.

"Well you never brought a man around, until now," Uncle Leroy said, pulling the chewed toothpick from his mouth. "I told Damon earlier there must be something real special about him." I could see

Damon smiling out of the corner of my eye.

"I think there is," Aunt Rachel cut in. She was right; there was something very special about Damon. My hand was now rubbing it through his pants under the table.

"There is something extremely special about Octavia," Damon smiled nervously.

Squeezing my hand under the table he stared at me with crystal clear eyes. My freak moment deteriorated and I suddenly felt like I was in the middle of a Kodak commercial.

Bill had been gone for a month but my mother didn't seem to mind. She was too busy re-living her childhood with my father. They spent every moment they could together. He took her roller-skating, on picnics in the park and out of town to the casinos. My mother had become a partying - gambling - adulterating, wild woman. To say I was having a hard time adjusting to her lifestyle change would be a small understatement. Nevertheless, I wanted her to be happy and if being with my father again made her happy; then so be it.

Damon had become an active part of my life and to be completely honest I didn't mind. I had all of the benefits of having a man without having to make an actual commitment. When my car needed a tune up, he took it to the dealership. When it needed to be washed he took it to get detailed. We went out, we laughed, we talked and we made crazy love. In my mind we were both content with the way things were. I'm a firm believer that if it ain't broke don't try and fix it.

Shontay on the other hand was trying her best to work things out with Kenny. I truly could not understand why. The man wasn't that good looking and as I remember from seeing him naked at the hotel, the family jewel could use a few extensions. Shontay was a dark-skinned, plus-size beauty. She was thick in all the right places and had never had a problem getting the attention of a man. She made more money than he did so she didn't need him financially. In my opinion, she was too good for Kenny but my opinion didn't matter because she loved him. She loved him so much she was willing to accept that he brought a child into the world with another woman.

Chapter 15

I had forgotten all about Beau until one day I was cleaning out my car and I found the crumbled piece of paper containing his number. Damon was in Atlanta for the weekend and Shontay was spending the weekend with her husband and his daughter. My mother and father had driven to Mobile to see my Great Aunt so I was left with nothing better to do than call him.

He answered on the first ring and sounded like he was underwater.

"Yeah," he said, inhaling deeply.

"May I speak with Beau?"

"Who dis?"

"Octavia."

"Who?"

"Octavia, we met after Erica and Tim's wedding."

He inhaled again. Let out a slight cough then asked, "What's up Ma' what took you so long?"

Smiling I told him," I've been a little busy."

"Word," He said, inhaling. "I feel that shit, baby"

"Anyways, what's up with you for the night?"

"It's whatever baby."

"What do you have in mind?"

"You."

"And?"

"Me."

"Doing what?"

He inhaled again then slowly answered," Whatever comes naturally, baby."

There was silence until he said," Why don't you meet me at Fatty's around eight?"

Fatty's was a hip-hop club on the south side of Huntsville where all the thugs and ghetto mamas go to party. I normally wouldn't step off in the place but I thought what the hell it's Saturday night.

"I'll be there," I told him.

"Tight, I'll be looking for you."

I stepped in Fatty's wearing my backless, body hugging, gold mini halter dress and my three inch open toe, gold stilettos. I decided to let my hair do its own thing so I let it air dry and ended up with a beautiful wavy bush. You know, the same hair styles females buy weave to have. The men in the club seemed to like it because I was turning far more heads than normal, time I stepped in the place. The club was packed with half naked women shaking their asses and men with their pants sagging watching the women shake their asses. I spotted Beau sitting with four other men at a table toward the back of the club near the deejay's booth. Making my way across the crowded dance floor, I kept my eyes on him as I approached the table. I was less than halfway there when a tall dark complexioned brother stepped in front of me.

"How you doing," He asked. He had the face and build of Shaq with the voice of Mighty Mouse.

"Fine." I attempted to step around him.

Placing his hand on my arm, he stopped my stride. "Where you going, beautiful?" He asked.

Looking from my arm to his eyes I frowned, hoping he would get the hint and let me go. He didn't because he continued to stand there smiling with his hand on me. Tightening his grip on my arm he looked from my head down to my toes.

"What's your name?" He asked.

Taking a deep breath I tossed my head back and softly said," My name is Octavia. Now please step off."

He let me go, but he continued to stand in my way. "What's the rush, baby?" He asked," Why don't you let me buy you a drink?"

"Thanks but I'm here to see someone."

"Fuck him."

I wanted to scream out *Fuck YOU, now get the fuck out of my face* but I decided to remain calm.

"Listen, I'm not interested," I said.

"You will be once you get to know me," He said. "So, how about that drink?"

"No, thank you," I said, again attempting to step around him.

Blocking my path again, He asked "Why not?"

Rolling my eyes I stepped back and crossed my arms across my chest.

"Because I fucking said so," I yelled. I was tired of playing with him and it was obvious the brother was not the type you could be nice to.

"Now please get out of my fucking way," I added.

"Oh, so you're too good for me?" He asked, raising his voice.

"You said it…not me."

"Fuck you, bitch!"

He stepped in so close to me I could feel his breath on my face. Before I could say or do anything, I heard Beau's voice coming from behind him. "You look like the bitch to me," he said.

"What the fuck did you say?" The brother asked, spinning round to face Beau.

Beau looked positively fuckable in his baby blue Ralph Lauren polo and dark denim jeans. His hair looked like it had just been unbraided. It had crinkles and was blown out wild, the way Ben Wallace of the Detroit Pistons sometimes wears his.

"I said, you the bitch," Beau said, crossing his arms across his chest.

"Fuck you!" the brother yelled taking a step towards Beau.

During the commotion I hadn't noticed that everyone had stopped dancing. All eyes were now centered on the three of us. The four brothers Beau had been sitting with pushed through the crowd.

"Trust me," Beau said seriously, "This ain't what you want."

"Whatever, muthafucker!"

The brother made a fist with his right hand and swung at Beau's face. Beau stepped back, causing him to miss. Just as the brother again attempted to make contact, Beau's table companions rushed toward him and knocked him to the floor. Stepping back, I watched as the four of them put an old school beat down on the brother's ass. I looked around the club and noticed three bouncers observing the ass kicking but they never moved in to break up the fight. After hearing the brother begging for them to stop I looked over at Beau and mouthed, "Make them stop."

He cocked his head to one side. Looked me up and down then licked his lips.

"That's enough," he spoke with authority.

The four men slowly pulled back. The brother lay in the fetal position on the floor. His entire face was bloody and swollen. "Get up," Beau said looking down at him. He never moved.

"I said get your ass up!" Beau yelled.

Slowly the brother rolled up onto his knees. Grabbing his side he struggled to get to his feet. The brother was having such a hard time I almost reached down to help him but considering the whole brawl started with me, I decided to leave him on his own. When he finally made it to his feet Beau stepped in his face.

"Get the fuck out of my club," he said. "And don't let me catch ya ass back in here."

The brother nodded and staggered toward the exit followed by two muscle popping brothers wearing t-shirts that read "Security".

Taking me by the hand, Beau asked, "You want to go somewhere

where we can be alone?"

I nodded my head.

Smiling Beau scanned my body with his eyes and smiled. "I forgot how sexy you are," he said.

Returning his glance I said, "You're looking good yourself."

"Come on," he said.

Still holding my hand Beau led me behind the deejay booth through a small passageway that lead to a steel door. Once we were on the other side of the door we were standing in a large room. The room was equipped with a wide screen TV, CD player with surround sound, leather sofa with a matching chair, and a fully stocked bar.

"Have a seat, Ma," Beau said, pointing to the sofa.

"So this is your club?" I asked, sliding back on the sofa.

Grabbing a bottle of Absolute and two shot glasses from behind the bar, Beau nodded his head and smiled.

"So that's why when your boys beat ole' boy to the floor no one bothered to stop them," I concluded.

"Yeah," he said.

He sat down next to me on the sofa, so close his leg was touching mine. After filling one of the glasses he handed it to me. "Thank you," I smiled.

He hadn't asked what I liked to drink or even if I drank at all which under other circumstances would have made me develop an attitude, but considering he had stepped up when the brother on the dance floor disrespected me I was willing to let him take charge for the moment.

Watching as he filled the second glass to the brim I swayed to the sound of Jaheim's "Anything" coming from the speakers in the room.

"Don't sip it," he said holding up his glass. "Take it straight to the head."

Locking my eyes with his I put the glass to my lips. Allowing my tongue to slowly dip in and then out of the glass I threw my head back and turned the glass up. I didn't so much as blink as I swallowed the liquid in one gulp.

Smiling, he said, "I like that."

Beau swallowed the liquid in his glass and then quickly began pouring us two more.

"Damn," I moaned throwing my head back against the sofa.

It was after our fourth round of shots and the dress I was wearing was hiked up around my waist. My lace thongs were dangling from my left ankle and Beau's head was in between my spread legs. He was on his knees with his tongue swimming in my kitty-cat. He was sucking and licking on me like he was trying to cure his munchies.

He told me he smoked weed on a regular basis and that's what he had been doing earlier when I called him. I told him I hadn't gotten high since high school and I didn't care if he did or didn't, just as long as he didn't whip out a crack pipe or a syringe. So he rolled himself one up took a few puffs and the next thing I knew he was eating all he could of me.

By the time Beau came up for air I had come so many times I thought I was going to be dehydrated.

"You taste like cotton candy," he whispered.

Pulling my dress over my head, I smiled and said, "You ate me like I was."

Standing, he pulled off his shirt. His body was the color of cocoa beans and his arms and chest were cut. Not as big as Damon but nice all the same. The one thing I loved the most about looking at Beau was the tattoos he was marked with. I love a man with tattoos. On his chest he had a pair of drama masks. One of the masks was smiling, the other was frowning. On his right arm he had a pair of praying hands holding a scroll with the words "Lord Knows". What really got my attention was the name tattooed on his left arm in calligraphy.

"Who is Brittany?" I asked, watching him drop his pants.

Stopping, he smiled and his rough exterior softened. "My daughter," he said. "My reason."

"Your reason?"

"No doubt," he answered, "for living."

I thought about my Daddy and when I was a little girl and he use to come in and kiss me goodnight. Long before the fights and before he left. He would always tell me he loved me and that I was his heart. The same look Beau had now was the expression I saw in my father. I suddenly missed the closeness we once had. "You okay, Ma?" Beau asked.

Snapping back to the present I looked at Beau. He was now completely naked with his cocoa dick pointing at me. I estimated that it was about eight inches. It wasn't as long or as wide as what I had been getting from Damon but it would do.

"I will be in a minute," I smiled," You have a condom?"

Picking up his pants Beau pulled out a single wrapped condom.

"I told you I'm ready for whatever," he said.

"Yeah, but I guarantee you're not ready for me."

Stretching out on my back I opened my legs wide. Stroking my clit with my finger I watched him put the condom on. When he had our protection secure he climbed on top of me, then slid his dick inside of my vagina. Beau delivered hard forceful thrusts inside of me. I wrapped my legs around him tightly pulling him in even deeper.

"Give me this pussy," he grunted, grinding harder.

I granted his request, throwing it back; I rotated my hips following his movements. He grabbed my breast then started sucking my left nipple while pinching the right one with the tips of his fingers.

"Is it good, Ma?"

"Yes" I moaned, while running my fingertips over his back.

"Shit…"

Beau grabbed my legs then pushed them back until my knees were up by my head. He rammed his dick inside of my wetness until he came. Slowly he withdrew, still shaking from his orgasm. He let go of my legs then collapsed on the couch next to me.

Chapter 16

When Mama called and asked me to pick her up for church I should have known she was up to something. Mama always makes it her business to make it to nine a.m. Sunday school. I get up just in time for the eleven a.m. Morning Worship Service. So when she called me asking if she could ride with me to service, I should have asked a few questions.

When I arrived at her home she was sitting on her front porch wearing the gold silk Donna Karin suit and matching gold pumps I bought her last Christmas. She looked beautiful as always.

"Hey, beautiful," I said, kissing her cheek.

"Hey Baby," she smiled. "You look nice."

I was wearing a cream crepe skirt with matching jacket. I had taken the time to straighten my hair and had it up in a nice French roll.

"So do you," I smiled. "You always do."

Our morning pleasantries were interrupted by the sound of a car pulling up her driveway. Deja vu. This time it wasn't my father but instead it was Bill's Cadillac Deville.

"Mama," I said, watching Bill step out his car.

He was wearing a cream suit with a gold dress shirt and matching gold and cream pinstripe tie.

"When did Bill get back?" I asked.

"Last night."

"Did you tell him?"

Silence.

Looking at my Mama I frowned. She was smiling innocently.

"Mama, you know bet…"

Just when I thought the situation could not get any more uncomfortable, my Daddy's F150 came flying up the driveway kicking up dust.

"Daddy!" I screamed, softly. "Ah, Hell Naw!"

I suddenly forgot where I was, but Mama was straight trippin'. Now it all made sense. She called and asked me to pick her up so I could play interference.

"Watch your mouth baby," she instructed me.

"But Mama!"

We both watched as my Daddy climbed out of his truck wearing the suit I had also bought him last Christmas. A black three button Ralph Lauren. He was wearing a white dress shirt underneath and a gold silk tie. The tie I bought him was royal blue.

"Nice tie," I whispered.

"Which one?" She asked.

"Both."

"I know," she smiled. "I have good taste."

"Mama."

I watched as Daddy and Bill shook hands then each headed towards us.

"Hey, Princess," Bill smiled kissing my cheek.

Not to be out done Daddy stepped in front of him and kissed my other cheek.

"How's my baby?" He asked.

"Hi Bill," I smiled nervously. "I'm fine, Daddy and you?"

"Never better," Daddy smiled. "You're looking beautiful, Charlene."

"She always does," Bill smiled.

"It's no wonder we have a beautiful daughter," Daddy added. He cut his eyes in Bill's direction. I was starting to sweat from the tension in the air. Mama on the other hand was smiling her ass off.

"Well gentlemen," Mama finally spoke." the ladies are ready to go."

I looked from Daddy to Bill then to Mama.

"Who is driving?" I asked.

"I think we should all ride in the Caddy," Mama suggested.

There was no way I was going to be caught up in Mama's little mess.

"You know Mama I have somewhere to go after church," I lied." It's probably better if I drive my own car."

I didn't care if I was putting her in a tight spot. Keeping her men from killing each other was not one of my assigned duties as a daughter.

"What do you have to do?" Mama asked. She was calling me on my lie.

"I have to go by the Ambiance and take care of some urgent paperwork," I lied again.

"Why don't we all go over after service," Mama smiled." It's been awhile since I had some of your chocolate cake."

"Mama, I'll bake you one," I said frowning at her.

"I want some today."

"Well, Mama I'll bring you one later today." I love my Mama but she was starting to irritate me.

"We're all going after service," Mama ordered." Case closed."

She crossed her arms across her chest and gave me her "you want your ass whooped look". I crossed my arms across my chest and gave her my "I wish you would look". I think her life crisis was causing her to have amnesia too because she had forgotten that I was not a child. I didn't care if she said, "case closed". The case was still very much open and her ass was about to be convicted. First of all she hadn't bothered to warn me that not only was Bill coming to church with us but so was my Daddy. She didn't tell me what she had told Bill about her and Daddy or if she had told him anything at all. Mama had pulled me into the middle of her daytime drama without as much as a damn warning. Now she thought she was going to tell me what I was going to do. I don't think so.

"Thank you Lord," I whispered.

As soon as I saw Faith Christian I gave thanks. I had endured silence during the thirty-minute drive from Mama's to the church in the backseat of Bill's Cadillac with my Daddy. Mama rode in the front passenger's seat while Bill played the happy chauffeur. I had my mind made up that I was not going to be the fourth wheel in Mama's love triangle but a daughter's loyalty is a serious thing. My Mama carried me for nine months and then went through thirty-six hours of labor to bring me into this world. She changed shitty diapers, wiped my snotty nose and kissed away my "boo boos". She gave me support and encouragement when I thought I didn't have what it took to open Ambiance. Mama was my biggest fan and my best cheerleader. She never asked me for anything in return, except for this. So because of all these things I ate my pride and let her have her way. Plus the fact that she told me I wasn't too grown for her to whip my ass. Lately Mama had nerves of steel, so I wasn't about to try her.

"Good Morning, Sister Ellis," Pastor Davis, greeted me with a handshake. He was standing outside on the front steps of the church greeting his members as he did every Sunday.

"Good Morning, Pastor," I smiled, flirting.

Pastor Davis was one of the finest ministers I have ever seen. At forty-eight he still had the physique of a twenty year old. Broad shoulders and toned arms. His skin was the color of honey and he had beautiful ocean blue eyes. He had only been the pastor at Faith Christian for a year but in his short reign the congregation had tripled. Bill said it was because Pastor Davis knew the "word" and could use it to move even the deadest of souls. Considering the majority of the new members were single, man hungry women, I would have to say it was because of Pastor Davis' good looks.

"Who is this young man?" Pastor Davis asked, looking past me at Daddy.

"Pastor Davis this is my father, Charles," I said, stepping to the side so the two men could shake hands.

"Nice to meet you, Pastor Davis," Daddy said.

"It's nice to meet you," Pastor Davis smiled." Please don't let this be your last time visiting with us."

Looking behind him at Mama, Daddy smiled. "Don't worry," he said." I have a feeling you'll be seeing a whole lot more of me."

Clearing my throat, I rolled my eyes.

"Praise God," Pastor Davis said, patting Daddy on his back.

"Sister Moore, how are you?" He asked, taking steps towards Mama and Bill.

"Fine Pastor and you?" Mama asked, shaking his hand.

"Blessed," Pastor Davis smiled," Brother Moore."

"Pastor," Bill smiled, shaking his hand.

I could hear the church pianist Antoine starting to play inside, signaling it was time for service to begin.

"Well, I guess we better get inside," Pastor Davis said, holding the door open.

The church was packed but I managed to find us a pew in the second row from the front. Smiling, I acknowledged Sister Emma, who was sitting with the other mothers on a set of pews to the right of the pulpit; facing the congregation.

Sister Emma was in her late sixties, a widow, and the mother of three. She was wearing a white dress with a ruffled collar and a big-feathered wide brim hat. Red curls from the wig underneath framed her forehead. She smiled at me then quickly looked away.

I slid onto the pew followed by Daddy, then Mama and finally, Bill.

Once we were all settled into our seats, the Faith Christian Mass Choir stood in unison and began to sing a soulful rendition of "Swing Low Sweet Chariot".

Pastor Davis' sermon brought tears to my eyes. He quoted a scripture from Psalms 51:" Have mercy upon me, O God, according to Thy loving kindness: according to the greatness of Thy compassion blot out my transgressions."

He spoke to us about trials, transgressions and the power of forgiveness. In the middle of the sermon, Daddy put his arm around my shoulder. I leaned against his body and rested my head against his shoulder. When I looked up at him he had tears in his eyes, too.

"Church it's time for forgiveness," Pastor Davis stood at the pulpit.

"Someone here needs to be healed," he said. "Someone needs to be forgiven."

I looked down the pew at Mama. She was sitting in between Bill and Daddy with her hands folded across her lap. She looked at me and smiled. I shook my head at her and focused back on the pulpit and Pastor Davis.

"Someone here," he continued. "Has been caring a weight around. The weight of sin."

"Someone here needs to confess," he said.

"Yes, Lord," Mama said.

I shot her an "I know you didn't look" out of the corner of my eyes.

"Church someone here is living a lie," Pastor Davis continued. His arms were extended open towards the congregation. "You need to confess," He said, scanning the congregation with his eyes.

Claps. Amens.

"It's time for confession," he said," So your path to forgiveness will be clear."

Amens.

I looked down the pew and noticed Bill fidgeting with his tie. He looked at Mama then down at Daddy and began to rub his hands together. He looked like he was going to snap at any moment. I crossed my legs nervously still watching him.

"Someone needs forgiveness!" Pastor Davis declared. "Today is your day!"

Bill sat forward on the pew holding his head in his hands. I cleared my throat to get Mama's attention. She looked at me, nodded her head and continued to watch Pastor Davis. Meanwhile Bill was moving and squirming in his seat like a five year old that needed to go potty.

"Help us, Lord," I said aloud.

"That's right, Sister," Pastor Davis said, pointing at me." Someone here needs your help, Lord."

Out of the corner of my eye I could see someone staring in our direction. I turned my head and saw Sister Emma. She was shaking her head and frowning.

I wondered if she knew about Daddy and Mama. It was definitely possible, after all Mama and Daddy have been running all over town together. The entire congregation probably knew. I suddenly felt like everyone was looking at us. Uncrossing my legs I slid down lower on the pew. The people in front of us turned around and started looking at us. Using my program as a fan I adjusted my collar. Lord, why is it so hot in here? I'm sure it's because these people are burning us with their eyes. I looked at Pastor Davis and he was watching us. The fifty members Mass Choir was staring! An-toine, the flamboyantly gay director of music was staring! I looked over my shoulder and the people behind us were staring! Finally I heard Bill clear his throat and I knew why they were staring. He was now standing.

"Brother, do you have something to say?" Pastor Davis asked pointing to Bill.

I sat up in my seat and adjusted my dress. *He's going to tell on my Mama!*

Stuffing his hands in his pants pockets Bill looked down at Mama. She sat looking straight ahead. I saw a single tear fall from Bill's eye. Why did Mama have to do this to a man like this? I looked at Daddy; he had shifted in his seat and was watching Bill intently.

"Brother Moore," Pastor Davis called. Wiping his face with his hand, Bill nodded his head.

"Pastor, I have a confession," Bill cried.

Silence.

"Go ahead, Brother," Pastor Davis said softly.

"I've been carrying a weight around for the last year," Bill said slowly.

"Let it go," Pastor Davis encouraged him. Sniffing, Bill looked at Mama. His eyes were full of tears.

"For the last year, an adulterer has been living in my home," Bill cried.

Oh Snap! Bill was about to bust Mama in front of the entire congregation and a whole lot of neighborhood visitors. There were whispers coming from every direction throughout the church.

Mama held her head high and stared Bill in the eyes. Daddy adjusted his tie and crossed his leg over his knee.

"The vows," Bill continued, tears flowing down his cheeks. "Made between me and my wife have been broken."

Don't do it, Bill! Please don't let the entire community via the church gossip network, know that my Mama is a two timing Jezebel! Please don't do it, Bill!

Bill let out a deep sigh and then shook his head at Mama.

"Charlene," he whined," Why?"

Lord, please send me a miracle. Something. Anything.

Mama cleared her throat and then said," Why."

Her voice was soft but strong. Mama was calm and collected. I, on the other hand was sweating harder than a two-dollar hooker in church on communion Sunday. Daddy looked like he wanted to beat Bill down at any moment.

"Why, Charlene," Bill cried. He wiped his eyes with the back of his hands and then exhaled. "I don't know why I did this to you," he said.

Come again?

Whispers.

"Charlene, I've been having an affair," He said," I'm sorry."

I almost fell off the pew. I would have if Daddy hadn't put his arm across me. There were "Lord have mercies" and "Um um umms" coming from every direction. I couldn't believe it. I was in a state of shock but not too shocked to blurt out, "With who, Bill?"

Looking at me Bill dropped his head," Sister Emma," He whispered.

Someone in the back of the church yelled out," We can't hear you!"

Someone else was kind enough to fill them in," He said Sister Emma!"

Whispers.

Lord, have mercies.

I looked at Sister Emma and saw that her face was as red as fire. She took her hat off and adjusted her wig.

Emma?

Whispers.

The thought of Bill bumping and grinding with five-foot four, three-hundred-sixty-pound sister Emma made me gag. Tears started running out my eyes and I was waving one of my arms in the air. One of the ushers must have thought I felt the spirit because she ran over to me and started fanning me.

Pastor Davis stood in the pulpit with a look of shock on his face. An-toine fanned himself with his hand," Lord have mercy," He said.

"I'm sorry," Bill continued," I need forgiveness."

I asked for a miracle and I got one. Not what I expected but beggars can't be choosers.

"Mama did you know about Bill and Emma?"

Mama and I were sitting in her kitchen finishing off slices of her homemade apple pie. After Bill's confession, Pastor Davis said a long prayer for Bill and Mama's marriage. He also asked the Lord to forgive Sister Emma for her involvement in the affair. After Pastor Davis dismissed the congregation, he offered to speak with Mama and Bill privately in his study. Mama declined and told him she had already prayed about it and that God had shown her the right path to take. Bill chose to stay and speak with the Pastor alone.

So, my parent's and I loaded up in the Caddy and headed home. They didn't mention the scene at the church and neither did I. They talked about their trip to Mobile and how beautiful the weather was. I sat in silence trying to think of a new church I could move my membership to.

When we made it back to Mama's and Bill's the three of us sat down and ate fried chicken, collard greens, macaroni and cheese and corn bread muffins. Mama had cooked earlier that morning. Her little show on the porch about going to the Ambiance was because she knew I was lying about having something to do. After dinner, Daddy left to go help Uncle Leroy with his car. Mama and I were alone and I was ready for some answers.

"No," She said, "Emma was a surprise."

"You didn't look surprised," I said.

"That's because I knew he was cheating," She said.

"Explain."

I sat in silence and utter disbelief as Mama explained that while she and Bill were in Vegas she found receipts for hotel rooms in his briefcase. The receipts showed that the rooms had two adult occupants. She told me all of them were for rooms in Boston. They were for the weekends Bill told her he was going to visit Opal. Mama said this made her suspicious so she checked Bill's cell phone. She found a number with area code six-one-seven that didn't belong to Opal. Mama said when she called from Bill's cell, a female answered the phone "Hey Baby". I listened as Mama explained that the female was a twenty- three-year-old stripper called "Desire" that Bill met at a strip club in Boston. Mama told Desire that she was Bill's sister and she was looking to hire entertainment for Bill's birthday party. During their conversation, Desire innocently informed Mama that Bill was fond of strippers and escorts. That was the night Mama called Daddy. She told me he listened as she explained the sudden discovery she made about Bill. Mama said she asked Daddy to come see her and without hesitation he caught a flight to Vegas.

"I have always loved your father," She told me.

Mama and I had moved outside to her front porch. The wind blew lightly as we rocked back and forth on her swing.

"And your father has always loved me," She smiled.

"He hurt you, too." I reminded her.

"How?" She asked looking at me.

"When he left you," I said softly. I said the words gently because for some reason I thought the reminder would bring her new pain.

"Baby, leaving us was one of the best things your Father could have done."

"For whom?" I asked. "Definitely not for me."

I never admitted it to Mama but I despised my Daddy for leaving us. I didn't love him any less but a part of me despised him.

"All I know is in the middle of the night I heard the two of you arguing and the next thing I knew my father was gone," I said, angrily.

"You cried every night for thirty days straight," I told her." I saw you Mama."

"Then after he walked out on you he had the nerve to file for divorce?" I laughed. I was trying to calm myself but my heart was racing and I could feel the tears in my eyes. I always cry when I get mad. "You cried for thirty more days after that," I said, looking in her eyes.

"You did everything you could for him," I continued." And he left."

Mama took my hand in hers. She sat quietly as I continued.

"He left his daughter," I cried." He walked out and never looked back."

"He called and came to see you," She reminded me.

"Like a stranger, Mama," I whispered." Not like a Father that spends time with his child."

My father would call or come by for fifteen minutes. His visits and phone conversations never lasted longer than fifteen minutes. Just long enough to bring Mama money for child support, give me my allowance, throw me a kiss and leave.

"Well I remember the holidays," Mama said." I remember the birthdays and your graduation."

I thought back to those times and Mama was right; Daddy made extra effort for special occasions. For my high school graduation he bought me my first car. When I graduated from Spelman College, Daddy gave me $3500.00 as a graduation gift and he paid off all of my student loans. By doing this he made me free to open my own business without any other debts. Financially Daddy was there but I needed more than his money.

"I had his money, Mama," I said. " But I needed him."

"He needed you too," Mama said. She squeezed my hand gently and I watched as tears fell from her eyes. "Charles left because he was sick," Mama told me.

"Sick?" I asked. In an instant my anger had been replaced by care and concern. "What was wrong with him?" I asked." Is he alright now?"

"He's fine now," Mama reassured me.

"What was wrong with him?"

"He was an alcoholic," Mama told me.

"Daddy?" I asked. "I never saw him drink."

"That's because he did it whenever he left the house."

"Remember when all the arguments started?" She asked.

"Yeah about a year before he left." Before that time I had never so much as heard my parents raise their voices at each other.

"Right after your grandfather Ted died," Mama said.

Ted was Daddy's father. They spent so much time together and looked so much alike you would have thought they were brothers. My grandmother Pearl died from breast cancer when Daddy was seventeen, and after her death Daddy and his father became as close as a father and son could be. When my grandfather died it was sudden and unexpected. He died in his sleep from heart failure.

"After Ted died, Charles started hanging out more," Mama continued." Drinking and partying."

"He'd come home later and later," She said. "I assumed it was because of another woman."

"Was it ever because of another woman?" I asked.

"Not with your father," She smiled. " He saw the way our fights were affecting our family."

"He knew he couldn't keep putting you and me through that," She continued." But at the same time he couldn't stop drinking. He loved us so much that he let us go. That's why he left."

"When did you find out the truth?" I asked.

"After I married Bill," She frowned. "Your Uncle Leroy told me."

"When did the drinking stop?"

"He's been sober for two years."

"So what happened between you two after that night in Vegas?" I asked

"Charles asked me to leave Bill," She said." But I had to wait."

"Wait for what?"

"I wanted to make sure Charles was completely sober," She said." He got upset and that's why I didn't talk to him for almost another year. But I couldn't go any longer without being with him."

"Why didn't you just divorce Bill?" I asked.

"I was going to but I wanted to wait until this house was paid for," She said. "I love this house and I am not letting that ho chasing dog have it."

"Bill would have given you the house," I said.

"I know," She said, rolling her eyes." But I wanted it to be paid in full."

I shook my head and let out a small laugh. Mama had always been a smart woman.

"He is not about to leave me with any bills," She added.

"So you and Daddy are a couple again?"

Giggling Mama batted her eyes," Yes, again and forever."

"Forever is a long time," I said.

"Not when you have a man who loves you."

"Like Daddy loves you," I smiled.

"Yes," She said," And like Damon loves you."

"Mama Damon does not love me," I said, smacking my lips.

"I know men Octavia," She said. " And Damon is a man in love."

"We've known each other four months, Mama."

"When something is right it doesn't take long."

"Damon and I are just..."

"Friends," She said, cutting me off.

"Yeah."

"Damon is a good man," She said." And good men are hard to come by."

"I'm not looking for a man."

"I know," She smiled." But you have one."

I thought about what Mama said for a moment. "Whatever happens-happens," I told her.

"Okay," She said. " I just hope you let it happen with Damon."

Laughing I rolled my eyes," So, how did you know Bill would confess?" I asked.

"I didn't," She said. "But I was hoping and praying."

"I thought he was going to bust you and Daddy in front of the entire congregation."

"I did too," She smiled. "But God does answer prayers."

"That he does," I smiled. "That he does."

The Ambiance was packed during lunch, with a thirty minute wait for a free table. My servers and bus boys were running themselves ragged trying to take care of the customers while keeping the tables clean. I put my payroll on hold and made an appearance inside the restaurant to make sure everything was flowing smoothly. They appeared to have everything under control so I returned to my office. Less than thirty minutes later, Amel knocked on my door and informed me that we had a party of twelve at the front door and nowhere to sit them.

"Apologize and explain that we're booked," I instructed her, continuing with my work.

"I did, but one of them asked me to give this to you."

I looked up and saw her holding a long stem red rose and a business card. She placed the rose on the only corner of my desk that wasn't covered with paperwork, then handed the business card to me.

"Nomad Investments," I read aloud. "Damon Whitmore, President." I shook my head and smiled.

"Are they still waiting?"

"Yes."

I tapped my fingertips on the desk trying to think of a solution.

Anybody else would have been shit out of luck, but Damon was different he was special to me.

"What about the lounge?" I asked, "Amel."

"There are a couple of people at the bar, but otherwise the lounge is clear," she said. "The problem is that we don't have any tables set up."

"I want you to grab one of the reserved signs out of the storage closet, then rope off the entire room."

"Okay, but these guys don't look like the hip hop type," Amel said, frowning. "And Scar is upstairs bumping Dem Franchise Boys."

"Tell Scar to put on some Billie Holiday, Kenny G., or something."

"I'll grab Horatio and Thomas from the back so that we can set up the tables," Amel volunteered. She was already headed for the door. That's what I loved about her, she was a go-getter. I never had to stand over her or spoon feed her directions.

"One more thing, Amel," I called out to her.

"What's that?" She asked, spinning on her heels to look at me.

"Thank you."

She gave me her signature sweet smile then left the room. I gave a lot of orders but I tried to always remember to show my gratitude. Before I went into business for myself, I worked for other people and they could be damn right nasty to deal with. They gave a whole lot of orders but rarely gave recognition. I made a promise that I would never be that type of boss, so I told my employees "thank you" on a regular basis and even gave them bonuses on days like today when I knew I was working them like a group of Hebrew slaves. I also tried to be flexible when it came down to family emergencies and time off. I would fill in for my employees myself if I had to. I was the boss but I had no problem with getting my hands dirty.

I removed my MAC compact from my purse along with my lip gloss. I freshened up my lip-gloss then checked my face for shine. Once I was refreshed I adjusted my linen, knee length dress then left my office. By the time I made my way upstairs to the lounge,

Damon and his party were seated and enjoying their drinks. It was like Damon sensed my presence when I entered the room; he stopped his conversation abruptly then gazed in my direction. The other men seated at the tables, who were all Korean with exception of one handsome brother with mocha colored skin, followed Damon's eyes.

"Excuse me, gentleman," Damon smiled, staring at me from my head down to my toes.

I smiled while walking across the floor to the center of the room, where my crew had pushed four rectangular tables together.

"I just wanted to welcome each of you to the Ambiance."

"The men smiled at me, nodding their heads.

"Gentleman, this is Octavia Ellis," Damon introduced me. "Ms. Ellis is the owner of the Ambiance."

"You have a lovely establishment, Ms. Ellis." One of the businessmen said. He gave me a smile then allowed his eyes to scan over my body. Men are the same no matter what race or nationality. They all have a way of thinking with the little head in between their legs!

"Very beautiful," he continued.

The other men at the table nodded their head in agreement. I looked at Damon and laughed.

"Thank you, gentlemen," I smiled, sweetly. "And please let me know if you need anything." I smiled at Damon then slowly turned on my heels and the left the room.

I sat at my desk calculating the lunch totals. Not including what we took in from the customers still outside dining, we had already made $8000.00 and it was only three o'clock. I made myself a note on my desk planner to do something special for my team, to reward them for all their hard work. I was in the process of checking my email, when someone knocked on my door.

"Come in."

Damon opened the door then walked in. I had noticed earlier but now that he was standing before me, I could see just how sexy he was in his dark suit and silk mint green shirt and tie.

"I just wanted to say thank you." He shut the door behind him them turned the lock. "It completely slipped my mind that I had promised my associates that we would come here for lunch."

"Um hum..." I said, smacking my lips.

"And when you remembered, did it cross your mind to call and make reservations?"

"It did, but I figured I'd take my chances."

"On what?"

"The fact that the sexy owner and proprietor would do me a favor." He smiled, slowly slipping his jacket off. He folded the coat neatly, then laid it on the back of one of the leather guest chairs.

"And so she did," I smiled seductively, and walked around my desk in front of him. "So, I guess you owe her one."

"I do... "

"So where are they now?" I asked, looking at my watch. It had been well over an hour since I left them upstairs in the lounge.

"On their way back to Atlanta," he said, moving closer to me. "From there to New York."

"So how did your lunch go?"

"Great but I'm ready for dessert."

"Well we have some great items on the menu."

"What I want isn't on the menu." Starting at my calves, Damon slowly ran his hands up my legs, to the inside of my thighs. He eased down to his knees then gently pushed my legs open. I pushed the paperwork on the edge of my desk back, and then sat down with my legs spread. Lifting my hips I allowed him to slip my panties off. Damon's warm mouth showered kisses on my lower lips before his tongue slipped into the warm crevice in between them. He licked around the inside of my vagina slowly, taunting my body with his tongue. I grabbed his head using him for balance as my entire body shook from pleasure. It felt so good I wanted to scream and cry! He sucked then licked my clit until I was sloppy wet and breathless. Damon stood up then adjusted his shirt and tie.

"May I use your bathroom?"

"Um hum." I moaned, trying to catch my breath. He smiled before stepping into my private bathroom to wash his face. I slipped my panties back on then smoothed my hands over my dress before falling back into my chair.

"I have to get back to the office," He said, stepping out of the bathroom. "But why don't we finish this tonight?"

"Dinner at my place?" Before he could respond, his cell phone rang from inside his jacket.

"Hold that thought." I paused while watching him retrieve his phone from the inside pocket of his jacket then flipped it open.

"Damon Whitmore."

"What?'

"You gotta be kidding me."

"What happened?" The expression on his face told me that he wasn't getting good news.

"Fine. Just stall," He ordered. "I'll catch the next flight out." He snapped his phone shut.

"Fuck!"

"What's wrong?"

"I've got to go to Atlanta," he said, quickly slipping his jacket on. "That was my associate, Tate."

"The brother you saw with me earlier." I nodded remembering the handsome man's face.

"Well it seems that somewhere between the limo and the damn airplane Mr. Chung Woo decided not to do business with me."

"Mr. Chung Woo?"

"The one that was checking you out." I remembered the man who had scooped me out from head to toe.

"Money wise what does this mean for you?"

"It means that if I don't change his mind and secure the contract..."

"I could lose out on a 4.5 million dollar development."

"You'll get it." I said, sincerely. "If anyone can change his mind, you can."

"Thanks baby." He gave me a simple but sweet kiss on the lips. "Sorry about tonight but I'll call you as soon as I can."

"Don't worry about it," I smiled. "Go handle your business."

Before leaving the Ambiance, I slipped out of my dress and heels and into a pair of running shorts, a loose fitting oversized t-shirt, and a pair of Nike Air Maxx. I hopped in my car, cranked it up then pulled out of the parking lot with my system bumping 50 Cents "A Lil Bit". Traffic was heavy but moving freely on the Interstate as I drove towards Ladies All Around Fitness. I'd been a member at the all female gym for over a year but could count on two hands how many times I actually used my membership. I work out when the mood hits me. If it doesn't hit me, I don't work out. I've never had to worry about my figure; I was blessed with good genes and a high metabolism. I can eat whatever I want and not gain a pound. However, I do try to watch what I eat because no matter what size you are you can't stuff your body with junk food all day everyday and expect it to run flawlessly. I hit my right turn signal then changed lanes. I bobbed my head to 50 as I approached my exit. Once on the exit, I looped around then turned off into the gym parking lot. I pulled my car into an empty space close to the front door, and then shut off my engine. I stepped out of the car with my Dooney and Bourke duffle bag in my hand, shut the door, and hit the security button on my keyless remote. I was walking towards the double glass doors when a white Mercedes Benz with dark tint pulled up to the curb. The driver's side window slowly crept down.

"What's up, sexy?"

"What's up?" I stopped my stride then walked over to the car. Beau was leaning back in his seat wearing a white wife beater and denim shorts. His hair was neatly corn rowed.

"What you doing here?"

"I came to work out." I said, stating the obvious.

"For what, Ma?" You're already fine as hell." I smiled.

"How you been?" He asked.

"I've been good and you?"

"Missing you." We hadn't seen each other since that night at Fatty's.

"Missing me when?" I asked flirtatiously.

"Every time my dick gets hard." He said, grabbing his crotch.

"So you miss me now?" I asked, looking down at his hardness.

"Yeah."

"That's good to know."

"What's up for tonight?" He was straight to the point.

"What do you have in mind?"

"You'll see, Ma," He licked his lips, causing electricity in the seat of my panties. "I'll call you later."

"Alright." I stepped back from the car.

"Peace." He pulled off then circled out of the parking lot.

I slid my membership card into the slot on the keypad then entered the gym. Ladies All Around Fitness was the biggest female only gym in the area. They offered a variety of classes, including: spinning, kick boxing, Tae Bo, and Pilates. Whenever I came I always focused on the elliptical, treadmills, or free weights. Today I planned to get an hour in on the treadmill. My planned changed when I saw that every treadmill on the floor was taken. I found a free ski machine by the window, sat my duffle bag on the floor, stuck my head phones in my ears then turned on my iPod. I started my workout with a five minute warm-up at a slow pace to get my heartbeat up then increased my speed and intensity for the next forty-five minutes. I spent the last ten minutes of my workout cooling down and bringing my heart rate back to a normal pace. When I finished I was good and sweaty but I felt good. I stuffed my iPod back in my bag, pulled out a bottle of Aquafina then headed for the door. I decided to try and work in gym time at least twice a week from now on. Even though I felt good from my workout, I could tell my "fine" ass was out of damn shape.

I walked through my front door and immediately my phone started ringing. I dropped my bag on the table then grabbed the cordless.

"Hello."

"Hey, beautiful." Damon sounded like he was on cloud nine.

"I take it you worked everything out."

"Not quite but I think we're at least back on track."

"What happened?" I balanced the phone on my shoulder while removing all my clothes from the waist down.

"Someone placed a higher bid."

"So you made a counter offer."

"Not exactly," he said. "My original offer was sweet enough."

"But this other guy matched it plus he offered to be a silent partner, leaving all major decisions in Woo's hands."

"So Woo wants someone to invest but he likes the thought of having all control."

"You got it."

"So what does he plan to do?"

"He told me he would reconsider my offer," Damon told me. "And if he's as smart as I think he is, he'll choose to do business with Nomad."

"This other guy is unknown," he said. "He claims that he heard about the development from a reliable source."

"That sounds suspicious," I said, plopping down on my couch.

"Exactly."

"Do you think someone from inside your company is a leak?"

"Maybe but I'm going to stay here until I have the contracts signed and sealed."

"I would do the same if I was you."

"But listen I didn't call to talk about business." He said, changing the subject.

"What did you call to talk about?"

"You and how good you tasted today."

"I wish you could have felt me today." I said, picturing him deep inside of me.

"So do I," He said, in a low voice. "But that will have to wait until I get back."

"Unfortunately."

"But I promise to make it worth your wait."

"You better."

"I'm a man of my word."

"We will see."

"Yes you will." He said, confidently. "I'll talk to you later."

"Bye"

"Bye baby."

I had just put the phone down when my cell started ringing. I pulled it out of my bag then checked the caller ID. It was Beau.

"Hello"

"What's up Ma?" The sound of his sexy voice made my panties wetter than they already were.

"Just about to jump in the shower."

"What's up for tonight?"

"You tell me."

"Dinner at DeAngelo's," He answered. "Get ready and I'll come scoop you in an hour." I hesitated for a second. I had only kicked it with Beau once and besides the fact that he ate my kitty like a pro and his sex good, I really didn't know much about him. I've always been cautious when it came down to letting men know where I stay. Okay, Damon was an exception. It looked like Beau would be exception number two because against my better judgment I gave him my address before hanging up.

An hour later I sat in the passenger side of the Chevy Avalanche Beau was driving. Much like the Escalade he was pushing when we first met and the Benz he was in earlier, the truck was customized with chrome wheels and tinted windows.

"Is this yours?" I crossed my legs, allowing my short pleated skirt to slide up to my mid thighs. Beau's eyes darted to my exposed brown legs then back to the road ahead.

"Yeah." He kept his answers short.

"It's nice."

"Thanks."

We rode in silence while Tupac's "I Ain't Mad at You" played through the speakers. Every once in awhile Beau would look over at me but he never said a word.

"Are you okay?" I finally asked.

"Yeah just got a lot on my mind." *Well, you need to get that shit off your mind or take me back home. Incoming Call.*

Beau's cell phone rang. He turned down the music before answering.

"Yeah."

"What?"

"Yo, I'll be there in fifteen minutes!" He slammed the phone shut, then made a quick u- turn in the middle of the street. I could hear brakes screeching and horns honking, while I held on to the passenger's side door to keep my body from slamming into it. The expression on his face showed his anger.

"Where are we going?"

"I have to handle some business at the club."

"Fatty's?" I asked, looking out the window. We were going in the opposite direction.

"Naw, Low Key."

"The strip joint?"

"Yeah, that's mine too." I had never been to the Low Key but I heard it was one of the hottest gentleman's clubs in the city. Jade mentioned it from time to time whenever I was in the salon.

"You can drop me off at home, if you want."

"Naw, this won't take long."

The parking lot of the Low Key was packed. I wondered how many husbands were up in the place spending their family's grocery money or child support money on someone else's woman. It's a damn shame! Beau pulled directly in front of the door then jumped out. To my surprise he walked around to the passenger's side and held the door open for me.

"Come on Ma." I took his hand then followed him through the doors of the club. Inside, two overly built guys sat on stools by the door. The shirts had "Security" printed on the front of them. They jumped up in unison when they saw Beau.

"If both of ya'll niggas are in here, then who's watching the outside of my club?" Beau asked, looking from one to the other.

"We uh…" one of them stammered.

"Don, get your ass outside!" Beau ordered him. He quickly exited out the door. "Turk, you don't move from this spot until I tell you to," Beau barked at the other man.

"But…"

"But what nigga?" He asked, standing in his face.

Turk looked from Beau to me.

"Man what if I gotta go take a piss?" He asked.

"You know my bladder is fucked up."

"Hold that shit!" I felt bad for the brother but, Beau ran his business as he saw fit. Besides, I was positive that anyone who chose to work for him knew what they were getting themselves into. Beau held my hand as he walked to one of the two bars in the club.

"Tina, where's Sasha?" He asked the tall, slender female working behind the bar.

"She left," she said, hesitantly.

"What do you mean she left?" His voice rose. "What did I tell your black ass on the phone?"

"She'll be right back, Beau," Tina explained quickly. "She went with Johnny to get her dancing gear."

"Cool." Beau cocked a half smile.

"Sit here and order whatever you want," He said to me. "I'll be back in a minute."

I sat down on an empty bar stool, while Beau exited pass another security guard through a pair of long velvet curtains located at the side of the stage. On stage was a dark-skinned sister, wearing a pair of clear stilettos, and a leopard print g-string. She hung upside down on the steel pole that came down from the ceiling and stopped in the middle of the stage floor. I watched in awe as she slid head first, down to the floor with her legs spread open. The men standing around the stage screamed, while some of them threw crumbled bills onto the floor. She flipped backwards off the pole into a handstand then did the splits until her toes were almost touching the floor. I felt like running up to the stage and throwing a couple of bills my damn self, I was so impressed. I looked around the room and noticed there were other girls in the room giving lap dances, or either trying to get the men to buy a lap dance. I can't understand why anyone would want to work so hard just to make a couple dollars.

"Can I get you a drink?" Tina asked me.

"I'll take a rum and coke, please." She gave me a pleasant smile then proceeded to fix my drink. Once she was finished, she placed a cocktail napkin on the bar in front of me, dropped a straw in the small glass then sat the glass on the napkin.

"Thanks." I took a small sip, immediately breathing in the alcohol. Tina hooked me up! I had more rum than coke, and that was just the way I liked it. She watched me for a moment then went down to the other end of the bar to check on her other customers. I swiveled around on the bar stool then continued to watch the crowd. I locked eyes with those of a handsome dark-skinned brother sitting at a table, in the corner near the side of the stage. The corner was dark but I still noticed him. He raised his glass up then flashed me a winning smile. He looked completely un-phased by the action surrounding him. In fact he looked out of place. I smiled at him then continued sipping on my drink. A few seconds later a beautiful girl came through the door followed by a short, overweight man. She had chestnut colored weave that stopped just above her ass, wearing a pair of fitted velour pants with a matching velour jacket that stopped just below her breast. A nylon gym bag swung from her shoulder. The girl didn't look a day over eighteen but the man had to be pushing fifty-one. She came and stood at the bar next to me, with the man standing closely behind her.

"Tina." Her voice sounded even younger than she looked.

"What's up Sasha?" Tina asked, walking down in front of her.

"Give me a shot of gin." I sat with my back against the bar, watching the next dancer, a tall brunette who could stand to gain a few pounds. What she lacked in size she made up for in skill. She was shaking her ass like she was on a Lil Jon video.

"Hey," Sasha spoke to me.

"Hello," I said, looking at her. She had a round baby face with wide set eyes and long curly lashes.

"Are you one of the new girls?" She asked, before tossing her shot of gin back.

"No, I'm just waiting for someone."

"Who?" She's a nosey little something.

"Be…"

"Sasha you're up next." The man she came with abruptly interrupted us. "Okay, Johnny."

"Hopefully, I'll see you later." She gave me a small smile before walking away. She walked pass security through the curtains with Johnny trailing right on her ass.

Beau's minute turned into thirty, while my patience went from thin to nothing. I decided if he wasn't back in fifteen minutes I was calling myself a cab. I was starting to get a hunger headache and the loud music in the club wasn't making it any better. I looked by the door and saw Turk squirming in his seat, doing the pee-pee dance. My own bladder started calling my name, so I asked Tina where I could find the bathroom.

"In the back, first door on the left."

"I'll be right back." When I got up, I noticed the stranger in the corner watching my every move. If he wasn't sweating me so hard with his eyes, I would have sworn he was gay. He didn't even blink towards the stage where two girls were bumping coochies. I shook my head, continuing my stroll. I walked up to the brother guarding the curtain.

"Excuse me," he smiled, displaying his gold fronts. I wanted to gag but chose to give him a fake smile instead.

"Where you going, lil mama?" He asked, licking his lips.

"To the ladies room." He stepped to the side, holding the curtain back for me. "Let me know if you need any help." I ignored his weak attempt at a come on, while walking through the doorway. I found the bathroom then quickly stepped inside and locked the door. After relieving my bladder I washed my hands, checked my hair in the mirror, unlocked the bathroom door then walked out. I looked down the hall and saw several closed doors. The closest one was right next to the bathroom. I could hear heels clicking and women talking so I assumed that it was the one that led to the dressing room. I turned going back in the direction from which I came, while wondering which door Beau was behind. I was halfway to the exit when Sasha came running out into the hallway, crashing into me. I stumbled but managed to maintain my balance. She on the other hand hit the floor face first. I reached down, helping her up. She looked at me and I noticed the entire right side of her face was red and swollen.

"Are you okay?"

"Sasha!" Johnny seemed to have come out of nowhere. He walked up to Sasha and grabbed her by her arm. She looked like a rag doll in his grip. He jerked her into his fat body then began dragging her off in the opposite direction.

"Leave me alone!" She screamed so loud a couple of the dancers came out of their dressing room.

"Don't ya'll bitches got something to do?" Johnny snapped. They immediately dispersed. Some of them brushing past us to go out into the club, and others went back inside the dressing room.

"Let me go!" She screamed.

"Leave her alone!" I yelled, following behind the two of them.

"Mind your own business, bitch." Johnny yelled, back at me.

"Fuck you!" I responded. He stopped in his tracks then spun around on his heels.

"What you say?" He asked, his dark eyes staring at me.

"You heard me." I said, with attitude.

He released his grip on Sasha then took a step towards me. I took one step back, preparing myself to plant my three inch heel in the middle of his legs. I figured somewhere among the rolls of fat were a pair of nuts and if Johnny attempted to put his hands on me, I was going to make sure my foot found them.

"Johnny!" Beau's voice commanded our attention. "Back off."

"Beau dis bitch..."

"I said back off!" Johnny slowly stepped out of my way. Beau stood in the hall facing the three of us.

"You alright, Ma?"

I cut my eyes over at Johnny. He looked like he wanted to reach out and choke me. I rolled my eyes at him then walked towards Beau.

"You okay Ma?" He asked, stroking my cheek with his fingertips.

"Hell no," I snapped. "First of all your minute is up!"

"Second, what happened to her?" I asked, pointing at Sasha. She stood against the wall, like a child getting ready to be punished.

"Third, who does that fat mother fucker think he is?" I turned around, staring at Johnny.

"Bitch…"

"I don't see your Mama up in here." I stated, cutting him off. Beau laughed.

"Johnny, chill out man." He said, looking over at him.

"And Sasha here had a little run in with one of the other girls," he continued. "You know how it is with females and money."

"Bitches get jealous of each other." Beau stated, cutting his eyes over at Sasha. "Johnny was just trying to calm her down is all."

"He just has an iron fist," Beau said." He lacks the gentle touch that I have when it comes down to the ladies."

"Ummph," Sasha sighed, loudly.

"Sasha, get ready to get on stage," Beau ordered.

"I'm not going out there looking like this," She whined. "Look at my fucking face, Beau." She pointed to the swelling, which was quickly turning into an ugly purple bruise.

"Slap some make up on that shit," Beau said, coldly.

"And what about this?" Sasha pulled the top of her pants down, revealing that she had on no panties, and displaying a long bruise on her ass cheek. The purple mark was the same shape as a footprint. Someone had literally put their foot in her ass.

"Slap some make up on that shit too." Beau said, seriously. "Hell those niggas out there don't care what your ass looks like as long as you're shaking it."

" But..."

"But nothin', get dressed and get on stage." Beau's voice was loud and firm.

"Matter of fact," He said. "I want you here every night shaking your ass."

"When the doors open."

"Till they muthafuckin' close."

"That's not fair, Beau!" Sasha whined. "You know I can't work no twelve hour days."

"Can you pay me the money you owe me?" Beau asked, stepping around me in Sasha's face. She looked close to tears as she shook her head no.

"Then you'll be here, all day, every day, till' you can."

"Who's gonna watch my baby?" Sasha cried, with tears flowing down her face.

"Find the little bastard's daddy." He said. "Better yet find that ho you call your mama." Sasha dropped her head. My heart went out to her. I didn't know how much she owed him but I was willing to give her the money. I couldn't stand seeing another black or any other woman in pain. Sasha raised her head looking up at me.

"What the fuck are you looking at?" She asked, wiping her face with the back of her hand. She was trying to be hard but I saw right through her. The same way I saw through Beau. I hadn't bought his bullshit line about having a gentle touch. He was foul and I could smell his ass a mile away.

Despite the fact that I knew Beau had done Sasha wrong, I climbed back in his truck with him. The two of us arrived at DeAngelo's just before ten o'clock. After the waiter escorted us to a secluded booth in the back of the restaurant we placed our orders. Beau ordered himself the stuffed lobster and me the crab salad with mixed greens. His etiquette and table manners surprised me. He went from hardcore to perfect gentleman in zero to sixty seconds. It was like he had split personalities. After we finished our meals we sat in the cozy leather booth in silence.

"I like the way you handled yourself back at the club." He spoke first. "You've got heart."

"I just don't like men who disrespect women."

"Johnny has a wife and three daughters," Beau informed me. "He loves women."

"So why does he talk to them like their shit?" I asked, with attitude. "Is it because he's trying to make up for some insecurity?"

"Like what?"

"I don't know…maybe he has a little dick." Beau laughed.

"I don't know about the size of his dick." He said. "But I do know in business you have to be tough."

"There's a difference between being tough and being an ass."

"You're right, but in my line of work you can't afford to show any sign of weakness."

"Weakness leaves room for takeover," He continued.

"Showing compassion isn't a sign of weakness." I said, staring into his dark eyes.

"It depends on the situation, Ma." Our waiter returned informing us it was closing time. Beau paid the check then left a fifty for the tip.

"You want me to take you home?" Beau asked, as we walked out of the restaurant.

"What else did you have in mind?"

"I'd like for you to come home with me." I wasn't big on the idea of the two of us going back to his place. Beau must have sensed this.

"Or we can get a room if you want." He said, quickly. "I just have to call Lisa to let her know I won't be home." Who in the hell is Lisa? Don't tell me he's married.

"Lisa is my daughter's babysitter." He said, reading my mind. The two of us got back into his truck.

"Your daughter lives with you?"

"Yeah, every since she was born."

"And how old is she now?"

"Four." Beau didn't seem like the nurturing type. It was hard for me to believe that he had raised a child for four years.

"Her mom died right after she was born."

"I'm sorry to hear that," I said, sincerely.

"Me, too," Beau's voice got low. He started the truck then pulled away from the curb.

"So where to?" He asked. I'm a sucker for a sob story.

"Your place." I said.

Beau's five bedroom brick rancher sat in a cul-de-sac in Thomas Hills. Thomas Hills is a restricted subdivision, where the homes go for 140,000 and up. His home was well decorated with dark leather furniture and wood accents. After stopping by his daughter's room to kiss her goodnight Beau led me to his bedroom. The master bedroom was equipped with a king size bed with matching dresser and nightstand, a sitting area with a sofa, loveseat, a 54" big screen TV, and a mini bar.

"Why you still single?" He asked, rubbing his fingers across my naked breast. The two of us lay naked stretched out across his silk sheets.

"By choice," I answered.

"Why are you?" I countered.

"Most women can't be trusted."

"Neither can most men." Beau rolled onto his back, then pulled me on top of him. I straddled his waist while looking into his eyes.

"You're not like most women," he said. "You're different from most females I meet."

"What do you mean?"

"You're not money hungry or sweatin' a nigga to marry your ass."

"I make my own money and I don't need a husband."

I eased down on his body until his rock hard dick was touching my lips. I kissed the head first, then slowly trailed my tongue from the head to the base.

"Umm…" he moaned, grabbing a handful of my hair.

"Tell me what you want…" he said.

"What you need…and I'll give it to you," he continued. I didn't respond.

I slid my mouth down over his dick until he was touching the back of my throat. I sucked him hard. I deep throated his dick while gently kneading his balls with my hands.

"Shit!" He moaned, pumping in my mouth wildly. I slid up to the head, sucked gently then took all of him in my mouth again. I stopped when I felt his body trembling; I didn't want him to cum, not until I got what I came for. I quickly tore open the condom I had him place on the nightstand before we got naked, and then slid it over his erection. Turning around, I sat down backwards on his dick. I rocked and rolled my hips to my own beat. Squeezing my nipples, Beau lifted his hips meeting my movements with fierce blows. I guided one of his hands down to my clit while the other one continued to grab and pull at my breast. He stroked my clit until it was engorged and my pussy was wet. So wet it made loud gushing sounds. I came hard. I turned around facing him, never allowing him to slip out of me. Slipping my tongue in Beau's mouth, I found his. We changed positions, with me on my stomach and him behind me. Before entering me again, Beau licked from the base of my neck down the center of my back to the curve of my ass. When he got to my ass, he used his hands to spread my cheeks then slowly slipped his tongue in my tight hole. He tossed my salad until I came again, and then slid his dick in me from behind. Beau fucked me hard doggy style, while pulling my hair. He was rough and hard and I was enjoying every single minute of it. I bounced back and forth causing his nuts to slap against my skin loudly.

"Dammmnnnn…"

He came, collapsing onto my back.

Chapter 18

I had every intention of sleeping in late. That changed when there was a knock on my door at eight a.m.. I drug myself out of bed, and then marched to my front door. I looked out the peep hole and saw a tall man holding a bouquet of long stem roses. Rubbing the sleep from my eyes, I unlocked the door.

"Yes," I said, clearing my throat.

"Delivery for Ms. Octavia Ellis," he was smiling at me, like he hadn't disrupted my sleep.

"I'm Octavia," he handed me the arrangement of pink and red roses.

"Thanks," I gave him a half smile, while pushing the door shut.

"Uh, ma'am." He better not be waiting on a damn tip. Although, I was receiving flowers, I was not happy about getting them so early. I didn't think the florist opened until nine!

"Yes?"

There's more.

"Okay." I stood by the door, while he ran back downstairs. He returned with two more arrangements.

"Put them over there please." I pointed to the coffee table. I followed him then put the arrangement in my hands on the table as well.

"Be right back," he said, hurrying out the door. I plopped down on the couch, and then pulled the greeting card out of the first bouquet.

Thinking of you, morning, noon, and night.

Always,
Damon

The delivery guy returned with two more bouquets, then two more after that until I had twelve dozen roses covering my living room and a smile on my face. After running up and down three flights of stairs, I decided the deliver had earned a tip. I went in my bedroom grabbed my wallet, and then handed him a fifty dollar bill. After seeing him out, I shut the door then picked up my phone.

"Hello," Damon sounded, half sleep himself.

"Good morning," I was beaming from ear to ear.

"Hey baby."

"I love the roses, they're beautiful."

"Just my little way of letting you know I miss you," he said, clearing his voice.

"I miss you too."

"I'm glad," he said.

"When are you coming home?" I asked.

"Home?" He sounded, confused.

"I mean back." My lack of sleep, had me confused my damn self. I forgot his stay in Huntsville was only temporary.

"I liked the sound of that."

"Of what?"

"Of you asking when I'll be home." I sensed our conversation was headed in the wrong direction. My palms were starting to sweat. I was something I had never been before, when it came to a man. I was nervous.

"Don't get nervous." He laughed, reading my mind again. "That's another conversation for another day. Anyway, I'll be back on Sunday."

"Okay." I wiped the perspiration on the legs of my pajama pants. "I'll see you then."

"Bye, beautiful."

"Bye, Damon."

After I took my shower, I slipped on a pair of my denim shorts and one of my Juicy couture fitted t-shirts. I slipped my feet into a pair of flip flops, and then cooked myself a vegetable omelet and poured a glass of OJ. After breakfast, I was wide awake. Going back to bed was not an option, so I decided to indulge in my favorite pastime: shopping. I picked up the phone and called Shontay, hoping she would be free to join me.

"Pick me up in an hour." She sounded relieved that I called.

"What's wrong?"

"Nothing, I just need some air." It was obvious to me that her new family arrangements were getting to her.

"I'll see you in an hour."

I wanted to buy Damon a little something to let him know I was thinking about him, without giving him the wrong impression. I found the perfect gift at Crown Jewelers.

"Diamond cuff links?" Shontay asked, staring at the one carat links. I handed the overly happy sales girl my American Express card, then smiled.

"What's wrong with diamond links?" The sales girl swiped my card quickly. I think she thought I would change my mind. I wasn't. I was confident that I had made the right choice. A $1,500 choice, but still the right one.

"Are you sure he's just a friend?"

"Of course I'm sure, 'Tay."

"With all the money ya'll are spending on each other and the time you've been spending…"

"You're trippin'." I took my bag from the salesgirl, then walked out of the store with Shontay following behind me. After we left the jewelers we stopped in Coffee & Tea, where I picked up Mama a hazelnut roast gift basket. We later hit up Charlotte Russe, New York & Co, and B. Moss. Shontay wanted to stop by the Baby Gap, so we did. She ended up buying her stepdaughter a Levi denim sundress. We had lunch at the American Cafe then headed back to my car. The two of us loaded our packages in my trunk, and then climbed inside my car.

Turning up my stereo, I grooved in my seat to the sounds of Jill Scott coming from my speakers. "So how is your stepdaughter?" I asked.

Shontay and I hadn't discussed the new edition to her family since that day at her house. Since then, she, Kenny, and his baby's mother had been trying to work out some form of understanding.

"Kiya is adorable," She said, looking out the window. "She looks just like Kenny."

"You're cool with that?"

"It's too late for me not to be," She said. "I wasn't given a choice."

"You have a choice of whether or not you want to be a part of their extended family."

"It's a package deal," She said, looking over at me." If you want the man you want the child."

"Why do you want the man?"

"I love him," she said." He's my husband."

"I know 'Tay, but is it worth all he's put you through? Is it worth sacrificing the happiness you deserve?" I asked.

"Kenny's made sacrifices too," she said, softly.

"What has he sacrificed?" I asked, angry. "Other women?"

Letting out a fake laugh, I concentrated on the traffic around me. Tapping my brakes lightly I watched in my rearview mirror as the car behind us slowed down and put some distance between us. They had been tailgating us for more than thirty minutes.

"No," she said, solemnly.

"Plus, he had a child with another woman," I added.

"I know that 'Tavia." "So what sacrifice?"

"You don't think I'm upset about all of this?" She asked, raising her voice.

"Are you?"

"I'm mad as hell!" She snapped. "I'm mad that I love him. I'm mad that I can't let him go. But most of all I'm mad that another woman gave him the one thing I can't."

I took my eyes off the road just long enough to look over at Shontay. Tears were rolling down her cheeks. "Tay," I asked," What do you mean?"

"I'm sterile, 'Tavia."

I focused back on the road in front of me. "How long have you known?" I asked.

"Since I was fifteen," she confessed.

"What happened?"

"I had PID," She said, sniffling. "And I didn't get the proper treatment." I read about PID, Pelvic Inflammatory Disease, and that if left untreated it could leave a woman sterile. But I had never heard of anyone as young as Shontay having it.

"Tay," I said softly.

"My fallopian tubes were severely damaged." She cried.

Taking one hand off the wheel I grabbed hers," I'm sorry Tay," I said sincerely. "Why didn't you tell me?"

"The only people who know are my mom and Kenny," She said.

"That's why you stayed with Kenny," I told her.

"He accepted me for me," She said," He loved me and wanted me even though I was damaged."

"You're not damaged," I told her." Not being able to have children doesn't determine who or what you are."

"That's easy for you to say," She said, wiping her face with her hands," You still can."

I never thought about my ability to conceive a child or the possibility that I couldn't. For me it had never been an issue because I've never wanted children. Shontay on the other hand always loved being around kids and always talked about starting her own family. Now knowing that she couldn't, I felt so much pain for her. But not as much pain as I felt for her because she didn't seem to realize that her physical condition didn't give Kenny justification to do what he did.

Letting go of her hand I wiped my face. "So are you bringing Kenny to Daddy's birthday party?" I asked.

"No, I know you don't like Kenny," she chuckled." I'm coming solo."

"Bring him," I said, hesitantly.

"You sure?" She asked.

Laughing, I said," Yeah I'm sure."

"Thanks 'Tavia."

"Welcome."

"So will I finally get to meet Damon?" She asked. Taking the I-565 exit I headed in the direction of Shontay's home.

"Of course," I said, smiling. "Mama invited him before she invited me."

"Ms. Charlene really likes him."

"Girl, yeah."

"She's probably already planning your wedding."

Throwing one of my hands up I shook my head, "Marriage is not in my vocabulary."

"That's the same thing you said about relationship."

"Don't go there."

Laughing, she said," Okay, but never say never."

I pulled into Shontay's driveway and put my car in park. We were walking up to her front door when a black Impala with dark tinted windows pulled in front of her house and stopped.

"Who is that?" I asked.

"I have no idea."

We waited to see if anyone was going to get out. No one did. I strained to see through the tint. I couldn't make out how many people were inside the car. Unlocking her front door Shontay stepped inside. Following her I shut the door behind me. Dropping her bags, Shontay walked over to her living room window.

"They're just sitting there," she said, peeping through the curtains.

Looking over her shoulder I watched as the car finally spun off.

"I guess they had the wrong house," Shontay stated, walking away from the window.

"Maybe." I stood in the window, staring into space. I had a bad feeling. I didn't know when, where, or how but something was about to go down.

Chapter 19

With Daddy's 53rd birthday approaching and her divorce pending from Bill, Mama had her hands full. I wanted to keep as much stress of her as I could, so I volunteered to help her with the party planning. I looked around the living room and that's when the reality of Mama and Bill's divorce set in. All of his belongs were gone. All the family pictures that included him were gone. He was gone.

"I'll be a single and free woman in sixty days," Mama said.

The two of us were sitting side by side on her sofa going over the details of Daddy's party.

"Ten days before your father's birthday," She said, smiling.

"I'm sure Daddy will be very happy with that present," I said, scanning the guest list. "Are you sure you want Pastor Davis to come," I asked, circling his name on the list.

"Do you know any other ministers we can invite?"

"Why do you have to have a minister present," I asked, scanning the other names.

"Because, I'm giving your Daddy this."

She slid a small covered ring box into my lap. Looking up at her I held the box in the palm of my hand. There was silence as I slowly opened the box. Once I had the box open, I gazed at the beautiful gold diamond cut man's wedding band.

"It's beautiful."

Smiling she reached into her pants pocket and pulled out another box. "It matches these," she said, holding open the other box.

Inside were a gold ladies band that matched the band I was holding and what I estimate as being at least a two-carat marquise cut solitaire.

"He gave me these last year in Vegas," she said." He told me to keep them until I was ready to be with a man who really loves me."

I looked at her smiling the beautiful smile I had grown to love and also missed during the time she and Daddy were not together. She smiled when she was with Bill too but it wasn't the same.

"So I guess we have a wedding to plan," I smiled.

Her expression changed to one of surprise. "You support this?" She asked.

"Yes I support it."

"No complaining about us just getting back together?" She asked. "No comments on how I'm getting out of one marriage and jumping into another?"

"Nope."

"What's gotten into you?" She asked, looking at me suspiciously.

Smiling I thought about Damon. "If something is right Mama," I said, smiling," Why question it."

"You have a point."

"Besides," I added. "I love you and Daddy. I want you to be happy."

"We love you too," She smiled. "And we are." There was a pregnant pause between the two of us. "So how are things with Damon?" She asked.

"Good."

"Good?" She asked," How good?"

"Real good," I laughed.

"So good you may finally give me a son-in-law?"

"Not that good."

"What are you afraid of?"

"What do you mean?" She gave me her "don't play with me look".

"I don't know Mama."

"Of having my heart broken, I guess."

"He can't break it if you never give it to him."

"Exactly."

"But..." I knew there was a but.

"You also can't experience the good that comes along with loving someone and having them love you. Why deprive yourself of that?"

"I pondered her question without answering.

"Besides, Damon's not the type of man who is going to settle for just sex.

Sooner or later he's going to ask you for the real thing."

"I'll deal with that when we get to it," I said. "But as for right now we have one wedding to plan."

"We could make it a double," She mumbled.

"Let it go, Mama."

Throwing her hands up in the air, she said, "Ok, have it your way."

Shaking my head I patted her on her leg and said, "Now let's get back to planning your dream wedding,"

A dream wedding is exactly what I wanted my parent's to have. The first time they got married they didn't have enough money for a ceremony so they tied the knot in front of a justice of the peace at our local courthouse. This time I planned to give them the wedding they deserved. Mama didn't care where the two of them got married just as long as it happened. I know the most important thing about getting married is pledging your eternal love and commitment to each other but there was no way I was going to allow my parents to make that pledge during some backyard countrified ceremony. Instead, I planned a mid-day wedding in the Rose Garden of the Botanical Gardens followed by a reception at the Ambiance.

By the end of the day, Mama and I had almost every detail of the wedding worked out. The only thing we didn't find was a dress for Mama that we both agreed upon. I wanted Mama to have something made especially for her so I called Marcella Cantrell, a friend of mine from Spelman. Marcella was a struggling fashion designer that could make a tablecloth look like a Vera Wang. I gave her Mama's measurements and told her to create something beautiful.

I was too tired to drive home, so I opted to spend the night with Mama. I thought I would get one of her good home cooked meals, but instead she handed me the phone and told me to call Dominos. I ordered us a medium veggie supreme and a small order of hot wings. We sat in front of the TV stuffing our faces, while watching the ten o'clock news. I can't remember the last time I watched the nightly news. There never seemed to be anything on, other than death and depression. I use to only watch for the weather forecast but now I don't even depend on that. Meteorologist are only guessing when they give the forecast, it doesn't matter how many radars or graphs they use. I figured that one out when our local weatherman predicted sunny skies and a high of 89, and we ended up with a foot of snow in the middle of April.

I bit into another wing while partially listening to the skinny blonde sitting behind the anchor desk, giving the latest news.

"Police have released the identity of a young woman, whose body was discovered this morning. The woman has been identified as nineteen year old Natasha Montgomery."

I dropped the half eaten wing on my plate, when a picture of Sasha appeared on the TV screen. She was smiling, holding a little boy who looked just like her.

"I know her." I whispered, sitting my plate down on the coffee table.

"What?"

I ignored Mama, while picking up the remote control. I turned up the volume and continued to stare at Sasha's picture on the screen.

"Montgomery's body was discovered in her Valley Bend apartment, by a neighbor. Authorities suspect a possible drug overdose. An autopsy will be performed to determine the cause of death. At this time there is no suspicion of foul play. Montgomery leaves behind a one year old son."

"In other news…"

I pressed the volume key again, turning down the sound. "You know her?"

"I met her."

"When?" Mama asked, looking at me.

"Last night." I was in shock. I had just seen Sasha, now she was dead.

"Met her where?"

"At the club where she works," I said. "Where she use to work."

"That's a shame." Mama said, clearing our plates from the table. "We're here today and gone tomorrow."

"She was just a baby," she said, shaking her head. "A baby with a baby." Mama left me sitting on the couch staring into space. I was trying to process the information the anchorwoman had just given. A drug overdose? There was nothing about Sasha that gave me the impression that she was into drugs. I know you never really know anyone but my first impressions are normally the right ones.

I kneeled at the side of the bed in my old room and said a prayer. I thanked God for my parents, my life, my health, and my strength. I thanked him for Shontay and even Damon. I asked him to bless Sasha's son and her family wherever they may be. I said, "Amen", and then climbed under the covers. I lay on my back in the darkness, unable to fall asleep. My thoughts shifted back and forth from my life to Damon to my parents back to Damon. I thought about Sasha and all the things she would never get to experience and all the times she would never get to share with her son. My thoughts were interrupted by my cell phone vibrating loudly on the nightstand beside the bed. I rolled over on my side and looked at the caller ID. It was Beau. I hadn't spoken to him all day and I wasn't in the mood to talk but I picked up anyway.

"Hello."

"What's up, Ma?"

"Nothin' much and you?"

"Chillin'." He inhaled, deeply then exhaled. I could tell he was on the other end of the phone getting high.

"I wanna see you."

"I'm already in the bed." I don't know what it was but something about hearing his voice at that moment annoyed me.

"Why don't you let me come by and join you?"

"I'm really tired." I felt no need to explain that I wasn't at home, because it was none of his business. In fact even if I had been at home I wouldn't have let him come over.

"I saw the news." I said, changing the subject.

"Me, too."

"They found Sasha dead?" I asked the question as if he had just reported the information to me.

"That's what they say." He said, nonchalantly. He inhaled then exhaled again.

"That's awful." I said, picturing Sasha's pretty face.

"That's life, Ma," he said. "We're born. We live. We die." He was telling the truth but it was the way he said it that further agitated me.

"Does she have any family here?" I asked "What about her mom and dad?" I paused, then asked,

"Who's going to take care of her son?"

"Hell if I know," he snapped. "What are you...the damn police?"

"I was just asking." I snapped, back. "You don't have to get an attitude." I was officially pissed off.

"Why you so concerned about that hoe?" He asked. "It's obvious she wasn't concerned when she was taking hits."

"And as far as her Mama goes... you can check the corner of 10th and 12th for her because the last I heard she was up north on the hoe stroll."

"And her dad...well that nigga could be any trick on the east side of Buffalo."

"As far as her son goes... the lil' nigga ain't mine, so I don't give a fuck what happens to him." Beau was cold and callous. I decided I'd had enough of him.

"Look I'm tired." I said, faking a yawn. "I need to get some rest."

"Yeah, you do that." He said, calmly. "I'll holla back.Night, Ma."

"Good night." I put my phone back on the nightstand, and then rolled back over. I closed my eyes and tried to clear my head. It didn't work. There was a new thought clouding my mind, I was thinking it was time for me to cut Beau off.

Chapter 20

Saturday I decided I needed a little rest and relaxation, so I treated myself to a trip to the Terrame Day Spa. I started with a facial, followed by a seaweed wrap and a full body massage. If I was into girls, I would have taken the pretty Vietnamese chick who gave me my rub down, home with me. That's how good she made my body feel. When she finished; kneading and rubbing my body I felt completely revived. After my massage, I got a fresh manicure and a pedicure. Once the top coat dried on my nails, I paid Minh then left the spa.

It was still fairly early so the flow of traffic wasn't heavy yet. That's one of my favorite things about living in a smaller city. You don't have to worry about forty-five minute waits on drives that should only take you ten minutes. I'm not saying during lunch hour or rush hour you won't run into a delay but it's nothing compared to the traffic you have to deal with in ATL or Los Angeles. I rode along I-72 listening to the R Kelly's greatest hits CD, Scar made me. Track 5, Sex Me, flowed through my speakers. I sung along with the R. while occasionally checking my rearview mirror. The car behind me had been riding my bumper for at least a mile. I tapped my breaks then redirected my attention to the road ahead. They eased off for a split second then started tailgating me again. I was not going to let one inconsiderate asshole on the interstate ruin my good mood, so

I checked my mirror to make sure the right lane was clear, put my signal on, and then got over. If he or she wanted my spot in the lane that bad they could have it. I waited for the car to pass me but it never did. Instead they got over behind me and continued to ride my ass.

I tapped my breaks again. The car slowed down but then started tailing me again.

"Freaking idiot," I yelled, looking in my rearview mirror.

"Where's a cop when you need one?" I got back in the left lane. The car followed. I eased on to the gas, hoping to put some distance between us, they sped up as well. I got into the right lane and floored it. I was blessed that there were no cars in front of me. The last thing I wanted was to have a collision, from trying to weave in and out of traffic. When I saw my exit coming up, I breathed a sigh of relief. The car suddenly swerved into the other lane, pulling up next to me. I slowed down preparing to exit and that's when they swerved into my lane. I swerved to avoid hitting them but ended up getting off on the exit too fast. My car jerked to the left towards the concrete divider going around the curve, and I scrambled frantically to straighten my sedan up but only made things worse. I slammed my foot on the brake pedal, as my Infiniti began to spin around recklessly. The sound of glass shattering and metal crushing echoed through my head as my car slammed into the concrete. My body attempted to jerk forward but my seatbelt locked slamming me back against the seat. My air bag deployed blocking my view. I had no idea what was ahead of me or what direction I was facing. I didn't care. The only thing that mattered was that I was alive. I was scared breathless but I was still alive. The entire driver side door was folded in against my body. There was a shooting pain running from my ankle up to my thigh. I tried to move my leg but it was pinned under crumbled metal. I looked down and saw a gash on my leg with a small stream of blood trickling out. I looked closer and saw the bone in my ankle sticking out under my skin; I knew my ankle was broken. Suddenly it became harder and harder for me to breath. I tried to take a deep breath in through my nose but my chest felt like it was caving in. I opened my mouth taking short quick breaths as everything around me faded to black.

Three days later, I was recuperating with a cast on my left ankle and twenty-one stitches just below my calf. When I saw the pictures of my car, which was totaled, I thanked God that my injuries were not worse. I passed out just before HEMSI arrived at the scene but according to their report they were called by the police. According to HPD, they received an anonymous phone call, reporting a one car accident. The police had a ton of questions about what happened but I was little to no help at all. The whole thing was a blur to me. The good thing is that there was another car on the road behind me who witnessed the other driver swerving into my lane. They gave the police a description of the car but unfortunately, according to what I was told, there was not a tag on the back of the car so they could-not provide a license plate number. It was like finding a needle in a haystack, so I charged the whole incident to the game. Meaning I took it as a loss and presumed the authorities would never find the psycho who had an obvious case of road rage.

The cast was an inconvenience in more ways than one. First of all I couldn't wear my cute stilettos or heels. Second, I couldn't walk up a flight of stairs, which meant that I could not stay in my apartment. There was no way I could make it up three flights of stairs while on crutches, without busting my ass. So, I had to find an alternate place to stay for six weeks. Naturally, Mama insisted that I stay with her. I willingly agreed. I loved being around my mother, especially whenever I was sick. I may be a grown woman but Mama always treats me like her little girl. The only downfall was that I wasn't going to be able to get my dick like I wanted to. I may be grown but Mama is not having any laying up in her house, unless she's the one doing the laying.

Damon returned from Atlanta early Sunday morning, and his first stop was by Mama's house to see me. I hadn't spoken with him since I had my accident but I presumed Mama or Daddy had. The three of them had become extremely close over the passing months. After reassuring Damon over and over and over again that I was alright, the two of us sat in my mother's den, stretched across her suede sectional, cuddling.

"What are you going to do about your car?" I didn't even want to think about my car. I had only two payments left, before having my car paid in full. Three years early! I had been making double payments each month since I purchased it and now I was going to have start all over. The fact that I had full coverage with Alfa did not make me feel any better. They were only going to pay the final two payments off. I was still responsible for buying a new vehicle plus my $250 deductible. They were getting off pretty damn cheap if you ask me.

"I'm going to rent a car, until I find another one I like." I said. I was laying on my back with my legs propped on the sofa and my head resting in Damon's lap. He stroked my hair gently.

"I was thinking that maybe you should stay at the hotel with me." He said. "I could rent out the corporate apartment for the two us." What? My facial expression must have been speaking for me because he immediately began to explain.

"The Hilton is only five minutes away from the Ambiance," He said. "And ten minutes away from my office."

"It's a forty-five minute drive from here to there." He reminded me.

"What if something happens at the restaurant?" He asked.

"Wouldn't you want to be closer?"

"Nothing's happened in the last two years," I said, looking into his dark eyes. " And nothing will."

"Maybe you're right," he said, shrugging his shoulders. "But I hate that your mom is going to have to drive you back and forth for the next few weeks. Especially with everything she has going on," he said." "And the fact that I'm willing to help in any way." He had a point, Mama had a lot on her own plate and I really didn't want to add any more to it. At the same time I didn't like the thought of being dependant on Damon or any other man.

"If I have to I'll take a six week vacation," I said. "But thank you for the offer." He kissed me softly on the lips. His lips lingered on mine, causing flutters in my panties.

"I want you to know…I'm here for you," he said, giving me that look of his. "And I'll do anything…anything for you." I smiled.

"Thank you," I said, sincerely. My eyes were becoming far too heavy for me to keep open. I snuggled into Damon's body then closed them.

I woke up three hours later, tucked safely in my bed, with my leg throbbing and my ankle itching at the same time. I sat up in the bed then slowly swung my legs off the edge. The itching, I could deal with at the moment but the pain was kicking me in the ass. I've never been big on prescription drugs but this time I was willing to make an exception. I grabbed the pair of metal crutches propped against my nightstand then slowly hobbled my way out of my bedroom, down the hall to the kitchen. As I approached the kitchen I could hear the voices of my mother and father. I entered the kitchen and found the two of them sitting side by side at the kitchen table, holding hands and laughing and talking. I smiled. This is exactly how family is supposed to be. Minus- your twenty-seven year old daughter having to move back in because she broke her ankle when some mysterious psycho ran her off the road and the fact that your mother and father are dating but can't officially get remarried until your mother divorces her current husband, who just happens to be addicted to strippers and escorts, and who also slept with the mother of the church. Other than those tiny little details, this is how family is supposed to be! I was thinking way too hard. The more I thought about it the more my life was beginning to sound like a ghetto soap opera.

"How you feeling?" Daddy asked, getting up from his chair. He walked around the table then held out a chair for me.

"Okay," I said, sitting down. "Just a little pain."

"I'll get your pain pills." Mama said, before getting up.

"You need to eat something first." She said, opening the fridge. She pulled out a foil covered plate. She removed the foil then walked over to the microwave.

"Damon told me to tell you, he'll check on you later." She said, sliding the plate full of food into the microwave.

"Yeah, he said he had some business to take care of." Daddy added.

"How'd I get in bed?" I asked, already knowing the answer.

"Damon." They said, in unison. I looked from one to the other, they were both grinning. I laughed, shaking my head.

Mama brought the warm plate of baked chicken, greens, and corn over to the table then sat it down in front of me, along with the bottle of Percocet the doctor had prescribed for me. Daddy got up and poured me a glass of orange juice then came back and sat back down. I popped one of the pills in my mouth then took a long sip of my drink. I bowed my head, said grace then dug into the meal Mama had prepared.

"Your mother tells me, you knew the girl they found dead in her apartment." I had forgotten all about Sasha.

"Yeah, I met her right before she died." I said, in between bites.

"They got the autopsy back," Daddy said. "They say she died from a heroin overdose."

"Really?" I asked, staring at my father.

"She didn't take me as the junkie type." I said. I remembered how healthy and beautiful Sasha looked that night at the club.

"She may not have been an addict." Daddy said. "Maybe it was her first time and unfortunately it ended up being her last."

"It's sad," Mama shook her head. "Our children are killing themselves with that poison."

"It's even sadder that there are assholes out there selling it to them." Daddy's anger was etched all over his face. He was passionate when it came down to the war against drugs. My father served on the Huntsville Police force for ten years then owned his own private investigation firm for another eight before he finally retired and opened up his own auto repair shop. In the years he served on the force he saw the cause and effects of drug abuse in our community. That's why it's still hard for me to grasp the fact that he was once an alcoholic. There was a brief silence between the three of us.

"So how is everything at the restaurant?" Daddy asked.

"Business is good," I said, proudly. "So good that I may expand."

"Open up another Ambiance?" Mama asked. I had barely finished eating before she stood grabbed my plate and began walking to the sink.

"Lene, I'll get it." Daddy said, following her. "After all these years your mama still doesn't know how to rest." I agreed.

"So where are you looking to expand?" Daddy asked, while motioning for mama to sit down. She reluctantly obeyed then came and sat back down at the table.

"Maybe a second location here," I said. "Then eventually some other cities."

"That would be good." Mama said. "Maybe you should sit down and talk to Damon."

"I'm sure he could give you some great advice on expanding." I gave mama the evil eye. Lately it seemed like every conversation we had, she slowly involved Damon.

"Don't give me that look.," she said, rolling her eyes. "I was only making a suggestion."

"Charlene leave my baby alone." Daddy said, wiping his hands on a towel. "If she wants Damon's help she'll ask him for it." I licked my tongue out at my mother then grinned. She shook her head and smiled.

"How about the three of us have game night?" Daddy suggested, walking back over to the table. "I'll run out and get some butter pecan ice cream and root beer." He suggested.

"We'll make us a couple of floats and play a couple rounds of monopoly."

"Just like the old days." Mama said, smiling. Memories flooded my head of the three of us having game night when I was a child. I smiled.

"What do you say baby girl?" Daddy asked, putting his hands on my shoulders.

"You can be the top hat." I leaned back, looking up into my father's brown eyes.

"Okay." I said. Daddy leaned down then kissed me on my forehead.

"I'll be right back." He kissed Mama's cheek, and then grabbed his keys before heading out the front door.

Chapter 22

When I told Damon nothing was going to happen at my restaurant, I may have been speaking a little too soon. Before I could get out of bed good on Monday my cell began ringing. It was HPD calling to let me know that the alarm had been triggered at the Ambiance.

"There's been a break in," the female officer told me. I hung up the phone before she could finish her sentence, took a quick wash up then threw on a pair of cut-off shorts and a t-shirt. Mama and I hopped in her Jeep Grand Cherokee then punched it on our way to the city. When the two of us arrived at the Ambiance, I thought maybe the officer on the phone was mistaken. The inside of my restaurant looked fine.

"There doesn't appear to be any damage." The tall slender red head said to me. "Other than the back door was pried open." I exhaled. I could have the door fixed in a matter of minutes. If there had been other damages things might have been worse. I hobbled to the back to check my office, with Mama right behind me. I held my breath as I unlocked the door. Everything was just as I had left it. I walked around my desk then pulled out my chair.

"Mama can you help me?"

"Sure baby." She came over to where I was standing. I pointed to the rubber mat underneath my desk.

"Pull that back for me." Mama got down on her knees then pulled back the mat, revealing the safe I had hidden in the floor. The lock and door looked un-tampered with, but I wanted to be 100% positive. I gave Mama the combination, then she opened the safe for me. All of the bank statements and the cash I kept stashed inside were still there. After Mama and I left my office we walked thought the kitchen, the lounge and even the bathrooms.

"I don't understand." I said, looking at the officers. "They didn't take anything."

"Probably just some kids pulling pranks." One of the officers said. "We've had a lot of those lately."

"Why would they go through the trouble of possibly getting caught without at least tearing up the place?" I asked. I knew that I should have been grateful that things weren't worse but it wasn't adding up.

"Ms. Ellis, who knows what goes through the mind of someone who is breaking the law." The female officer looked annoyed with my questions but I didn't give a damn.

"Maybe they had a change of heart." Mama said.

"Maybe." I shook my thoughts off then called Overhead Door Company to come replace the back door. I chalked the entire incident up as bad luck. Little did I know my bad luck would continue to come.

*****

Two days later Amel called informing me of yet another problem at the restaurant.

"The men's bathroom is flooded," she said. "Water is everywhere."

"What do you mean everywhere?" I asked, praying that she would not say the dining area.

"The water ran out of the bathroom into the hall." She said. "The floor is covered with water and…"

"And what?"

"Feces."

"Tell me you're kidding!" The thought of shit floating in the hallway made me sick!

"We got most of it up but the odor is awful." Amel continued.

"Did you block off the area?" I asked.

"Yeah, but there is one more problem."

"What now? What is it?"

"The Health Department is here." The image of the Health Department shutting me down and the restaurant score card running all over the news made me want to scream.

"Has the inspector already seen the mess?"

"Not yet," Amel said quickly. "He's still in the kitchen."

"Okay, grab some deodorizer or something ASAP," I instructed. "And call Roto Rooter."

"I already did but the guy said it would be another thirty minutes."

"I'll be there as soon as I can." I said. "Just do what you can." I hung up before Amel could say another word. I was stranded at Mama's house with no transportation. Mama was gone to the florist to give the final approval on the flowers before the wedding and Daddy was out on the boat with Uncle Leroy. My next thought was Damon.

"Damon Whitmore."

"Damon I need a huge favor." I cut straight to the chase.

"Anything."

"There is a problem at the Ambiance and the health inspector is there." I began quickly. "Amel says there's water and shit floating around."

"As in human shi…"

"Yes," I cut him off. "And I'm sure if the inspector has his way I'm going to have to close for the day, plus I'll have to wait a month for another inspection and he'll give me a low score..,"

"Don't worry," Damon interrupted me.

"Did Amel call a plumber?"

"Yeah but it's going to be another thirty minutes."

"I'll see what I can do," He said. "I can meet you at the restaurant in about twenty minutes."

"That's the favor," I said. "I'm stranded."

"Where's your mom?"

"Out taking care of some things for Daddy's party."

"And Charles?"

"With Uncle Leroy.. .fishing."

"I'm only a few minutes from there," He said. "I can come by and get you."

"I'll be ready when you get here."

"I'm on my way."

It took Damon less than ten minutes to make it to my mother's house and after breaking the speed limit less than thirty minutes to get me to the Ambiance. The two of us walked in just as the health inspector was coming out the front entrance.

"You can't have customers here with only one working restroom." The familiar face said, handing me the inspection sheet.

"What about the places who have unisex bathrooms?" I asked, looking over the sheet. He had given the Ambiance a seventy, a failing score.

"They're called unisex because they're built for both men and women," he said, looking at me like I was crazy.

"Sir, the plumbers inside working on the problem." Damon interjected. After our phone call, Damon managed to get the plumbing company who handled his office to make an emergency visit by the restaurant.

"And what are your gentleman customer's going to use in the meantime?" the inspector asked.

"The employee restroom," I answered.

"The one in the back of the kitchen?" He asked, staring at me over his wire rim glasses.

"Yes."

"That would be cause for another violation," He said. "You

can't have your customers running in and out of your kitchen...it's unsanitary."

"And what about liability?" He asked. "What if one of them was to trip and fall?"

"Do you really want a possible civil suit on your hands?" Did I ask him to give me legal advice?

"Okay, I can close just for today but you can't give me a failing score," I pleaded.

"Do you know what that'll do to my image?"

"I'm sorry," he said. "You'll have a month to make the improvements and I'll be back."

"A month?" Damon asked.

"Yes, a month," he repeated himself.

"Maybe there's something we can work out." Damon said. The man looked from my head down to my low cut blouse that framed the slope of my breast.

"Like what?" He asked, smiling. If I wasn't on crutches I would have crossed my arms blocking his peep show. Damn freak! I don't know what he was thinking but sex was not an option.

"Maybe you and I can work something out," Damon said.

"Baby, why don't you give me and Mr.."

"Horatio," the inspector answered.

"Give me and Mr. Horatio a moment alone." Damon continued. I watched as the two men walked through the parking lot with their heads together engulfed in conversation. A few minutes later I watched as Horatio went over a new check list, and then handed it to Damon. Damon took the sheet then passed the man what appeared to be three crisp, one-hundred dollar bills.

"He said for you to keep your old rating posted until a different inspector comes." Damon said, handing me the new score sheet. I smiled at the bright red 94 on the page. My current posted score was a 100 so leaving that up was fine by me.

"Money talks," I said.

"Sometimes," Damon said. "It just depends on who's listening."

Chapter 23

After all the little incidents at the Ambiance, I finally decide to take Damon up on his offer and agreed to stay with him in the corporate suite until I had the cast taken off. He offered to get me my own suite but I didn't see any point in the two of us staying at the same hotel in different rooms besides, we would have ended up in the same bed either way. Damon catered to my every need and I do mean every. He gave me sponge baths being extra careful not to get my cast wet. He helped me get dressed and chauffeured me all over town like my name was Miss Daisy. I'll admit I was getting too spoiled for comfort. Damon was taking such good care of me that I hadn't thought of any other men. That was about to change.

"Hello." I answered my cell without checking the caller ID.

"What's up Ma?" Beau's voice was still smooth and sexy.

"How are you?"

"My dicks hard…so what does that tell you?"

"You miss me."

"You know it." I laughed lightly.

"Why haven't you called me?" He asked.

"I've had a lot going on."

"You ain't gotta lie to me, Ma," he said. "I know you weren't feeling me after our last conversation." I didn't deny it.

"It's not that I don't feel bad about what happened to ole girl," He said.

"I do have a heart."

"It's just that she got on a nigga's bad side....and that was the wrong thing to do."

"I'm a grudge able muthafucka." He said. His voice was soft but I was fully aware of the honesty in his words.

"I understand that." I said. "But there's a time and a place for everything."

"No doubt." He said. There was a pregnant pause between the two of us.

"So what do I have to do, to see you?" He finally asked.

I can't..."

"Don't make me beg Ma."

"It's not that," I said. "But I don't have a car right now."

"What's wrong with your ride?" He asked.

"I had an accident...it's totaled."

"Damn...you alright?" There was a hint of concern in his voice.

"Yeah but I broke my ankle."

"I can come to you." He said.

"Actually, I'm staying with a friend," I said, quickly.

"Well tell me how we can make something happen." He pleaded. "I need to feel you Ma." As much as I wanted to resist, I couldn't. My pussy had a mind of her own.

"Name the time and the place," I said.

"My place at eight."

"Okay."

I was clueless to how I was going to work it out but I had the will, so I knew there was a way.

Damon picked me up from work a little after five. I had my plan and my lie together before my butt settled in the passenger's side of his Mercedes.

"I'm going to go spend some time with 'Tay tonight."

"You two going out?"

"Yeah, one of the girls from the Hairtip is having a saucy ladies party." The lie rolled off my tongue like water.

"What's that?" He asked

"An adult toy party." Damon's face lit up like a tree on Christmas.

"Are you going to buy any toys?" He asked, grinning. "I may." I laughed.

"So you want me to drive you?" Why did he have to be so considerate?

"Shontay is going to drive." I said, quickly. I had already worked out the details with Shontay. She would pick me up from the hotel then drop me off at Beau's. There was no way I was going to let Damon drop me off at 'Tay's house. You never know when a brother might do a ride by. I'm not saying Damon is the type to follow a sista or check her whereabouts but you never know.

"Alright," he said.

"I can't believe you're using me as an alibi." Shontay complained. She arrived at the hotel at exactly seven-forty-five to pick me up.

"Why are you even doing this?" She asked.

"According to you Damon is all that a woman would want in a man."

"He is." I was wondering where she was going with the conversation.

"Okay, so why are you fucking with this guy, Beau?"

"Because he's good at what he does," I said.

"Why is everything about sex with you?" She asked. She sounded genuinely annoyed.

"When are you going to realize there's more to life?"

"Do you really want to spend the rest of your life alone?" She continued, before I could answer.

"I'm just not ready to be committed to one man." I said, looking over at her. "If and when I am…I will."

"It's not like you're getting any younger," she preached.

"You sound just like Mama and Aunt Rachel," I said, rolling my eyes.

"So what 'Tavia," she said. "They're right."

"I don't want to hear it Tay."

"Fine," she said. "But just think about this..."

"Maybe everything that's been happening to you is for a reason."

"Like what?" I asked.

"Maybe, God is trying to tell you something."

"God doesn't have to *try* and tell me anything." I said. "He just says it."

"Maybe he is and you're just too stubborn to listen."

"I could say the same about you." I said, sucking my teeth.

"What is that suppose to mean?"

"He's been showing you that Kenny is a dog, for how many years now?"

"But yet you're still clinging to his trifflin' ass." I said, folding my arms across my breast.

"Why is that?" I waited for her answer.

"I'm not clinging." She said. "I'm standing by him."

"No, you're getting walked over." I said, sarcastically.

"Call it what you want." She said. "At least I'm woman enough to try to work it out with my man."

"Oh, I'm woman enough," I said. "I'm just not that stupid!"

Even though I was pissed by Shontay's judging me, I immediately felt bad for what I said. I had never asked Shontay to lie for me, or do anything else for me. So I knew her frustration was channeling from someplace else, probably from something that had happened with her and Kenny.

We rode in silence until she pulled up in front of Beau's house.

"Call me when you're ready." She said, not looking at me.

"I can call a cab." I said, opening the passenger's side door.

"I brought you and I'll pick you up."

"Thanks." I maneuvered my way out of the car, then balanced myself on the crutches.

"Octavia."

"Yeah?"

"It's just that you have so much going for yourself," She said, leaning over looking at me. "I just think it's sad that you don't want to share that with someone."

"You really think I got it going on?" I teased, cocking my head to one side.

"Yeah, trick," she laughed.

"Thanks, girl." I smiled. "But so do you…I just wish you knew." I shut the door to the car, then blew her a kiss.

"I'll call you when I'm ready."

Beau and I didn't waste any time with conversation. The moment I walked through his front door, we were all over each other, kissing and exploring one another's bodies. He removed my fitted t-shirt and denim shorts at his door then carried me off to his Master suite.

Inside his bedroom he had burning candles, sitting on small mirrors all around the room and R Kelly's "Imagine That", playing in the stereo. He re-acquainted himself with every inch of my body, by rubbing my skin with KY warming massage oil. Afterwards, he took each of my fingers in his mouth and licked, then sucked them teasingly. By the time he rolled the lubricated condom over his dick and entered me, I was halfway to ecstasy. My pussy was warm, wet, and purring. Beau sucked on my chocolate nipples, while he moved slowly inside me. In the beginning his rhythm was slightly off. At first, it was difficult for him to position himself on top of me; my cast kept getting in the way, but then he lifted my legs so my ankles were resting on his shoulders and from then on, the two of us were straight fiickin'. He pushed his dick in and out of my pussy, each time stopping just before he hit my g-spot. Finally, he drove his head into my hot spot, setting of a chain reaction. One heat wave of pleasure followed by another shook my body. I came long and hard. I kissed his lips then sucked on his tongue, savoring its warmth and wetness.

"I love this phat pussy Ma." He moaned, in my ear.

"This is my pussy... my pussy."

"My pussy…" he chanted over and over again.

"Awww…fuck!" He yelled. "I'm cummmminng…" I felt him. I

held him inside my walls until his orgasm was complete.

Beau climbed off me then sat on the edge of the bed, trying to catch his breath. He took a deep breath in through his nose then out through his mouth.

"Damn you're good," he said, looking over at me. I gave him a small smile, before easing off the bed.

"Do you mind if I use your bathroom?"

"Naw, not at all."

"The towels are on the shelf by the sink," he said. "There's soap in the top drawer."

"Thanks." I grabbed my purse then slipped inside the bathroom. I turned on the water in the sink then called Shontay to tell her I was ready for her to pick me up. After taking a quick wash up, I walked back into the bedroom to get dressed. Beau was sitting on the sofa with a lit blunt in between his fingers. He took a long pull, inhaling slowly, held his breath then allowed the smoke to bellow out through his mouth. I moved across the room then sat down on the love seat facing him.

"You want me to fix you a drink?"

"No thanks," I said. "I'm fine."

"How many other niggas are you fucking?" His question caught me completely off guard.

"Why?"

"I just wanna know." He said, looking at me strangely.

"Does it matter?"

He took another pull before putting the half smoked blunt out in the ashtray sitting on the coffee table.

"When I'm gettin' something...I want to be the only one gettin' it." He said, seriously.

"The shit you do to me, I don't want you doin' it to nobody else."

"We both agreed to keep this strictly sexual." I said, looking him in the eyes.

"I don't care how many women you have," I said. "As long as I'm protected."

"I'm not like the rest of those punks you've been dealing with," He said, leaning forward on the sofa. "I'm a grown ass man."

"And I don't share." He said. Before I could respond my cell phone rang.

"Hello"

"I'm outside." I had never been so relieved in my life to hear Shon-tay's voice.

"I'm on my way out." I closed my phone then dropped it down in my purse. I put my purse on my shoulder then grabbed my crutches.

"My ride is here." I said, standing.

I walked to the front door with Beau trailing behind me. I opened the door then turned around to look at Beau.

"I had a good time tonight." I said, honestly. "But this was our last." I looked him in the eyes to gauge his reaction. He laughed.

"Whateva, Ma." I didn't respond. I moved as fast as those damn crutches would allow, down the driveway to Shontay's car. Shontay got out, helped me in, then hopped back in on the driver's side.

"I take it you had a good time," she said, pulling away from the curb.

"I did," I said.

"I guess if you're going to creep…it should be worth it." I didn't respond to her statement, instead I looked out the window thinking to myself. I had no intention of ever creepin' with Beau again. Our situation had run its course. I guess it's true what they say: all good things truly must come to an end.

"I thought you were going to buy some toys." Damon asked, after I made it back to the hotel.

"I didn't see anything I liked." I lied. Lately, I was telling more lies than I had in my entire life. It was an ongoing cycle. One lie led to another one then to another then to one more.

"Oh." He looked somewhat disappointed. I laughed.

"You are a freak."

"You like it.," he said, pulling me down on the sofa on top of him.

"I do…I really do."

He gave me a quick peck on the lips then rubbed his nose against my neck, smelling my hair.

"Have you been smoking?" He asked, pulling away then looking at me.

"No, why?"

"Your hair smells like smoke," he said, sniffing me again. "Like weed."

"You know how girl's night out can get," I said, sweetly. "A couple of the girl's were smoking in the bathroom.

"I had to pee…I ended up walking right in after they had left."

"Oh, okay." He looked a little suspicious but I didn't give a damn.

"Why don't the two of us take a nice hot bath?" He suggested.

"I'll even wash your hair." What I really wanted was to go to bed. Shit, I was tired! Then I thought about all the lies I had told him. *Damn!*

"I'll wait here while you get the water ready."

Chapter 24

Damon and I decided to drive to Memphis for the weekend. We agreed that we needed a change of scenery. The two of us were worn out mentally. I, from everything that had happened in the past few weeks and he, from the deals he had going on with Nomad and Gold Mortgage.

The two of us were standing on the deck of the Creole Queen enjoying a midnight cruise. Wrapping his arm around my shoulder, Damon kissed my cheek softly. I settled into his arm and continued to stare at the half moon in the sky above us. The stars surrounding the moon sparkled like tiny diamonds.

"I have something to tell you," he whispered.

Wrapping both arms around his waist I turned to face him. Looking me in the eyes he bit his bottom lip nervously.

"I don't know how to tell you this," he said.

In the months Damon and I had been kicking it I had dismissed the notion that he had something to hide. I had slowly accepted that maybe just maybe he was one in a million. Well, I have a feeling reality is about to bite me in the damn ass. I bet you he has a wife and crumb snatchers tucked away back home in Atlanta and I'm willing to bet, Wifey told him to get his shit together. I took a deep breath and said nothing.

"I didn't intend for this to happen," he said.

"What is it, Damon," I asked. I was starting to get a little pissed. The man brought me all the way to Memphis to confess. He could have done this back in Alabama.

Swallowing he ran his fingertips down my cheek. "Octavia, I'm in love with you," he said.

"What?" I asked. I wanted to make sure I heard him correctly.

"I am in love with you," he repeated himself.

I stood there looking into the eyes of one of the finest men I had ever touched and I smiled. I don't know if I smiled because I was relieved he didn't have a wife and kids or if it was because he had just professed his feelings for me. Either way I could feel myself smiling. When he saw my expression he began to smile too.

"I can't get you out of my mind," he said. "I want to make you happy."

Kissing my forehead lightly he continued," I love you and if you give me the chance I'll do everything I can to prove it to you."

He took my face in his hands and he kissed me slowly and gently. I felt my heart flutter. Pulling back he kept his hands on my face. "Will you give me the chance?" He asked.

I thought about my track record with men. Even if I had been ready for a relationship most of the men I've known still had some type of issue. Baby Mama Drama! Bad credit! Lazy! Little dicks! No ambitions! There was always something. Damon didn't fit into any of those categories, but yet if he was asking for the chance to prove his love for me, I knew that he would be expecting a commitment in return. I wasn't ready for that.

"Damon, what exactly are you asking me?"

"I want us to be together," he said. "Exclusively."

"I want to know that you want me the same way I want you." He said. I looked away without saying a word. I wanted Damon but I wasn't completely sure it was on the same level he claimed to want me.

"You don't feel the same."

I could hear the disappointment in his voice. For the first time in my life I felt bad for not being willing to give a man my heart. "I'm just not ready…"

"I understand," he said, cutting me off. "But you will be and when you are I'm going to be right here waiting." He stroked my cheek with his fingertip then pulled me into his arms.

"I'm not going anywhere," he said.

Damon acted like he was cool with me not wanting to commit to him but I could tell from the look in his eyes that he was not. Mama had warned me that he was not the type to settle for just sex and I knew in my heart she was right. I could have and should have just let him go, walked away from him, but I couldn't. It was like there was some force pulling me to him. I could say that it was selfishness. I didn't want to give him what he needed but I didn't want to let him go.

Chapter 25

It only took six weeks for the gash on my leg to heal and for my cast to be removed but for me it seemed like forever. I was ecstatic to see that aside from a small scar from my cut, my leg looked exactly as it had before the accident.

Alfa paid my car off but I had yet to start looking for another one. Mama offered to let me drive her car, rather than me having to go through the trouble of paying for a rental. I accepted her offer, even though Damon assured me that he was fine taking me from A to B. The day my cast came off, I packed my overnight bags and told him I was going home.

"You don't have to leave," He said. "I love taking care of you."

"Thank you for everything," I said, sweetly. "But I need to go back to my own place." The truth was that I felt like I was using him. He was giving me more than I had ever allowed any other man to give me, but I wasn't giving him what he needed in return. My conscience was eating me up! Sexually, I'm all about my own needs but I'm far, far from being a gold digger.

I woke up at three a.m. to the sound of the wireless remote on Mama's keychain beeping. I opened my front door and heard her car alarm screaming. After throwing on a pair of sweats and some tennis shoes I ran downstairs to check on her Jeep. Walking from the driver's side to the passenger's side I inspected all the windows and doors. Kicking the tires I looked for signs that they had been tampered with. All of them looked fine.

Running my fingers through my hair I ran back upstairs to my apartment. Locking the door behind me I kicked my shoes across the living room floor. All the lights were off in my apartment. I stumbled around until I finally found the lamp sitting on one of my end tables. Reaching for the switch I felt a sharp pain go from the top of my head to my neck. Someone was pulling my hair. Screaming I struggled to break free. They grabbed me by my neck then placed a gloved hand over my mouth. My heart was beating like crazy as I fought to break loose.

Thump!

I heard the end table and lamp hit the floor. I was next.

My attacker threw me on the floor and slammed both of my arms down above my head. My wrists were burning from the pressure being applied to them. Raising my knees I kicked wildly. I moved my head from side to side attempting to get their hand off of my mouth. But the intruder was too strong. It was at that moment that I knew it had to be a man. My heart continued to pound inside my chest like a drum as I struggled to get up. I was screaming but my screams sounded more like whimpers under his hand. He was on top of me in between my legs. *He's going to rape me! Please God, don't let him rape me! Please don't let him kill me... please!* He applied more pressure to my arms, pressing them harder against the floor. So much pressure my wrist felt like they were going to snap. He spread my legs with his then ripped my pants down. I tried to focus my eyes in the darkness but there was no use I couldn't see a thing. I heard him unzip his pants and that's when I knew it was now or possibly never. I stopped struggling underneath him and his body weight lightened.

"That's right," He moaned. His voice was distorted but it sounded familiar to me.

"Give me this pussy." *Beau?* My adrenaline began to pump through my body like the blood flowing through my veins. I fought with all my strength, kicking until I finally landed one good blow to his dick.

"Aughhh!" He hollered, falling off me. I scrambled trying to get up on my feet but he managed to find my ankle, then pulled me back towards him.

"Help me!" I felt across the floor for something, anything that I could use in my battle. My hand landed on the base of the lamp. I quickly flipped over on my back and without any sense of direction; I swung but managed to hit my target.

"You bitch!" He screamed, releasing my leg. I struggled to get up, stumbling over the table until I was finally on my feet. I ran, bumping into the wall, until I finally reached my bedroom. I didn't waste any time trying to find the light switch. I could hear him in the other room struggling to get up. I dropped to the side of the bed, closest to the door and quickly felt underneath the bed. I found the metal box I kept hidden for safe keeping and quickly pulled it out. I popped the latches open, then pulled out the birthday gift Daddy had given me for my twenty-first birthday, a chrome .9mm. I steadied my hand then slipped the safety off. I heard my intruder hit the doorway to my bedroom. I focused in the darkness then squeeze the trigger. The loud clap from the shot echoed in my ears as the spark glowed like a tiny firecracker.

"Augh!" He screamed. My bedroom door cracked as he fell into it. I cocked my gun allowing another bullet to fall into the chamber. I aimed ready to fire again. I didn't have to. I heard him stumble, then fall until finally light came into the living room as he opened the front door. I sat with my back against the bed and my weapon clutched to my chest, my heart pounding fiercely.

Moments later the police arrived. One of my neighbors had called them reporting gun shots coming from my apartment. I was shaken up but I managed to sit through their questioning. I called Mama and despite my protesting, she came over with Daddy right by her side.

"Ms. Ellis you're sure you didn't see anything?" Officer Todd asked me again. I looked at the young uniform officer like he was stupid. *What part of, it was dark, doesn't this ass understand?*

"Didn't you hear her say the lights were off?" Mama snapped. She sat on the couch with her arms wrapped around my shoulder.

"Yes, ma'am but this is just basic questioning." Officer Todd explained. Mama sucked her teeth then looked across the room at Daddy.

"Calm down Charlene." Daddy said, coolly.

"Whoever he was, you grazed him." Brown said. Officer Brown was one of three other officers who had responded with Todd. He stood in my bedroom doorway staring at the bullet lodged in the wall. There were tiny blood splatters surrounding the hole and across the wall. I looked at Daddy, and he was smiling proudly. I knew if he had his way I would have killed my intruder. Daddy was an ex-cop but he was a father first.

"Ma'am is your gun registered?" Todd asked me.

"Of course it is." Daddy finally interjected.

"Just basic qu…"

"I know all about basic questioning." Daddy said, walking across the floor. "I served on the force."

"Right along with Chief Rowland." Daddy continued. "Whom I'm sure would be real happy to know that you're in here badgering his goddaughter rather than out there looking for the bastard who attempted to rape her." *Goddaughter?* I didn't have a Godfather.

"By the way tell Steve that I said we're still on for golf on Friday." Daddy said, crossing his arms. Daddy was pulling rank and it worked.

"I'm sure we've got enough information." Todd said, quickly.

"We'll be in touch."

"Are you sure you're okay?" Damon asked, holding me in his arms.

After the police left my apartment, Mama insisted that I come home with her. I didn't want to be alone but I also didn't want to endure the questions I knew she and Daddy had for me. We all agreed that the car alarm had been intentionally set off to get me out of my apartment. Not only did I take the bait but I left my front door wide open. Careless! Daddy asked if I had any idea of who might want to hurt me. I immediately thought of Beau but I lied and told Daddy that I couldn't think of anyone.

After I packed a few clothes, I had my parent's drop me off at the hotel. I didn't bother to call him before I came; I just took the chance that he might be alone. He opened the door and smiled at the sight of me. I had taken the right one! I brought along the cuff links, I had yet to give to him. To be honest, I had contemplated several times returning them to the store but I bought them with him in mind, therefore I wanted him to have them. I was just waiting for the right time.

"I'm fine," I said, looking at the bruises on my wrist.

"I want you to move back in here with me for awhile," Damon said, kissing my forehead.

"Damon you barely have room for yourself here."

"You're right," he said, pulling me onto his lap," That's why I think it's time I look for a permanent place to live."

"Permanent?"

"Yeah," he said," I've invested too much time in the new office to let someone else take over."

"What about your home in Atlanta?"

"I'll work something out," He said," Besides you know what they say."

"What's that?" I asked.

Wrapping his arms around my waist he pulled me closer, "Home is where the heart is."

"And where is your heart?"

My heart is with you."

"How do you know, Damon?"

"When I opened the door and you told me someone attacked you," He said, his eyes watering. "All I could think about was what if he hurt you or what if he had done more." He took both of my wrists in his hands and softly kissed the black bruises on each one at a time.

"He didn't," I whispered, watching the tears fall from his eyes.

"I know but I keep thinking "What if," He continued,"I went my whole life without you and now that you're here, I never want to let you go."

I searched his eyes and expression to find some sign of insincerity. I couldn't find one. I then replayed the scene at my apartment in my head. What if that man had raped me? What if he had taken my life? It's amazing how your life can change in an instant for the better or for the worse.

'Maybe God's trying to tell you something. "Shontay's words echoed in my mind.

Brushing his tears away with my fingertips, I paused to gather my words.

"Damon until I met you," I began. " I never let a man get close enough to know me. Never let a man stay the night and definitely did not let one meet my family."

"That's why your Aunt Rachel thought you were gay." We both laughed when he said that.

"Yeah," I smiled," That and plus Aunt Rachel is full of shit." I still could not believe she told Uncle Leroy I was a lesbian.

"I've never wanted to be in a relationship," I said, watching him. " Then I met you and everything just seemed to fall in place. I still think you may be too good to be true."

"I'm the real thing."

Running my fingers across his smooth head I said sincerely," I sure hope so because I want to try and make us work. I'm willing to try if you can be patient with me."

"I can," he smiled." And I promise I will." I took a deep breath then exhaled. I had made the first step towards commitment and I was nervous as hell.

Smiling I wrapped my arms around him.

"I have something for you." I said, getting up to get my bag.

"What is it?"

"You'll see." I pulled the velvet box from under my clothes, then handed it to Damon.

"I bought these a little while ago," I said. "I was waiting till the right time to give them to you." He opened the box and smiled when saw the diamond studs.

"I love them!" He said, kissing my cheek. "Thank you baby."

"You're welcome." I said, proudly.

"What are they for?" Damon asked, pulling me into his lap.

"Just to say thank you for everything." I said, sincerely.

"You don't have to thank me." He said. "Just love me." We held each other for what seemed like forever. Finally Damon picked me up and carried me to the bathroom. We showered together then we crawled into bed soaking wet.

We held each other in silence. As the sun came up I closed my eyes and slowly fell asleep, praying to God that I was doing the right thing.

After all my drama Mama spoke of postponing the wedding.

"Just until the police get a lead on the person who attacked you," she said.

"You're not canceling the wedding Mama." I had told her. It had been two weeks since the incident at my apartment and in my mind it was an open and shut case. I wasn't going to put my life on hold for the psycho who was obviously out to get me nor was I going to allow my parent's to put off their life together any longer.

The wind blew lightly as I walked my mother down a path of white and red rose petals. She looked breathtaking, and indescribably beautiful in her gold and ivory chiffon off the shoulder gown. Marcella had created a masterpiece of a dress complete with a four foot pearl and sequined train. As we approached the center of the rose garden, I smiled at my father. He looked so handsome in his cream tuxedo. He stood in between Pastor Davis and Damon watching us. Shontay stood opposite of them wearing an ivory sleeveless A-line gown. Marcella made both of our dresses. The only difference between the two was that mine was gold with a slit that teasingly showed my thigh.

My cousin, Darlene's voice rang out through the garden as she sang Brian McKnight's *"Still in Love with You."* That's one thing that girl can do. Sing. That and make babies.

Holding a rose bouquet with her left hand, Mama held my hand tightly with her right hand. When we reached the center of the garden I placed her hand in my father's," I love you both," I said, sincerely.

"We love you too," they said, almost in unison.

Among a garden of red roses and our family and friends, my parent's exchanged their vows.

"Your parents are so happy."

Damon and I swayed to Anita Baker's *Sweet Love* at my parent's reception. My parents were dancing beside us on the dance floor. The two of them were smiling and gazing into each other eyes.

"They deserve it," I smiled." This has been a wonderful day."

"Thank you for sharing it with me," Damon said, pulling me closer.

Laying my head on his shoulder I closed my eyes. The day had been perfect in every way. I was happy. My parents were happy. Opening my eyes I watched Shontay and Kenny slow dancing. Looking at me Shontay gave me a huge smile. Even my best friend was happy.

"May I cut in?" Daddy was standing besides us with his arms open.

"Only if I can dance with the beautiful bride," Damon told him.

Smiling, Daddy said," Only because you're my best man."

Kissing my cheek, Damon let me go. Smiling at my Daddy I extended my hand.

"Hey, baby girl," Daddy smiled, taking my hand in his.

"Hi, birthday boy."

Scar changed up the music and put on the old school track "My Girl" by the Temptations.

"You look beautiful," Daddy said, smiling.

"And you make a handsome groom," I smiled, looking at him.

"I can't believe that I just got remarried."

"Were you surprised?"

"Surprised," He said his eyes wide. "I was blown away."

That was a part of the plan. Daddy thought he and Mama were meeting Damon and me for a picnic lunch for his birthday. Damon and I had a limo pick the two of them up as a part of Daddy's birthday gift. When they arrived at the Botanical Gardens, Damon and I were waiting and dressed for the ceremony. When they stepped out of the limo, Mama asked Daddy to marry her.

"I'll never forget the look on your face when Mama asked you to marry her," I told him.

"I wasn't expecting it," He laughed.

"You looked so terrified I thought you might say no."

Daddy shook his head then laughed." It took me a minute to absorb everything but there was no way I was going to say no," He said.

Looking across the dance floor Daddy nodded at Uncle Leroy and Aunt Rachel. "How did you get those two to keep the secret?" He asked.

"They didn't know," I informed him. "We didn't want to take any chances on them blabbing their big mouths. So we told them we entered Darlene in a talent search for American Idol."

Laughing Daddy shook his head. "Is that why she kept singing to the videographer?" He asked.

"Yes, Sir."

We both laughed. Daddy kissed me on my forehead then stared at me. "I love you Octavia," He said.

"I love you Daddy," I said, fighting back tears," And I'm sorry."

Frowning, Daddy asked, "For what?"

"For being mad with you for so long," I said, looking down at my feet. "I'm the one that should apologize," He said. "For not being honest with you."

Looking up at him I asked," Why didn't you tell me you had a problem?"

"A father is suppose to be strong," He said, his voice shaky." I was fighting a demon that made me too weak. I couldn't let you see me like that. I had too much pride baby."

"Daddy your human, not Superman."

"Baby girl, that's just it," He said. " In his daughter's eyes a man should always look like a hero."

Smiling I said," Daddy you are a hero. You fought your own personal demon and you won."

Smiling he kissed my forehead again. "Thank you, baby girl."

I watched Damon and Mama talking and laughing as they danced.

"You love him?" Daddy asked me, watching them too.

Smiling I confessed," Yes, Daddy I do."

"You want me to run a background check on him? He asked, seriously.

"No, Daddy" I laughed. "I got this one."

"Besides, I'm sure you've already got the results from the first check."

"You know me so well baby girl." He said, smiling.

"Damon's a good guy," He said. "And if you love him...you should tell him."

Looking my father in his eyes I said sincerely," I will."

"Don't let other people's mistakes keep you from the love you deserve."

Hugging my father I let what he said sink in. Daddy was right, I let fear paralyze me for too long. What I thought had been my own personal rules had really been fear. Fear of loving a man. Fear of having my heartbroken. Fear. Fear. Fear.

Damon and I stood outside the Ambiance waving goodbye to my parents. They were headed for the airport. We had given them a seven day honeymoon to Anchorage, Alaska. Once the limo was out of sight, I turned to Damon. Adjusting his tie I licked my lips. He looked phenomenally sexy in his black tuxedo. He accentuated his look with the diamond links I gave him.

"Baby, you are so fine," I purred. Running his fingers across my cheek he scanned my body from head to toe.

"Not half as fine as you," He said. " You are wearing that dress."

Spinning around on my high heels I put my hand on my hip. With my back to him I looked over my shoulder. "You like?" I asked, batting my eyes.

"I love," he smiled. "I love."

Wrapping his arms around my waist Damon hugged me from behind. Slowly grinding up against his crotch I moaned. Turning around, I faced him. Wrapping my arms around his neck I gave him a slow passionate kiss.

"Damon," I whispered, pulling away.

"Yes baby?"

"I love you."

Stepping back he looked at me closely," You love me?" He asked, as if he hadn't heard me correctly.

Smiling I nodded my head," I love you," I said.

"I love you too," he smiled.

I breathed a sigh of relief," There's only one thing that can make this day more perfect," I said.

"Whatever it is, just say it and it's done."

"The two of us," I said sweetly," Making love."

Taking me in his arms Damon kissed me. "Your wish is my command."

Chapter 27

Falling in love should be a wonderful experience when you're falling in love with an extraordinary man who is already in love with you. But when you're looking over your shoulder because your psycho, pot head, ex-fuck friend won't leave you alone, it's somewhat hard to enjoy the process.

Beau was becoming the thorn that pierced my ass. One minute he was calling me leaving me explicit messages on my voicemail of how he wants to be with me and fuck me. The next minute he was sending me text messages calling me a bitch or a trifling slut because I was avoiding his calls. It wasn't like I hadn't explained to him what I was trying to do with my life. I politely sat down with him and told him that I was seeing someone and that I was in love with that someone. He told me he understood and that it was fun while it lasted. We even had one last good fuck as a parting gift! Then not even five days later he was trippin'. The brother had me convinced that he had multiple personalities. Dealing with his compulsive phone calls and trying to keep Damon from finding out about them was driving me crazy. Plus I wasn't 100% sure that Beau wasn't behind the incident that occurred at my apartment. I finally decided I had to do something.

Shontay told me about filing a harassment communication warrant. She and Kenny had filed one a year ago on one of his flings;

some broad who kept calling their house playing on the phone. Shontay told me after the police picked her up and she had to pay a $5,000 fine, she finally stopped calling. I figured I should give it a try.

I called the restaurant and let Amel know I wouldn't be in then headed downtown to the fourth precinct to speak with Officer Donald Jones.

Officer Jones was a slim, balding brother who appeared to be in his late forties. When I explained my situation he was nice and told me that hundreds of men and women deal with the same thing I was going through every day. After showing him my call log on my cell phone and the text messages, a warrant was issued for Beau's arrest. Officer Jones explained to me that once Beau was picked up he would be processed then bail would be set and he would be given a date to appear in court. He told me that Beau would probably plead guilty and end up with a fine but more than likely after having to deal with the court system he would adhere to the restraining order the judge would issue and cease from contacting me.

I filed the complaint at eight a.m.. Officer Jones called me at one-thirty p.m. to let me know Beau had been picked up. I hoped that he would finally get the message and leave me alone.

It had been weeks since I slept in my own apartment or bed. After Damon volunteered to have the wall repaired, everything was back in order and I finally decided it was time for me to go home. When I did, I asked Damon to come with me. After cohabiting with Damon I had grown accustom to him lying next to me. Damon accepted my invitation without any hesitation and we were officially living together. I wanted Damon to know that I appreciated him and that he wasn't the only one committed to our relationship. I wanted him to have more than just his clothes at our place so I decided to have some of his personal belongings sent from Atlanta. He mentioned to me that he had a maid named Christina who came every Tuesday to clean. With today being Tuesday I hoped I could catch her at Damon's house. I wanted Damon to be surprised so I waited until he left for work to give Christina a call. Damon had given me his home number last time he went to Atlanta for a meeting just in case I couldn't reach him on his cell phone.

The phone rang three times until a woman answered. "Hello," She said.

"Is this the Whitmore residence?" I asked.

"Yes," she said. "And this is Mrs. Whitmore."

Come Again?

Placing my hand on my hip I asked with attitude," Did you say Mrs. Whitmore?"

"That's correct," She said. She sounded like one of those rich stuckup sistas.

"Mrs. Damon Whitmore?" I asked.

"That is correct," she said, sounding annoyed," This is Mrs. Damon Whitmore."

"And who are you?" She asked.

I hope I'm dreaming because if I am actually having this conversation with this woman I am going to snap to the damn crazy when Damon gets home. After everything he's married? And to add insult to injury she sounds like one of those high maintenance bitches who can't give decent head! I can't believe this. I bet you he has some plaid skirt and khaki pants wearing, boarding school attending, spoiled badass kids too. I paced back and forth across my living room floor.

"Hello," she said." I asked who was calling."

"This is Octavia," I snapped.

"Octavia?"

"That's right," I said," Oc-ta-via."

"Octavia," Her voice softened. "I have heard so much about you."

I stopped pacing and looked at the phone. Don't tell me they're one of those married couples who likes to swing. I'm freaky but not that freaky.

"Octavia…"

"I'm still here," I said.

"Darling this is Ilene."

Oh shit… It's his mother!

"Ilene," I said.

"Yes darling. Damon's mother."

"Mrs. Whitmore I am so sorry," I said, embarrassed. I was tempted to hang up the phone and pretend the whole thing never happened but there was no way I could convince Damon that his mother was going crazy and that I had never called. I was willing to try but I was almost positive Damon had caller ID so either way I was busted.

Laughing lightly she said," I understand, darling."

"It's just that when you said Mrs. Whitmore I."

"No need to explain," She cut me off. "You probably thought I was wifey."

I couldn't deny it, "Yes Ma'am," I said.

"Don't worry darling," She chuckled." There is currently only one Mrs. Whitmore in this family and that's me."

Letting out a light laugh I tried to regain my composure, "What about little Damon's or Damonettas?" I asked. "Any of those running around?"

Laughing loudly she said, "Excuse my French but hell naw." That made me laugh so hard tears started coming from my eyes.

"Damonettas," she said. "Darling the day I allow a granddaughter of mine to be called Damonetta is the day I stop wearing Jimmy Choo shoes and Vera Wang dresses." I laughed.

"And on that day there better be some mourning," She said." Because obviously I'll be dead."

Plopping down on my sofa I laughed again," Mrs. Whitmore you are too much."

"Thank you, darling," she said. "And please call me Ilene."

"How are you Ilene?"

"Wonderful and you?"

"I'm fine," I laughed.

"How is my baby?"

"Damon is great," I said, smiling. " Actually he's the reason I was calling Christina."

"I let Christina have the rest of the day off," She said. "Was there something I could help you with?"

"I think you can," I said. "I wanted to have some of Damon's family pictures and personal items sent here."

"How sweet of you."

I didn't know how much Damon had told her so I decided it would be best if I didn't mention that the two of us were living together.

"Damon told me the two of you were living together," She said.

"He did?"

"Yes and his father and I think it's great," She said. "You never really know a person until you live with them."

"I don't want you to think I do this often," I said. "Damon is the first man I've ever lived with."

"Darling I believe you," She said. "And just for the record, this is the first time for Damon too."

I hadn't thought to ask him how many women he had lived with, in the past. It just never came up but now hearing from his mother that I was the first I felt extremely special. I talked with Ilene for over an hour. Damon had told her everything he knew about me. Ilene turned out to be a really nice woman. She told me she would over night some of Damon's favorite things to me. Before I could hang up she also made me promise I would come to visit as soon as I had the chance.

"Oh Octavia darling," She said.

"Yes, Ma'am?"

"Don't break my baby's heart."

"Yes, Ma'am."

The next day I received the package Ilene promised me. She sent a photo album full of pictures along with awards Damon had received. She also sent a black leather recliner that she said was Damon's favorite chair. The recliner had a few nicks and peels in the leather and stood out like a bad seed among my furniture but I didn't care. Damon explained it belong to his grandfather, Bryant.

It meant a lot to him therefore it meant a lot to me. When I saw the expression on Damon's face when he saw all of his things I knew sacrificing my space was worth it. He told me no other woman had ever done anything that nice for him. He hugged and kissed me for what seemed like a hundred times. Then we made love right there on his grandfather's raggedy ass recliner.

Chapter 28

Settling in the passenger's seat of Damon's Mercedes, I adjusted the blindfold that was covering my eyes.

"No peeking!"

"I'm not," I whined, impatiently.

Earlier that day he called me at the Ambiance to tell me he was coming by to pick me up. When I asked where we we're going he told me it was a surprise. Like a kid on Christmas Eve I was so anxious I thought I was going to bust.

"I spoke with Mama today," he said.

"My Mama or your Mama?"

"Both actually," he laughed.

"How is Ilene?" I asked.

"Fine. She made me promise to bring you to Atlanta next weekend."

"I can't wait to meet her," I said, honestly.

"She keeps saying the same thing."

Smiling, I laid my head back against the headrest. "Mama didn't mention she talked to you today," I said, remembering my conversation with my mother.

"She didn't?" He asked.

"Nope."

"It probably slipped her mind," he suggested.

"Probably," I agreed." Every since she and Daddy returned from Anchorage they've been conjoined at the lips."

Laughing, Damon said," They are so in love."

"Did they tell you they're going to sell the house?" I asked.

"Yeah," he said, seriously." I was surprised. Your Mama loves that house."

"I know but she loves Daddy more."

On their honeymoon Daddy convinced Mama to put her house on the market. Daddy owned a beautiful ranch home of his own. It was smaller than Mama's but it sat on six beautiful, well kept acres of land. Daddy got Mama to agree when he told her it was going to be hard being married and living in two different houses. Daddy said there was no way he was going to live in another man's home. It didn't take Mama long to realize Daddy was not bullshitting. So as soon as their feet struck Alabama ground she contacted a realtor.

Damon made a left turn and then stopped. I heard his driver's side window go down. I heard him pressing some numbers on what sounded like a key pad, and then heard what sounded like a gate moving. He waited a few seconds then the car started moving again. We went a few feet then the car stopped. I heard him shift into park then cut the engine off.

I unfastened my seatbelt. "Can I take this off now?" I asked, touching the blindfold.

"Not yet," He said.

Exhaling loudly I crossed my arms across my chest to indicate how impatient I was. I listened as Damon got out of the car. Within seconds I heard the passenger side door open. Damon held my hand as I stepped out of the car.

"Where are we?" I asked, anxious.

"You'll see."

We took a few steps forward and then Damon swooped me up in his arms.

"Um, you smell good," I whispered, kissing his ear lobe.

"You feel good," He said, moving one hand down to cup my ass.

He held me tight as he took steps up. I counted in my head a total of five.

"Hold on," He told me.

Doing as he said, I locked my arms around his neck. I heard him fumble with some keys and then a door opened. Damon took a step then we were no longer outside. I heard the door click shut and then he put me down.

"You can look now," He said.

I anxiously slid the blindfold over my eyes and off my head. I sighed as I looked around me. We were standing in the marble floored entry way of a huge house.

"Damon?"

"Not a word," He said. "Until you've seen every room."

Damon led me through every room of the two story mansion. I loved every inch of it! Everything about the home was beautiful, from the crystal chandlers to the winding maple staircase. The first floor included a state of the art, fully equipped kitchen with a breakfast bar and all white cabinets and appliances. There was a large family room with a stone fireplace and a bay window with a window seat built for two. Outside of the family room there was a full bath that adjoined the family room and the study. The sunken den included a sixty inch high definition TV that lowered from the ceiling and a theater surround sound system.

The winding staircase led to the second floor, which housed five bedrooms and six full baths. When Damon led me to the Master Suite my bottom lipped popped open. The Master bedroom was as big as our living room and bedroom put together. There were French doors that led out to a balcony that overlooked the manicured lawns. Two huge walk in closets with electric rotating racks and a full size bathroom that included his and hers sinks surrounded by marble counter tops. Plus a shower that could hold up to six people with a built in shower seat and an in-floor whirlpool bath tub.

After I practically drooled over every square foot of the house, Damon took me outside and showed me the swimming pool with a disappearing edge and the grotto with a built-in Jacuzzi.

The house even had a five-car detached garage and a guest house. All of it was wired with a full security system, including cameras.

"So what do you think?" Damon asked.

"Unbelievable."

"Do you really like it?"

Nodding my head I allowed my silence to be my answer.

"Good," He said, smiling. "Because it's ours."

I looked at him to see if he was serious. The expression on his face told me that he was. "You bought us this house?" I asked, in disbelief.

"Yes."

"I-I don't know what to say," I stuttered. We had discussed getting a bigger place but what he had purchased was far better than I could have ever imagined. Stepping back, Damon looked at me and smiled. "There's one more thing," He said.

"Baby there is no way you can top this," I said, looking around at the beautiful property.

Damon reached into his pocket and pulled out his keys. Pressing the small black clicker that hung from his key chain he aimed at the garage. All five doors started to go up. All of the bays were empty except for the third one. Parked inside the third bay was a shining, cranberry red Mercedes CLK 55 convertible.

"The keys are inside," he told me. I looked at the car then at Damon then back at the car.

"Go look," he said, gently giving me a push.

I opened the door and was immediately greeted by the fresh new car smell. Sliding into the driver's seat I rubbed against the camel colored leather. I was a kid on Christmas morning that had just opened all her presents. Turning the key in the ignition, I started the engine. She purred. I couldn't stop smiling as I turned the key to turn the car off. When I slid the keys out of the ignition I saw it. Holding the key ring up in front of me, I gasped. Sparkling in my hand was a huge platinum, emerald cut diamond.

"Octavia."

I didn't answer Damon as he reached for my hand. I was too busy staring at the ring! Taking the key ring from me, Damon slid the rock off. Kneeling down beside me he held my hand. I sat unable to move as I watched him. Somewhere deep inside of me fear was scratching trying to get to the surface. Making me want to stop him before he started to speak, but above that fear there was something bigger and greater. That something was love, and love made me want to listen.

"I love you," he said, his eyes wide and clear." With every ounce of me, I love you. There is nothing I won't do for you but there is something I need you to do for me."

My heart felt like it was beating a hundred beats a minute when I said, "Anything."

Damon lifted my hand to his lips. I can't remember a kiss ever being sweeter. "Octavia," he asked, "Will you marry me?"

I didn't want to, but I cried anyway. I looked him in his beautiful eyes and cried. Then somewhere in between my falling tears I gathered my words and I said," Yes."

"Yes?"

"Yes."

Damon slid the ring on my finger so fast I almost didn't feel it. He kissed my face until all the tears were gone then pulled me out of the car into his arms.

Chapter 29

Damon Senior and Ilene stood outside their Stone Mountain mansion smiling as Damon and I stepped out of his car. Damon Sr. was a handsome older version of his son. Same caramel skin, same dark eyes, and the same bald head. Ilene was a beautiful, mocha complexioned woman with gray eyes. Their family portraits had not done either of them justice. Standing side by side the two of them were a remarkable pair.

I was beyond nervous meeting Damon's parents for the first time but they immediately let me know my feelings were unjustified. Throwing their arms around me they hugged me at the same time.

"Finally," Ilene sighed, stepping back to look at me. "Octavia how are you darling?"

Smiling I said," I'm fine and you?"

"Outstanding," she said.

Touching my face, Damon Sr. looked at me carefully. "Son, you did not do this sexy young woman justice," he smiled. "She is Ewe We!" Looking at the man, I blushed.

"I have to agree," Ilene smiled. "We are going to have some beautiful grandbabies."

Looking at Damon I raised my eyebrows. We hadn't set a wedding date and much like my mother, his mother was already talking about babies.

Throwing her hands in the air she let out a soft scream. "Is this the ring?" She asked.

Holding out my hand, I wiggled my fingers in front of her. "Yes Ma'am," I smiled, proudly.

Holding my hand Ilene examined my diamond. "Seven carat platinum Cartier," She cooed," Nothing but the best."

Seven carats? My knees got weak. I held my hand up in front on me and looked at the ring like it was my first time seeing it. I knew it was banging, but damn!

"Mama is an expert when it comes to diamonds," Damon laughed, stepping between us to kiss Ilene's cheek. Looking at the boulder on her finger and stones glistening from Ilene's ears I chuckled.

"So I see," I said.

"Whitmore women deserve a little bling-bling," she said, reaching for my hand." Come on darling let's go inside." "DJ, do you and your father need help with the bags?" She asked, looking over her shoulder

"No, Ma'am," Damon answered, watching his mother walk through the doors of their home with me tagging behind.

Damon and Damon Sr. decided to go for a drive leaving me and Ilene behind. The two of us sat on the second story balcony of her three story home, stretched out on a matching pair of velvet chaise loungers.

"Do you really love Damon?" She asked, looking at me. Her expression told me that she was waiting to analyze my answer. Turning on my side to face her I looked her directly in her eyes. "Yes Ilene. I do," I said, confidently.

"Why?"

Her question caught me by surprise. I knew I loved her son but I had never broken down the reasons. I didn't want to take too long answering her but I also didn't want to give her an answer just to satisfy her curiosity.

"Because he loves me," I said. "He loved me first and that made me love him."

Ilene's eyes widened. I cleared my throat preparing for a war of words. I respected the woman but I was ready for whatever.

"When I met Damon Sr. I wasn't looking for love," She said. "I was happily single but then he came along and everything happened suddenly."

"That's what happened with me," I confessed. "One day I was happily single then the next I was in love."

"It's scary isn't it?" She asked, running her fingers through her hair.

"Knowing a man can come into your life and change everything, including the way you feel and think."

"How did you deal with that fear?"

"Honey, I still am," she laughed.

"After thirty years of marriage?" I asked, surprised.

"Yes," she smiled. "But now I wouldn't call it fear. It's more like I'm…I'm amazed." She paused for a moment then continued, "Amazed that every day he gives me a reason to love him more and more."

I smiled at the thought that after being with Damon for thirty years I would feel exactly like Ilene did.

"Next time the two of you come to visit bring Charlene and Charles," She said, referring to my parent's as if she knew them.

"We will."

"Damon told me they recently remarried."

Thinking back to my parent's wedding day, I smiled, "Yeah after all those years."

"Real love never dies," Ilene said, smiling at me.

The two of us sat under the Georgia sun laughing and talking until Isabella, Ilene's plump Italian housekeeper, interrupted us.

"Excuse me, madam," she said, with a thick Italian accent. "Mrs. De-voe-Whitmore is here."

I watched Ilene's eyes roll into the back of her head. "Not today," She mumbled," Not today!"

Confused I looked at Isabella," Who is Mrs. Devoe -Whitmore?" I asked.

Looking from me to Ilene, Isabella said, "You'll find out soon enough!"

Turning on the heels of her white Dr. Scholl's, Isabella marched back thru the open French doors. I watched Ilene as she massaged her temples with her manicured fingertips.

"There are a lot of great things about being married into the Whitmore family," She said, exhaling loudly. "Then there's the one reason you want to pack your shit and run!"

"What's that?" I asked, curious.

"My mother in law."

I was confused to say the least, so I asked, "Didn't you tell me you were the only living Whitmore woman?"

"In this family darling," She answered, "I don't consider her a part of this family."

I followed Ilene downstairs to the family room. Sitting on the Italian leather sofa was a tall, thin, light-skinned woman with curly short gray hair. She was wearing an expensive looking white pants suit much like the gold one Ilene had on and white heels. Looking up, she stared Ilene down from her head to her open toe Jimmy Choos. Then she cut her eyes in my direction. "Who are you?" She asked. She had a look of disapproval stamped on her wrinkled face.

Staring her in the eyes I said, with authority, "I'm Octavia Ellis, Damon's fiancé." Her eyes narrowed to slits. "No one told me my grandson was engaged," She said, staring at Ilene.

"That's because we haven't talked to you," Ilene said, nonchalantly. Walking over and taking a seat in the wing chair facing her mother in law.

"That is until you showed up here today," Ilene corrected herself. "Unannounced." She put emphasis on unannounced. Both of the women watched as I sat down on the far end of the sofa.

"I didn't know I needed an appointment to see my son," She snapped.

"It's common courtesy to call before you come," Ilene snapped back.

"That didn't occur to me!"

"It should have when you made your arrangements to fly from New York to Georgia!"

I looked from one woman to the other waiting for the next come back. There was a pregnant pause until the older woman asked,

"Aren't you going to introduce me?"

"Darling," Ilene grunted." This is Damon Jr.'s grandmother, Odessa."

"Odessa Devoe hyphen Whitmore," Odessa corrected her.

"It's nice to meet you," I lied.

She turned her nose up and then asked, "What is it you do?"

"I am a restaurant owner," I answered.

"Um," she grumbled, sucking on her teeth." How long have you been dating my grandson?"

"Nine months," I answered. I was getting a little annoyed with her tone of voice.

"Nine months," She frowned. "That's not very long."

"Long enough," Ilene jumped into the conversation.

Smirking at Ilene Odessa crossed her bony legs. "That's what, five more than it took you to sleep your way into my family?"

Letting out a sinister laugh Ilene smiled at me. "I was in after the first two weeks."

I smiled and Odessa cut her eyes in my direction. "What happened to Nadia?" She asked." The pretty ballerina from Los Angeles."

Rolling her eyes, Ilene looked at me. "Nadia was a gold digging tramp that Damon dated two summers ago. She was nothing and she meant nothing."

I nodded my head. I didn't give a damn about Nadia, I was the one with the ring.

"I favored Nadia," Odessa said, sucking her teeth.

"I guess so," Ilene laughed." She's your best friend's granddaughter."

"She may be but it was a total coincidence that the two of them met."

"Let's not dwell in the past," Ilene said, throwing her hand up in Odessa's direction. "This is my future daughter in law's first visit and I won't allow anything to ruin it." Ilene put her hand down and frowned at Odessa. "Anything or anyone," She added.

The three of us were completely silent until Odessa blurted out, "You're pregnant, aren't you!"

I looked at her like she had lost her damn mind. "What?" I asked, pissed.

Ilene crossed her legs and shook her head. "Unbelievable," She laughed."Odessa you are unbelievable!"

Leaning forward on the sofa, Odessa turned to face me. "Well are you?" She asked.

She was treading on thin ice and I was ready to push her old ass thru.

"No, I'm not pregnant!" I said, loudly. "Why would you think that?"

"You don't seem like my grandson's type," She stated." But Damon is an honorable man and he would compromise his standards if there was a child involved."

I know she didn't just say Damon compromised his standards.

"Odessa don't be rude," Ilene snapped. "And how would you know my son's type? If you knew his type you wouldn't have arranged that meeting with that tramp, Nadia."

"I told you that was a coincidence."

"Well it was a helluva coincidence."

"The past is the past," Odessa said, nonchalantly.

"Do you know me?" I asked, staring at Odessa. I didn't care who she was. I was not going to allow her to talk to me like I was beneath her.

"What do you mean?"

Looking her directly in her eyes I spoke slowly," Do you know me?" I repeated.

"Before today I didn't know you existed," She laughed.

"Well you do now," I said, with an attitude." However, keep in mind you still don;t know me."

"I…"

"Therefore do not assume anything about me," I cut her off. "It matters not to me whether or not you think I'm Damon's type and I promise you it won't matter to Damon either."

Daring her to say something, I paused. She didn't. "What does matter, however," I said, crossing my legs." Is that Damon is in love with me and I am in love with him."

"Love didn't buy that ring on your finger," She said, pointing at my hand. "Damon's money did."

"They don't accept love at Carrier's," Ilene whispered.

Never looking in Ilene's direction, Odessa frowned," Nor did love pay for all the shit my son has provided for Ilene. But if you really love my grandson please try to remember this one thing; his money is his money and your money is your money."

I watched as the withering old woman stood adjusted her pants legs and walked out of the room, leaving Ilene and me alone.

"What's her issue?" I asked Ilene, still annoyed by Odessa assumptions.

"Darling, she is a bitch," Ilene stated, bluntly." She hates anyone who doesn't kiss her ass."

"I guess she'll hate me forever," I said, shaking my head." Because I'm not kissing anyone's ass."

Laughing Ilene told me, "You just better hope she stays healthy until she dies. Because if she ever needs someone to take care of her, she's moving in with you and DJ because I am not allowing her to stay here!"

I didn't have to pray about that one because if the black Cruella Deville ever got sick, I planned to drop her ass off at a nursing home and never look back.

Odessa managed to avoid us until Damon and his father returned home. When she saw them she immediately started frontin' like everything was perfect and the three of us were getting along like old girlfriends. Ilene and I just listened to her lie on and on, each of us giving her a look that let her know we wanted to strangle her ass.

The rest of the weekend went great. Damon took me to P Diddy's restaurant, Justin's, Ilene took me shopping, and Damon Sr. and I went horseback riding at his stable. Odessa managed to stay out of my way and that only made the weekend even better.

Despite my run in with Odessa, I felt welcomed into the Whitmore Family. I knew Odessa was going to be an obstacle but I knew that together there was no obstacle Damon and I couldn't overcome.

Chapter 30

There is a difference between overcoming an obstacle and running into a damn sync hole in the middle of a one way overpass! That's exactly how I felt when I strolled into Damon's office Monday afternoon. I wanted to surprise Damon, so I showed up unannounced wearing a sexy pink slip dress and a pair of four inch open toe heels.

"Good Afternoon, Miss Ellis," Damon's assistant, Louisa greeted me from behind her desk.

"Good Afternoon, Ms. Louisa," I smiled.

Louisa had been working for Damon every since his office opened. I liked her. She was sweet and old. Ms. Louisa was the perfect woman to work with my man on a daily basis.

"Mr. Whitmore is in his office," she said. "He's wrapping up a consultation with a new client."

"Maybe I should wait here."

"Don't be silly," Louisa said, looking me up and down. "You and that dress may be the motivation his client needs to get him to do business with us."

Laughing I winked my eye at her," I'll do anything for my baby," I teased.

"And he'll do anything for you," She said, leaning forward on her desk, "If I would have known you were going to stop by, I would have worn sunglasses."

"Why is that?" I asked, puzzled by her statement.

Pointing at my left hand she covered her eyes, "You're blinding me with that rock!"

"You are too much, Ms. Louisa," I laughed.

Holding her hand over her eyes, she said, "Go on back there. I'm an old woman, I need what little eyesight I have left."

Shaking my head I headed towards Damon's office. When I reached his closed door I knocked and waited until I heard him say "Come in."

Smiling I opened the door and immediately saw Damon sitting behind his desk looking delicious in a cream dress shirt and mint green silk tie. His eyes were wide with surprise and approval as he looked from my head to my toes. Then I glanced to my left and almost passed out. He was sitting in one of the leather arm chairs wearing a dark suit with a red silk, button front shirt with no tie. Low haircut and well groomed goatee. He looked at me and a small grin crept across his face.

"Baby," Damon said, getting my attention.

I pulled my eyes from the man nervously and looked at Damon. I watched as Damon rose from his chair and walked around his desk to me. He kissed my cheek and then wrapped his arm around my waist.

"You look beautiful," He whispered in my ear. When he let me go he stepped back and looked at me then smiled.

"Octavia, I want you to meet my newest client." he said.

I watched as he stood and adjusted his jacket.

"Broderick," Damon said. "This is my fiancé, Octavia."

Our eyes locked as he extended his hand to me. "It's nice to meet you, Octavia," He said, looking at me seductively. "And please…call me Beau."

Everything about him was different; from the way he was talking to how he looked and was dressed, but it was Beau. The same Beau I had been fucking. The same Beau I had arrested for harassment.

Beau. Now Beau was standing in my husband-to- be's office, smiling at me.

With his hand still extended to me he looked at Damon and smiled.

"You're right, she is beautiful."

I extended my hand to him slowly and gave him a weak handshake. He held my hand a little too long for my comfort, then he finally let go.

"You look familiar," He said, stroking his goatee. "Have we met?"

My heart felt like it was going to jump out of my chest and run for cover. I shook my head in slow motion.

"Are you sure?" He asked, coolly.

"Probably from the Ambiance," Damon said, proudly. "Octavia is the owner."

Beau cocked his head to one side. "Is that right?" He asked.

"You have some of the best food in town. Especially the chocolate cake." He licked his lips slowly. "I love it," He said. "Almost as much as I love cotton candy."

Damon laughed but I wanted to slap the shit out of Beau's trif-flin' ass.

"Well Damon, I better get going," He said, reaching for Damon's hand. "I look forward to doing business with you."

I watched the two of them exchange a friendly handshake while my stomach boiled.

"Octavia, it was a pleasure meeting you." He smiled, mischievously. "I hope to see you again."

He exited Damon's office shutting the door behind him. My heart continued to beat hard inside my chest. I felt like I was going to pass out at any second. Damon wrapped his arms around me and kissed my lips. "Your heart is pounding," He said. "Are you okay?"

A part of me wanted to tell him everything but a bigger part told me not to mention my connection with Beau. "I'm fine," I said, smiling weakly. "You just have that affect on me."

Placing my hand on his stiff crotch, Damon kissed me passionately.

"Look what affect you have on me," he whispered.

I squeeze the stiffness in his pants trying to pretend that I had not just seen Beau in his office. "Um," I said, not wanting to appear distracted.

I was with Damon but I was worried about Beau's crazy ass. Even after Damon told Ms. Louisa to go home for the day and we made sweet love right on his desk, I still couldn't get Beau's image out of my head.

Chapter 31

I knew there was no possible way Beau's meeting Damon was just a coincidence. He was playing games with me. He confirmed my suspicions when he called me at the Ambiance the next day.

"Hello."

"It's a small world, huh, Ma?"

"It ain't that damn small." I snapped.

"How did you find Damon?"

"That was pure luck."

"Why are you fucking with me?" I asked.

"You fucked me then you fucked me over by running to the mutha-fucking police," He said, inhaling.

He was on the other end of the phone getting high. I was starting to believe that he was into more than just weed.

"You fucked yourself by acting like a fifteen year old, that had his virginity stolen, "I snapped." And who gave you permission to call me?"

"The way I see it Shorty, is that I don't need permission," He said, inhaling then exhaling slowly. "I can do whatever the fuck I want. I've proved that time and time again."

I decided to take another approach with him because my previous methods were obviously getting me nowhere.

"So what are you going to do?" I asked, calmly. "Tell Damon that we hooked up? Go right ahead sweetheart the ball is in your court." I was calling his bluff. I knew this whole thing was not about Damon. "Besides," I said." Damon and I weren't together then."

He laughed," Your man Damon doesn't have shit to do with this, Ma. This is about us."

"There is no *us*, Beau," I said, irritated. "Move on."

This time he laughed so hard and loud I had to hold the phone away from my ear. "You can't possibly think that this is all just about the pussy. You got me fucked up, Ma! I plan to put my name on that, no doubt, but right now the way I see it is you owe me."

"I don't owe you a damn thing!"

"You brought charges against me, causing me to be in the spotlight," He said, anger in his voice.

"Normally that's an unforgivable sin in my eyes but I'm making an exception for you. You violated, but I'm willing to let you make it up to me."

"You put yourself in the spotlight," I snapped. "The two of us have nothing to work out."

"Have it your way for now," He said, calmly." But I'm telling you Ma, I'm a man who always gets what he wants." Then he hung up.

Chapter 32

I was going over my payroll for the week when Amel came bouncing into my office and told me Damon was outside in the dining area. I was surprised because he hadn't mentioned he was stopping in, but I was always happy to see my man.

He was sitting in the VIP section but he wasn't alone. Beau was right there with him. The two of them were talking and laughing like two old friends. Just the sight of Beau made me want to scream. They both greeted me with smiles as I slid into the booth next to Damon.

"Hey baby," I said, giving him a small peck on his cheek. Looking across the booth at Beau I frowned, "I'm so sorry," I said. "I'm trying to remember your name."

He gave me a smirk and said with an air of arrogance, "Beau."

Snapping my fingers I shook my head, "That's right - Beau," I said. "How are you, Beau?"

"Fine."

Amel came to the table, her gray eyes shining bright. "Are you gentlemen sure I can't get you anything?" She asked, smiling at Beau. It was obvious she was flirting.

"No, thank you," Beau said, never looking in her direction.

A look of disappointment went across Amel's face as she looked at me and said, "Let me know if you need anything."

Giving her a sympathetic smile, I nodded. I couldn't blame her for her interest in Beau. The brother was fine. However, his not showing interest was actually a point in Amel's favor because I seriously doubt I was the first woman he'd ever been obsessed with.

After Amel was out of our sight Damon leaned in against the table. "What's up, man, it's obvious she's feeling you," He said, to Beau.

Leaning back in the booth Beau looked at me, "You think so?" He asked.

"Damon, how do you know this?" I asked, knowing I had felt the same thing.

Looking at me seductively Damon smiled, "Because she was looking at him like you always look at me."

"And how is that?" I asked, sweetly.

"Like you want me."

I could see Beau out of the corner of my eye, he was fuming with jealously. "So Dam you think ole' girl wants me?" He asked his voice cold.

Looking across the table, Damon said," No doubt."

Beau didn't respond he just cut his eyes at me and gave me a wicked smile.

"I'd better get back to work," I stuttered, squeezing Damon's hand gently. "I'll see you at home, baby."

"I love you, Baby."

Kissing Damon's lips quickly, I whispered, "I love you too."

I left without saying a word to Beau. The two of them sat in the booth for another twenty minutes, shook hands and got up to leave. Damon walked out first with Beau following close behind but before Beau left he stopped to talk to Amel. She was smiling a perfect ten smile as the two of them had a brief conversation. When Beau saw me watching them he smiled and gave Amel a slow kiss on the cheek. Then he turned in my direction and blew a kiss at me.

That night, Damon and I lay in bed naked with him holding me.

The two of us had shared a candlelit dinner at home followed by a long hot bath. After we bathed we decided to just hold each other. I was too distracted to do anything more so I gave Damon an excuse that I was tired.

"Are you asleep?"

"No, baby," He said, running his warm hands across my bare back.

"What business are you handling for Beau?"

"None now," Damon said, exhaling.

"What happened," I said, pretending to be concerned.

"That's why we were at the Ambiance today," He said." He called and asked me to meet him there. When we first met, we discussed that he wanted to sell a waterfront property that he owns in Miami."

"Miami?"

"Yeah, about twenty acres," he said. "A nice area for development."

"He changed his mind?"

"Yeah, he said he decided to sell to some commercial developer."

Raising my head I looked at Damon," You're disappointed?"

"Yeah I could have helped a lot of families with that type of property."

Rubbing his soft face, I said, "Maybe it's for the best."

"I know," He said. "I just hate to lose out on a good opportunity."

Rolling up on my knees I straddled him. "Then I guess you better take advantage of the one you have right now." Giving him a warm wet kiss on the lips I felt him rise underneath me.

"I thought you were tired, baby," He said, entering me.

I got wet instantly. Slowly I began to rotate my hips. "I just got a sudden burst of energy," I moaned.

Following my lead, Damon began to grind with me. "Let me see if I can help you use that energy."

That's exactly what he did. We made love for hours until my body ached. Afterwards, we showered then returned to our bed naked. For the moment, I was no longer distracted with thoughts of Beau. Knowing that he was not doing business with Damon put my mind at ease.

Chapter 33

Amel's appearance had changed dramatically. It was like she had won the lottery overnight. Every day she was wearing something designed by Gucci. I normally wouldn't be alarmed, but considering she was a struggling nursing student who only worked part time for me, I knew there was no way could purchase those things on her own unless she had found herself a hustle. I normally wouldn't get involved in my employees personal life but when I saw her in the parking lot of the Ambiance climbing into a new cream colored Cadillac Escalade instead of her Toyota Camry, I decided to get a little nosey. It's not that I thought Amel was stealing from me; I knew she wasn't, I kept a close eye on my money but I had an unsettling feeling about how she was getting all of her new things.

The two of us were setting up for our lunch rush when I brought up the subject of her new car. "I like your new ride," I said, straightening a tablecloth.

"Thanks, Octavia," she said, beaming from ear to ear.

"When did you get it?"

"Two days ago," she smiled.

"The payments must be outrageous," I stopped, looking at her.

Placing a folded linen napkin on the table she looked at me, "Actually, no," she said, still smiling. "It's paid for."

Raising my eyebrows, I said, "I didn't know I was paying you that well."

"You're not," she giggled." My man bought it for me."

"Well, congratulations," I said, sincerely. I was relieved that she wasn't shaking or selling her booty to pay for her new vehicle.

"Thanks," she smiled.

"You'll have to have him stop by one day so you can treat him to a free lunch," I said, moving to the next table. "Compliments of me."

"Thanks, Octavia," Amel said, cheerfully. "I'll be sure to tell Beau you said that."

I almost fell on my behind when I heard her say his name. "Did you say Beau?" I asked.

"Yeah," she said, "That's who I'm dating."

I watched her smiling and bouncing from table to table as she continued to set out the linens. Amel was a smart, beautiful, twenty-three year old woman with a bright future ahead of her. Under other circumstances I would have been happy for her but deep down inside I know Beau's motivation for dating her had something to do with me.

Amel's attitude had slowly begun to change and so was the quality of her work. She had been late four times in the last week and yesterday afternoon I could have sworn she came in smelling like weed. Her relationship with Beau was obviously keeping his mind off me because he had stopped by a couple of times to take her out to lunch on her break and each time he saw me, he barely acknowledged me. That was fine by me, but I couldn't get down with Amel getting contact and then coming into my establishment smelling like a bong.

On top of all that, a couple of the other employees had been complaining about her. They told me she was no longer pulling her weight when I was not around and that she had gotten confrontational when they mentioned it to her. None of these things fit the description of the Amel I knew. She had always been a quiet and somewhat shy employee who was always eager to help out and was great at her job. I couldn't have a hostile working environment so I decided to pull her to the side and ask her what was up.

"They're jealous of me," she said, sitting in the chair across from me.

I watched her run her fingers through her long chestnut weave.

"What makes you say that?" I said, watching as she pulled loose strands of her hair from her fingers.

"I can tell by the way they look at me," she said, dropping the strands on my maple desk.

"Maybe that's because they feel you're not pulling your own around here."

She looked at me like I was from another planet then asked, "So what do you want me to say?"

Giving her the same look I said, "I don't want you to say anything. I want you to start doing your job."

"I do my damn job," she said, standing and putting her hand on her hip.

Standing myself, I crossed my arms across my chest. "If you were doing your job we would not be having this conversation," I said, calmly. I didn't like the direction our conversation was going in but I couldn't have Amel disrespecting me either. "So I'm giving you a verbal warning that I need to see some improvement," I said, firmly.

Sucking her teeth she turned to walk away. "Fuck this job," she said, looking back at me. "I don't have to work here."

I was pissed by her demeanor, "Who do you know is going to let you work part-time and get fulltime pay?" I asked, angry.

"My man," she said, before she slammed my office door behind her.

Two days later, I was still pissed about the way things had gone down between Amel and me. In the year that she had been employed by me I had never had to reprimand her once, and now after a five minute conversation I was looking for a replacement for her. I didn't want to blame Beau because Amel was still a grown woman and she was fully capable of making her own choices but in my opinion he was the bad influence behind Amel's bad attitude. Then again it could have been the money he was throwing her way. Some women get a man with money and lose their minds, along with their self respect.

Chapter 35

A month had passed since Amel stomped out of my office and my new waitress, Tabitha was working out just fine. Tabitha was an older, white woman who was trying to get back on her feet after a messy divorce. She had been married to her husband for eighteen years when he decided to leave her for a beautiful, black twenty-one old that he met on the Internet. Her story was rare to me because normally it's the sisters telling me that their man left them for the white woman half their age. Tabitha was proof that the game had definitely changed.

Amel had never returned to pick up her final paycheck and when I attempted to mail it to her it was returned by the post office stamped "un-deliverable". The home phone number I had for had been changed to an unpublished number, so I decided to just lock her check up in my office safe. I liked to keep loose ends tied so if she ever popped in the restaurant, I wanted to have her check ready. I didn't like the thought of owing anyone anything; especially when it came down to business.

I was gathering my things together to leave for the day when my office phone rang. I started to ignore it but considering it may be Damon or one of my parents I thought again.

"Ambiance, this is Octavia."

"Hello, Ms. Ellis?" a nervous sounding woman asked on the other end.

"Yes this is Ms. Ellis."

"Ms. Ellis this is Betty Fletcher," She said. "Amel's mother."

"How may I help you, Ms. Fletcher?"

"I'm looking for my daughter."

Confused, I told her, "I'm sorry Ms. Fletcher Amel no longer works here."

"Do you know where she is?" I sensed panic in the woman's voice.

"No, ma'am," I said, calmly.

"I hate to disturb you Ms. Ellis," She said, quickly." But I haven't talked to my daughter in weeks and her number has been changed."

Despite what had gone down with Amel I hoped that she was alright.

"She dropped out of school," she said. "And when I contacted her landlord he said she moved out more than a month ago and she didn't leave a forwarding address."

That would explain why her mail was returned undeliverable. "What did she sound like the last time you spoke to her?" I asked, concerned.

"She told me she had met someone," She said. "She didn't sound like herself. She was talking differently and when she told me about all the new things he had bought her I let her know that I didn't approve."

She took a deep breath then continued," I told her any man who was so happy to give so quickly had to want something in return," She said. "We argued and then Amel hung up on me."

"I'm sorry, Ms. Fletcher," I said, sympathetically. "I wish I could help you."

"Amel has never gone this long without calling me," She said, sniffing." I just want to talk to her Ms. Ellis. I can't stand not talking to my daughter."

"I'm sure she's fine," I said, trying to sound convincing. "If I find out anything, Ms. Fletcher, I'll be happy to give you call."

"Please do Ms. Ellis," She cried. "Please do."

I scribbled down the woman's number on my calendar. She explained that she lived alone in Selma and would come up to Huntsville if she could, but she was too sick to make the drive. She told me Amel's father died when Amel was six years old. I thought about my own mother and how she would feel if she couldn't get in contact with me. My mother had my father but all Ms. Fletcher had was Amel. Before we hung up I promised that I would help her get in contact with her daughter.

I knew that I only had to go as far as Beau to find Amel. However I wanted him to be my last resort, so I went thru my employee information and found Amel's application. On the back, she had two people listed in case of an emergency. The first was her mother, and the second was a Nikki Cole. I hoped Nikki's number hadn't changed and that she and Amel were still friends as Amel had listed on the back of her application. Sure enough, Nikki's number was the same and she knew where I could find Amel. After I gave her a story about trying to mail Amel a few items she left in her employee locker, Nikki gave me Amel's new home number and the number for her cell.

After the phone rang several times Amel finally answered.

"Yes," she said, sounding agitated.

"Amel this is Octavia from the Ambiance."

"Hi Octavia," she said, sounding happy.

"How are you?" I asked, relieved that she sounded alright.

"Good and you?"

"I'm fine," I said." Thanks for asking."

"How is everyone down there?"

"They're fine," I said, wondering if she really cared.

"Good."

"Listen, Amel," I said, getting straight to the point." Your mother called."

"How is she?" She asked, quickly.

"Not good. She misses you."

"I miss her, too," she whispered.

"She wants you to call her."

"I- I want to but..."

"She's not mad with you," I said, reassuring her." She just wants to hear your voice."

"I wish I could, Octavia but I can't," She whispered.

There was something not right about the way she was acting. I decided to find out what was really going on.

"Listen Amel I want to mail you your final paycheck," I said, changing the subject." Why don't you give me your new address?"

"Something is wrong with my mailbox," she said, hesitantly. "I'm want to get a post office box but I keep forgetting."

"Would you rather I drop it off?" I asked.

There was silence on the other end of the phone for a few seconds then she said softly," Yes, please."

"What's the address?"

"Seven eighty-five Montclair," she whispered.

I wrote the address down next to her home number. "When is a good time?" I asked her.

"Today," she said quickly." After five."

"I'll be there at five thirty..."

"Goodbye," I said, hanging up the phone.

I pulled up to the beautiful town home at seven eighty five Montclair at exactly five thirty that afternoon. Amel's Escalade was the only car in the driveway, so I figured that Beau was gone.

When Amel opened the front door I was taken aback by her appearance. She was wearing a pair of black worn sweats with no shoes. Her weave needed to be redone desperately. I could see the threads and the tracks. She wore it pulled back in a sloppy ponytail. She still had the same round, almond colored face but her skin was chaffed and ashy. She greeted me with a hug and told me to come in.

I followed her into the living room of the well decorated home. Sitting on the small plush loveseat, I watched as she sat down on the matching sectional in the room.

"How are you?" I asked.

"Okay," she said, fidgeting with her short fingernails.

"Are you sure?"

"I guess."

"How is Beau?"

She looked down at her nails and then looked at me with tears in her eyes.

"Fine," she said, softly.

There was a pregnant pause between the two of us. "Why haven't you called your mother?" I asked. Shrugging her shoulders, she looked away from me.

"Is it because of him?" I asked, trying to get her to open up. She continued to stare off in space not answering the question.

"Amel what's wrong?" I asked, concerned.

Looking at me with tears streaming down her face she said, "I'm real fucked up right now. I don't even know who I am anymore."

She pushed the sleeves of her sweatshirt up then crossed her arms across her chest.

"I can't help you Amel if you don't tell me what's wrong," I said, gently.

Her eyes searched mine as if she was searching for sincerity. Then she held her arms out with her palms up. My heart saddened as I looked at the purple bruises and small scars. They were from the needles she had been using to shoot up.

"Heroin," she mumbled.

"Beau gave you heroine," I stated.

"I didn't say that," she snapped, her eyes wide.

"I'm asking."

"I didn't get it from Beau."

Bullshit! He probably was supplying her with the crap. I looked at her letting her know I knew she was covering for him. "Is he living here?" I asked.

"No but he comes over a lot," She said, fidgeting with a piece of lint on her pants.

"When is he coming back?" I asked.

"I don't know," she said sadly. "He told me he was going out of town for a little while."

"What would he do if you weren't here when he came back?"

She stared at me with childlike eyes and then said, "I can leave if I want."

"Then why don't you?" I asked, firmly.

"Because I love him," she said, without hesitation. 'And if I leave he'll move on without me."

"If he does then maybe it's not meant to be." I countered.

She wiped her eyes with the back of her hands. "He's good to me," She sniffed. "Better than any man's ever been."

"I understand that but you can't keep messing with that stuff," I said, referring to her drug habit. "It can kill you."

"I know," she mumbled, rubbing the marks on her arms. "But I'll kill myself if I have to live without him."

I took a deep breath and then exhaled slowly. The look of desperation in her eyes frightened me. I had no idea what she saw in Beau but whatever it was it had her trippin'.

"A man wants a woman who has her shit together," I told her. "You won't keep him if you keep living like this."

We talked a little longer until she finally agreed to admit herself into a rehab program. During our entire conversation she kept saying that she didn't want to disappoint Beau. She said she didn't want to let him down. That he was so good to her and that he took care of her. It was like the girl had been brainwashed. I hoped and prayed that my intervening would help her see that she didn't have any of her current problems until she met him and that she was better off with him out of her life.

Despite my better judgment, I agreed to pick up Amel on Friday. I wanted to persuade her to check herself in that same night but I was afraid that if I pushed her too hard she would change her mind. I also agreed to wait until Friday on the condition that she would call her mother and let her know she was alright. She kept her end of the bargain so I gave her a hug and told her I would see her on Friday.

I couldn't shake the feeling I had about Beau treating Amel's problem. I knew that she was too loyal to him to see who he really was. I knew the only way I was going to get information on him was if I went through another source.

I figured that if I met him at Erica's and Tim's reception then one of them should be able to tell me what I wanted to know.

"Octavia, how are you?"

"I'm fine Erica and how are you?"

"Wonderful," she giggled." I love the married life."

"That's good," I said, sincerely. I smiled when I thought about Damon and I getting married one day. "How is Tim?" I asked.

"He is the best husband ever!"

"I'm glad everything is going well," I said." But there is a reason I'm calling."

"What's that?"

"There was a guy at your wedding. He was dark-skinned with braids."

"Beau." Her happy upbeat tone went cold when she said his name.

"Yeah," I said, sounding clueless. "He wanted me to cater a party for him. He's been calling my office leaving me messages to call him but I've misplaced his number."

"Don't do it," she warned me." He is bad news." I waited for her to elaborate. She didn't.

"What do you mean?" I asked.

Clearing her throat, Erica said in a low voice," Octavia, I don't want to start anything."

"You won't be," I tried to reassure her." But if there is something I should know." I waited for her response.

"Okay," she said." His real name is Broderick Malone and he's my sister Stephanie's ex-boyfriend." I wasn't aware that Erica even had a sister.

"Was she at the reception?"

"No," I heard the tears in Erica's voice." My sister died four years ago."

I felt a rush of sympathy for the woman on the other end of the phone.

"I'm sorry to hear that," I said.

"He killed her, Octavia." Her words almost knocked me out off my chair.

"What did you say?" I asked.

"He killed my sister."

"What…what happened," I stuttered.

"They found her body in a dumpster in Brooklyn."

Silence.

"The two of them met while Stephanie was a sophomore at NYU," She continued." At first, Stephanie wanted nothing to do with him. She was all about her education and he-well he was all about selling."

"She sensed he was trouble," she said, "But she was young and he had money, you know how that goes."

"Yeah," I said, thinking of Amel.

"For the first month, everything was cool," She said. "But then Beau became too possessive. He wanted to consume all of Stephanie's time, he was obsessed with her."

"So she broke it off," Erica said." She told him they were moving too fast."

"How did he take it?"

"He lost his mind," She said, her voice shaking." He started calling every hour on the hour and following her around. Then one night he broke into her apartment and beat her up."

"Did he go to jail?"

"No the police couldn't prove it was him," She cried. "But I know he did it."

The incident in my apartment replayed in my head. I was lucky that he only scared my ass.

"What happened after that?" I asked. I hated to take Erica back through all of the pain she must have felt but I had to know the truth.

"He stayed away for a few weeks but somehow he convinced her to take him back. They started dating again and that's when she got pregnant."

Erica cleared her throat; then continued. "She was twenty years old, pregnant, and miles away from home. I tried to convince her to move back here but she said that's not what Beau wanted."

"It was like everything revolved around what Beau said," she said. "Then one night when Steph was six months pregnant, she called me and said she was coming home."

"She left him," I assumed.

"I thought she had," Erica said, sadly." But when she left New York, he came too. Steph said she thought the move would be good for the two of them. She said they would have a fresh start with their new baby. Beau even claimed he had changed. He bought them a brand new house and started working on opening up his own club."

"But in my mind," she said," I knew he was the same person. I just thought with having Stephanie here I could get her away from him. Every day I tried to convince her to move in with me but she wouldn't. That is until one day he saw her out talking with an old friend from high school and Beau went off."

"What did he do?" I asked, hanging on her every word.

"He beat the guy unconscious," she said. "That's when Stephanie left him and came to live with me. Everything appeared to be going well. She agreed to go back to school after the baby was born and she was happy. I thought I finally had my sister back but one day I came home and found a note from her stating she was going to New York with Beau for a few days."

"Not forty-eight hours later, "She said, crying. "Beau called to say she was missing. The very next day a homeless man found her body in a dumpster outside of a crack house." Chills ran across my body as Erica explained. "Her stomach was cut open. They took her baby and left Stephanie to bleed to death."

My stomach was churning and I felt like I was going to throw-up. "Did they find the baby?" I asked my voice low.

"Yes, she was with a known crack head they called Brenda," She said." Brenda came forward and said she killed Stephanie and was going to sell her baby but her conscience wouldn't let her do it."

"Did the baby die?" I asked, slowly.

"No, she survived," she said. "She's four now. Her name is Brittany and she looks just like Stephanie."

"Beau has full custody," Erica said, angry. "He brought her back to Huntsville with him. The fucking police didn't even look at him as a suspect. He's here with a new life raising my sister's daughter and it's not fair. They even made Stephanie out to be a druggie."

"What?"

"When they did the autopsy they said they found traces of crack in her body," she said. "They said that would explain why she was on the wrong side of town late at night, but I know if anything was in my sister's system it's because he drugged her."

"I even went to see Brenda in jail," she continued," She told me she didn't do it and that she was framed."

"Was Brenda convicted?"

"No, she never made it trial. She overdosed on heroin in her jail cell."

I talked with Erica for another hour. During that time, she explained that Beau claims his current business is legit but she's almost positive that he's still dirty. I had no idea who I was dealing with but if Beau was the person Erica made him out to be then he would own up to his words; *"I'm a man who always gets what he wants."*

I was not going to sit around and wait for him to make good on his promise, so I called the only person I knew that could help take care of the situation.

Chapter 36

"Why didn't you come to me when this all started?"

I felt like a little girl sitting in front of my father. The two of us were sitting in my parent's dining room. I had made sure Mama wouldn't be home so that I could tell Daddy about my problem without her getting all worked up.

"I don't know," I said, sincerely. "I thought I could handle it." The truth was I didn't want my Father to know that I had let Beau tap my ass.

Rubbing the hair on his chin, Daddy gave me a stern look. "So this brother, Beau was once a hustler on the east coast?" He asked.

"That's what Erica said."

"And she thinks he killed her sister?" I nodded my head. "And Sasha use to work for him?" I nodded again.

"And she allegedly died from a heroin overdose."

"Yes."

I watched as his brown eyes got dark and cold.

"I know some people," he said. "From way back."

"Let me see what I can find out," he said.

Reaching across the table for his hand, I smiled.

"Thank you, Daddy," I said.

Taking my hand in his he asked," Does Damon know about

this?"

Frowning I shook my head and slowly said," No."

"It's better if you tell him," he said." You don't want him to find out the wrong way."

"I know."

I knew Daddy was speaking the truth, but I had no intentions of telling Damon anything about Beau. What Damon didn't know wouldn't hurt me.

Chapter 37

Damon left for the airport early Friday morning to catch a flight to California. He was going to be gone for two weeks, working in Nomad's LA office. I started feeling lonely just thinking about not having him next to me, but business was business.

I planned to handle some business of my own while he was gone. For one, I planned to start looking for furnishings for our new home. I also wanted to start planning our wedding. The two of us had yet to set a wedding date mainly because Damon was giving me time to decide when I was ready. The truth be told I was already ready; I just had to make sure Beau was out of our lives. But first, I was going to get Amel checked into Harper Recovery Center.

Harper was the best substance abuse treatment center in the city. They were also the most expensive, but I wanted Amel to have the best possible help available.

I held my breath as Amel opened the door to her townhouse to let me in. She looked much better than she had the last time I saw her. Her hair looked fresh like she had just left the salon and she was wearing a figure flattering white pants suit with a pair of gold Gucci pumps. If I hadn't already seen the scars from her using I would have thought she didn't have a problem. I saw the two Gucci suite cases sitting by the front door and I exhaled. I had been afraid that she was going to change her mind about treatment.

"I'm ready," she said, timidly.

"Are you sure?"

"As ready as I'll ever be," she said.

The ride to Harpers was a quiet one until Amel's cell phone rang. She looked at the caller ID and then answered. She had a huge smile across her face. The first person who came to my mind was Beau.

"Hello."

"Where are you, Boo?" She whined.

"I thought you were going to come with me."

"Why?"

"You promise?"

"Okay."

"I love you."

"Bye."

I stared ahead at the road wondering if she had told Beau I was with her.

"Beau says hi," she smiled, looking over at me. *Question answered.*

"How is he?" I asked.

"Fine," She said, cheerfully." He promised to come visit me every week."

I looked at the happiness on her face and smiled, knowing that Beau had made her a promise he probably never intended to keep.

The faculty and staff at Harper assured Amel and me that she had made the right decision by choosing their facility. She signed up for an intense ninety day rehabilitation program. They told me at some point in time during her treatment she would hate me and probably anyone who wanted her to get clean. I told them I didn't care if she hated me for the rest of her life. If being in Harper was going to help Amel rediscover herself and stay clean that was all that mattered.

Chapter 38

That night Damon and I made love, long distance. After two hours of phone sex I needed a long hot bath. I sat in my tub surrounded by bubbles scented with lilac, the lights dim, and Heather Headley pumping from my living room speakers. I felt drained from everything that had been going on lately and I just wanted to relax.

"He is…the mind objector."

"The heart protector."

"The soul defender of anything I fear."

I listened as Heather sang and I thought about Damon. He was everything she was singing about and then some. I sang along with Heather feeling her words and understanding the love I imagine she felt when she wrote those lyrics.

The sounds of the music and my own voice prevented me from hearing anything outside of the room.

I was still singing as I strolled out of the bathroom and bumped right into Beau. "Ahh!" I screamed, stumbling backwards. My heart beat so hard I could hear the echo in my ears. He smiled as he looked at me standing in front of him wrapped in a thick white bath towel.

"What's up, Ma?" He asked, eyeing me.

"How did you get in my house?"

He stepped towards me backing me into the hall wall. "I used the front door," He said, placing one hand on the wall.

"Get out!"

"Come on boo, don't act like that," she said, leaning in close to me.

Putting my hands on his chest I pushed him back. He stumbled, and then regained his balance. "What's wrong?" He asked, laughing. " I know your man won't be home soon, and a freak like you can't wait two weeks."

I hadn't told Amel about Damon's trip so the only other way Beau could have known was if he had spoken with Damon himself. He must have known what I was thinking because he smiled.

"That's right, I called your boy to see how he was doing," He said. "We conversed for a moment and he told me he was in LA handling some business. We had a nice little conversation. But don't worry Ma, I didn't tell him about us."

I felt relief and fear running through my body at the same time.

"He'll find that out soon enough," he said. He threatened me with his eyes.

"I'm asking you nicely to please leave," I said, my body shaking.

"Drop the towel," he commanded, ignoring my request.

I stood still anticipating his next move. Heather was on another track but I could no longer hear her. The only thing I could hear was Beau and the sound of my heart beating. I held onto the towel wrapped around my body like it was my lifeline and attempted to run past him. He grabbed me by my arm and slammed me hard into the wall. I screamed as my head hit the wall and I, along with the towel, dropped to the floor.

Grabbing me by the throat, Beau climbed on top of me and pinned my legs down with his knees. Applying pressure to my neck he looked me in my eyes, "I told you I always get what I want," He said, his eyes heated. I felt tears running from my eyes as I struggled to get up.

"Please stop," I begged him.

"I'm just getting started," He smiled, kissing my lips. A hundred thoughts ran through my mind as I dug my fingernails into his arms as a weak attempt to pry his hands from my neck. "Okay," I choked out.

"Okay."

I prayed as his eyes scanned over my naked flesh. "You win baby," I whispered. "You win."

"You want this?" He asked, grinding in between my spread legs.

"Yes," I said, rubbing my hands up his arms.

His eyes softened as he slowly loosened his grip. "How you want it, Ma?" He asked.

"Just like last time."

Sliding his hands down my neck to my breast, Beau squeezes each of them so hard I thought they might bleed. "Um," I moaned. I felt him grow hard through his jeans. I lay still as he moved down my body until his face was in between my legs.

"Not tonight, baby," I said, rubbing his head." Remember I owe you."

His face lit up as he stood and looked down at me. Propping myself on my elbows I licked my lips seductively. "Take off your clothes," I said, sweetly.

As he slowly began to lift his shirt over his head I eased up on to my feet. My legs ached from the pain of his body on top of mine and my head throbbed as I watched him. His shirt hit the floor then he kicked off his shoes and started unbuttoning his jeans. "Let me help you," I said, walking up to him slowly.

"Damn you are so sexy," He whispered, as I slowly unzipped his zipper.

I watched as his pants dropped to the floor. "Lay down," I ordered.

"Whatever you want, Ma."

I carefully watched him as he eased down to the floor and stretched out on his back. "Damn baby you're fine," I smiled, standing next to him.

He licked his lips as I stepped in between his legs and began to ease down to my knees. I looked him in his eyes and smiled then I straightened my legs and planted both my feet down hard on his dick.

"Fucking bitch!" He screamed, as he brought his knees to his chest. "You fucking bitch!"

Lifting my leg high, I delivered my bare foot to his face over and over until I heard my toes crack. Ignoring the pain, I ran to the kitchen and grabbed a knife from inside the cabinet drawer. Then I slowly walked back through the living room with both hands firmly on the handle. I watched as Beau eased up the wall on to his feet. I stopped and waited for him to move towards me.

"Fuck you, bitch!" He screamed, taking a step forward.

"Think about little Brittany," I said coldly. "It'll be hard on her growing up without a Daddy."

Then there was nothing but silence as we looked at each other. My heart continued to beat fiercely as I waited for him to move. When he finally did it was to put on his clothes. I held the knife in front of me until he walked into the living room and out of the front door.

My body ached all over and I hated Beau for it. I should have cut his ding-a-ling off when I had the chance. I was afraid and furious at the same time. After Beau left, I slipped on a pair of sweats and my tennis shoes and started to pack an overnight bag. I was going to check into a hotel, but then I decided I was not going to be afraid to be alone in my own home. So instead I lodged the sofa against the door and slept on the living room floor with the knife under my pillow. I was scared but at least I was still home.

Chapter 39

When Daddy called that morning I was standing in my closet going through my selection of scarves. I was trying to find something to hide the burgundy bruise Beau's hands left on my neck.

"Good Morning, Baby Girl."

"Good Morning, Daddy." I said, trying to sound cheerful.

"What's wrong?"

Hearing the concern in my father's voice made me feel worse than I already did. I walked out of my closet and stretched across my bed with the phone still pressed to my ear.

"Beau was here last night," I said, softly.

"Did he hurt you?" Daddy, asked angrily.

"I'm okay," I assured him. "Just tired."

"Tell me what happened."

I went over the details of the previous night's events with my father. I could hear and feel his rage on the other end of the phone.

After I talked him out of going to Fatty's and seeking street justice he told me the reason why he was calling me so early.

Daddy informed me that Beau had been involved and was still currently involved in all types of illegal dealings, including everything from car theft to drug trafficking and distribution.

"He's dirty, Baby Girl," Daddy said, "But I know we can take him down."

"If he's been getting away with all these things for so long, what makes you so sure?" I asked.

"He made two mistakes," Daddy said his voice cold. "One he forgot to repay his debt back in Queens. He owes this supplier, Montay over a half a mill."

Damn. "What was the second mistake?" I asked.

"He touched my daughter."

"I love you."

"I love you, too."

"What about Stephanie?" I asked, "Do you think he killed her?"

"I wouldn't put it past him," Daddy said. "He's been known to harass a woman or two. The word on the street is that he has no problem with taking or breaking what he wants."

"So what happens next?"

"I'll call you once it's been taken care of," he said. "The less you know the better."

Chapter 40

I don't know how Daddy did it but he did. I was sitting in the living room flipping through the latest issue of Bride's magazine when Daddy called and told me to turn to channel 11.

There was a crawl on the bottom of the screen that said: "Breaking News." The scene was total chaos. There were unmarked police cars everywhere. The night sky glowed from the blue and red flashing lights. I turned up the TV volume to listen to the skinny, blonde news reporter.

"This is Sarah Brazier reporting for WFFZ Channel 11 News," she said, speaking into the wireless microphone. "We're on the scene of what is being called one of the biggest drug busts in Madison County in over fifteen years. Tonight, undercover agents raided the home and office of this man…" She paused as the cameraman zoomed into the scene. There he was wearing nothing but boxers with his hands handcuffed behind his back.

"Twenty-nine year old Broderick "Beau" Malone." Sarah continued." Malone was inside the home at the time along with an unidentified woman and Malone's four year old daughter." I watched as one of the officers assisted Beau into the backseat of a patrol car.

"Agents found an undisclosed amount of marijuana in Malone's home, along with more than two hundred and fifty thousand dollars.

But the raid didn't end there. Just a few hours later agents raided Fatty's a local nightclub and the Low Key, a local strip club - both owned by Malone. It was inside the club's that authorities found a number of drugs including cocaine, ecstasy, and heroin. There they also compensated an undetermined amount of cash. Agents say the items were found in a hidden closet inside Malone's office. Now, inside this office were several hidden cameras. Officers will be reviewing the surveillance footage over the next few days and then it will be determined whether or not other arrests will follow."

The camera zoomed back in on Sarah. "Stay tuned to WFFZ for more updates," She said. "Now back to you, Gill."

I pressed the power button on the remote and watched as the picture faded to black. Daddy was still on the other end of the phone. The two of us had not spoken a word through the entire broadcast.

"Where is Brittany?" I asked, concerned," Is she okay?"

"She's fine," he said." She's with her Aunt Erica."

I hated that the child had to see her father being handcuffed and read his rights but I was selfishly happy that Beau was behind bars.

"Beau has a rap sheet out of this world," Daddy informed me. "Along with enough warrants to last a lifetime. Now that he's in custody, there's no way the authorities are going to set him free."

"I guess he'll be living the rest of his life locked up," I said, relieved.

"Not for long," Daddy said." I give him eight months if he lives that long."

"Why is that?"

"Montay has connects on the inside," he said." I'm willing to bet they'll be all over Beau before he gets a chance to memorize his inmate ID number."

I told Daddy I loved him and told him to give Mama a kiss for me then I hung up and called Damon. I told him that I missed him like crazy and that I couldn't wait for him to come home so that we could set a date for our wedding.

Chapter 41

Damon was home again and the two of us were so in love it almost made me nauseous. We had our new home completely furnished even though we agreed we would not move in until after our wedding which was not going to be for another six months. When he first returned home, Damon and I had taken an entire week off to spend with each other. But we had made up for all that phone sex in the first night. Beau was charged with a number of counts, including: drug trafficking, robbery, assault, and tax evasion. They were also holding him on suspicion of murder but daddy figured that count may not stick due to both Stephanie and Sasha having traces of drugs in their systems. Daddy was almost positive, Beau was linked to other drug related murders but without witnesses it was going to be hard to prove. Nonetheless, they had frozen all of his assets and he was looking at possibly serving thirty years to life.

Amel, on the other hand, was doing well in rehab. I made it my business to call her or go see her at least once a week and just as the counselors had warned me she was pissed off with me for several weeks. She called me a nosey bitch at least a hundred times and told me it was my fault she wasn't with Beau when he needed her most. That was until she read in the newspaper that the unidentified female in Beau's home the night of his arrest was her best friend, Nikki. It turned out Beau had been getting with Nikki behind Amel's back. After hearing that and finding out the Escalade Beau gave her was stolen, Amel sung like a bird and confessed that Beau had been the one who turned her on to heroin. I promised to help her get back into school once she completed her treatment and to hook her up with a job. I felt partially at fault for her getting involved with Beau in the first place.

Chapter 42

It was a beautiful August day and I had just made it home from a day of gown shopping when I strolled into my apartment and found Damon sitting in front of the TV staring into space.

"Hey Baby," I smiled, bending down to kiss his lips. He turned his head and I ended up kissing his cheek instead. I sensed something wasn't right. "What's the matter?" I asked, sitting down next to him on the sofa.

Running his hand over his face, Damon sat silent. Then he handed me the remote to the TV. "Turn it on," He said, his voice low.

Confused, I took the remote and pressed power. The TV was on channel three, the local programming channel. I looked at Damon with raised eyebrows and waited for him to say something. Picking up the remote to our DVD/VHS combo he pressed play. I felt my stomach flip when I looked at the screen. There I was naked with my legs in the air with Beau deep inside of me.

"Beau sent this little wedding present Fed Ex to my office," Damon said, looking at me with a cold stare. "He said he thought we might enjoy it."

Standing Damon turned to look at me. Seeing the tears in his eyes made my heartache.

"Baby," I said, softly.

"Why didn't you tell me?" He asked, angry.

"I didn't want…"

"You didn't want what!" He snapped, cutting me off," Didn't want me to know you were fucking around on me?"

"I've never cheated on you," I stated, calmly." That happened before us."

"Then why didn't you tell me?" He asked," If it happened before us then why didn't you say something."

I turned my eyes from his, unable to give him an answer.

"That's what I thought," He said, his voice raised." Did the two of you enjoy playing me for a fool?" He asked.

"No one played you."

"That day in my office," He said, staring at me." The two of you acted like you had never met." Looking back at the TV, Damon watched as Beau turned me over into the doggie position. "It's obvious that the two of you were old friends," He said, sarcastically.

"We were not friends!" I snapped." He was stalking me!"

Laughing Damon snatched the remote from my hand, aimed it at the TV and pressed mute. The room was filled with sounds of Beau and me moaning. The picture sped up as Damon pressed fast forward then released the button so that the video went back to normal play.

"This my pussy?" Beau asked, groaning.

Silence.

"Is this my pussy?" He asked again.

"This your pussy baby," I moaned. There was silence again as Damon pressed mute again.

"It doesn't sound like he was stalking you," he stated.

"I can explain," I said, nervously.

"Explain what?" He screamed. "I don't need a damn explanation. I see it all right there!" He pointed at the TV.

"Tell me this…" He said, staring at me.

"Out of all the fucking men in Huntsville…"

"Why did you choose him?"

"I don't know…" I said, sadly.

"You don't now?" He looked like he wanted to slap my ass but instead he turned, giving me an evil glare then walked away.

I watched as he walked out the room down the hall. When he returned he had his bags in his hands. No words were spoken as he slid the key to our apartment of his key ring then threw it on the couch beside me. I stared at the ring on my fingers as Damon walked out slamming the door behind him. My heart told me to run behind him and beg him to listen to me. My pride held me on the sofa allowing him to leave.

Chapter 43

I always promised myself I would never cry over a man. I lied. It had been two weeks since Damon left me and I had become an emotional wreck. I cried in the morning. I cried at night. I was miserable without him. I felt like a part of me was missing and I had no idea how to get it back. I was use to being the one everyone came to for man problems and now I was having problems with my own man. A part of me wanted to write him off and let him go but I couldn't; I was stuck in love with no place to go.

After hearing Mama and Shontay say "Talk to him" for what seemed like a trillion times, I decided to go see Damon. I pulled up in front of Nomad just in time to see Damon walking out with a tall, slim, light-skinned female. They were holding hands as they walked laughing and talking. I felt my blood pressure rise as she touched her hand to his face and slowly kissed his lips. He stopped walking when he saw me climb out of my Mercedes with my keys in my hand. I stomped up the sidewalk ready to slap him down and ripe the weave off the female.

"Octavia," he said, dropping her hand.

"What's going on here?" I asked, with attitude.

"Nadia and I were just…" *I know he didn't just say Nadia.*

"Nadia?" I asked, cutting my eyes at the woman.

She took a step away from Damon then offered her hand to me.

It's nice to finally meet you," she said. I wondered if she was going to feel that way after I stumped her a new booty hole with my three inch heels.

I left her hanging and looked at Damon. "You didn't waste much time," I said.

"This is not what you think," He said, stepping towards me.

"That's right," Nadia jumped in." After what happened in LA I thought it was better for me to come here and try to work things out."

"What happened in LA?" I asked, still heated.

"You didn't tell her?" Nadia asked, looking at Damon.

"No," he said, guilt written on his face.

Looking from Damon to Nadia then back to Damon I asked," Tell me what?"

"I came on to him," Nadia said." When I found out he was going to be in town I went to see him and all those old memories came fading back and before I knew it."

She didn't finish her sentence she just stood there looking at me with a pitiful expression. I looked at Damon feeling a lump in my throat. I was angry but I refused to cry in front of him or the hoe he had obviously cheated on me with. I stared him in his eyes as I slowly slid the ring from my finger. I held the ring out.

He didn't move to take it so I grabbed his hand and laid the ring in his palm.

"Octavia, wait," he said, watching as I turned to walk away.

"Octavia!" He screamed.

I closed the door—started the engine and pulled away crying. I hadn't asked him about Nadia while we were visiting with his family because I assumed there was nothing going on. Now I was the one feeling like a fool.

That night, I climbed into bed and contemplated on calling Tony. I hadn't spoken to him since I had been with Damon but I knew he was on call if I needed him. I didn't call him. I wanted Damon and if I didn't have him then I just wanted to be alone. Instead, I curled up in the fetal position and cried myself to sleep.

Chapter 44

I was in a daze as I attempted to work. I couldn't understand how everything could be so good between me and Damon then quickly turn so bad. I wanted to call him and at least attempt to work through our problems but pride is a bitch, a bitch that was holding me back. The day passed like a blur but I somehow managed to make it to five without breaking down. At exactly 5:01 p.m., I locked my office then hopped into my Mercedes. I didn't want to go home but at the same time I wanted to be alone. I drove aimlessly with my future on my mind, while Floetry's "It's Getting Late" flowed through the car stereo. I thought about Damon and our home.

I pulled up to the gate then entered my pass code. After pulling around the circular driveway, I parked directly in front of the main entrance. I got out of the car with my Gucci bag on my shoulders. I checked to make sure I had my gun inside then dropped in my keys. Since the break in at my apartment, I never left home without my piece. I walked through the door, deactivated the alarm then locked the door behind me. Inside I slipped my jacket off then laid it on the glass table in the foyer. I looked around at the beautiful glass and marble frames Damon and I had picked out just weeks before. Everything in the home displayed mine and Damon's personal style and taste. I was catching hell just looking at the furniture and the decor. *God, why did I have to fall in love?* I walked into the family room then settled into the large Italian leather sofa. I kicked my heels across the Oriental rug then tucked my feet underneath me. I sat in the darkness debating on whether or not to call Damon. The sound of glass breaking disrupted my thoughts. I slowly eased off the sofa, grabbing my purse. I clutched my purse close to my body with one hand then slipped my other inside the fold, clutching my gun. I tiptoed slowly into the kitchen and found Damon down on his knees picking up fragments of the crystal glass, he had evidently dropped.

"Damon…"

He stood slowly, then turned and looked at me. He looked fine as always, wearing his denim shorts and white wife beater. He stared at me and I saw "the look" was still there. I watched him while he opened the drawer that concealed the trash bin, and then dropped the glass in.

"I didn't think you'd be here." I said, watching as he continued to sweep up the glass. "I didn't see your car."

"I'm parked in the garage," he said.

"What are you doing here?"

"I wanted to get away," he said, leaning against the kitchen island. "I wanted to be alone."

"Oh…well, I'll leave," I said quickly, turning on my feet. I didn't want him to see the tears forming in my eyes.

"Octavia."

"What?"

"Nothing happened with Nadia." I turned back around facing him, trying hard to force away my tears.

"I don't care, Damon." I said, softly. "It's over and done."

He rubbed his hands over his head. "Just like that?" He asked, staring at me.

"Just like that," I said, tears now streaming down my cheeks.

"After everything we've been through," He said, taking steps towards me.

"You want to just walk away?" He asked. I looked at him with my eyebrows raised. He stood in front of me with a mixture of confusion and anger on his face.

"No Damon," I said, wiping my face with the back of my hands. "I don't care what happened with *you* and Nadia. I love you and I want you." I said. "Only you." He pulled me into his strong arms.

"I love you, too," he whispered, running his fingers through my hair. He cradled my face in his hands then kissed me as if it was our last kiss on Earth. He slid his hands up my skirt then caressed my round, firm ass. I stepped back, then removed all of my clothing. He looked at my naked body, with shear lust illuminating in his eyes. I quickly helped him take off his shirt then his shorts and finally his boxers. His beautiful dick stood out like a hungry serpent ready to devour its prey. My kitty got wet just from the thought. I wrapped my arms around his shoulders as he lifted me up around his waist. He carried me the short distance to the wall then pushed my body up against it. I moved my lips from his then down to his neck then back up to his earlobe. He entered me with full force, causing my back to slam against the wall. I held onto his shoulders tightly with my arms and held his dick tightly with the walls of my throbbing pussy. Damon pulled my back off the wall, and then bounced me up and down wildly on his dick.

"Oh…yes…" I moaned. "Harder baby…harder!" I wanted him to knock the pain I had been feeling for the past weeks out of body. I dug my nails into his shoulder blades. At the same time I wanted him to feel my pain and know just how hard my life had been without him. He carried me over to the kitchen island and laid me down. He dove as far inside of me as our bodies would allow then began pounding my pussy harder. He moved inside my body like a new man. It was at that moment that I knew our relationship would never be the same. It would be better! He was showing me that he was all I needed emotionally and sexually. Tears of joy and pain rolled down my face as I arched my back and released my hot sticky wetness.

"I love you!" He screamed. He came, filling my body with his warm juices.

Damon pulled me into his arms, then we eased down to the floor. "I missed you so much." I said.

"Let's not talk about that," he said, kissing my forehead. "Let's just talk about our future."

"Do you still want to marry me?" I asked.

"Of course I do." He said.

"I'm not going to run at the first sign of trouble," he said. "And if we expect to make this work, you can't have one foot outside of the door."

"I'm not going to," I assured him. "I'm here and here is where I want to be."

He brought my hand to his lips then kissed each one of my fingers.

"Wait right here," he smiled. I watched while he began to put on his clothes.

"Where are you going?"

"Out to my car," he said. "To get your ring."

"I'll be upstairs in our bedroom waiting." I said, seductively.

"Round two?"

"Round two."

He gave me a seductive smile then exited through the French doors that opened out to the patio. I slipped my panties and shirt back on then headed upstairs to our bedroom.

I stretched across the satin damask comforter thinking about how good it felt to be back in Damon's arms. I won't lie: I was a mess without him. It's crazy how life takes unexpected turns; some are for the good; others are for the worse. The thing is you have to keep moving, and take every day, one step at a time.

Minutes passed and Damon had yet to return. I decided to go down and see if he needed some help. I ran down the winding staircase, taking the stairs two sets at a time. I leaped off the last one then headed for the kitchen. There was a familiar aroma coming from inside. I walked through the doorway and stopped so quickly, I almost fell on my ass. My heart began to beat hysterically.

"What's up, Ma?" Beau blew a long ring of smoke out through his nose. "Did you miss me?" Beau stood leaning against the kitchen island, wearing khaki pants, Timbs, and a wife beater. He held a freshly rolled blunt in between his fingers. I stared into his bloodshot eyes.

"Where's Damon?"

He took another hit, coughed, then blew smoke out through his mouth.

I scanned out of the corner of my eyes and saw my purse lying on the opposite end of the floor.

Beau laughed. "He went for a swim," he said.

"What?"

Beau nodded in the direction of the patio. I ran past him to the open doors and saw Damon floating face down in the pool.

"No!" I screamed. I jumped in then water then swam to him. I wrapped my arms around his shoulder then kicked my legs until I reached the pool's edge. I climbed out, then using all the strength in my body pulled Damon out. There was blood trickling from the side of his head just above his temple.

"Damon, please wake up," I cried. Beau stood watching me.

"He can't hear you, bitch." He laughed. I ignored him, then began performing CPR. *Please Lord, please don't let him die.* Seconds passed but it felt like days before Damon began to toss and turn. He coughed uncontrollably as water flew out of his mouth. *Thank you Lord!* I rubbed Damon's face as tears poured from my eyes. Beau walked out onto the patio, standing over us.

"Good job, bitch," he said. "Now that nigga can live long enough to watch me kill your black ass."

"Why are you doing this?" I whined, looking up at him.

"Because I can." He grabbed a hand full of my hair.

"No!" I screamed, kicking my legs. Beau dragged me soaking wet back into the house. My skin felt like it was on fire from being pulled across the concrete. Inside the kitchen, he flung me across the floor. I landed ass first against the cabinets.

"Get up…" he ordered. I didn't move.

"I said get up!" He marched towards me then planted the heel of his boot swiftly into my stomach, knocking the wind out of me. I was doubled over in pain but I didn't so much as groan. I used the wall as support, then slowly eased myself up onto my feet. I stared at Beau. He looked purely evil as he continued to take pulls. *How'd he get out?*

"A nigga posted bond." He said, as if he was reading my mind.

"1 mill." He paced back and forth across the floor then stopped in front of me.

"You were waiting on that, weren't you?"

"What are you talking about?" I asked, lowly.

"Don't play stupid with me!" He screamed. "I know you set me up!"

"I don't know what you're talking about..." He pulled back his hand then literally slapped the taste out of my mouth. I grabbed the left side of my face, trying to sooth the throbbing.

"You're just like the rest of those bitches," he said. He dropped the lit roach on the floor then stomped it out.

"Money hungry hoes."

I nonchalantly looked past him outside by the pool. Damon was struggling to get up on his feet. It hurt me to see him in so much pain. Pain that I knew was caused by me. I made a promise that if we survived Beau's wrath, I would spend the rest of my life making it up to him.

"That bitch I use to call my baby's mama was a hoe." He continued.

"I'm a good girl..." He mimicked a woman's voice. "Bitch please."

"She was letting niggas run in and out of her like a corner store."

"Sasha was hoe..." He continued. "But I knew that..."

"Any broad who will let a nigga smell her pussy for a couple of dollas is *definitely* a hoe!" He laughed.

"But she fucked up when she stole from me." He paced back and forth.

"I can't stand a thief or a liar." He looked at me with a smug grin.

"Amel...well she's a good bitch," He said, scratching his head.

"That hoe's trainable."

"But she's a dumb hoe." He laughed again. "I threw her country ass a couple of Gs and she lost her mind."

"Money...hungry...hoes."

"She would have faced the same fate as the other two but... " He pointed at me. "Captain save a hoe here, stepped in."

"Then there's you..." He said, sucking his teeth. "We could have been somethin' together."

"But you're a sneaky hoe." He said. "You can't be trusted."

He reached into his pocket and pulled out a vial containing a white powder.

"One taste will make the best hoe a fiend." He said, holding up the vial. He unscrewed the cap, poured some of the substance on the counter top, then snorted it straight up his nose. He snorted then rubbed his nostrils with his fingers.

"This some good shit!" He said. "Heroin, in its purest form." He rubbed his unshaven face with his hand.

"Ma, you gotta try this shit." I knew if I had a chance, I'd better take it then. I faked like I was going to move towards him then dove for my bag. Beau jumped on top of me like a man possessed.

"Where you goin'?" He asked, slapping me in the back of the head.

"I told you...you were a sneaky bitch!" He pulled my hair then flipped me onto my back. He looked like the devil himself as he stood over me.

"You're still sexy." He said, wickedly. His eyes traveled down to my open blouse. He was completely deranged. His demeanor continued to change from one degree to another.

"See what you do to me?" He asked, gripping his hard on. If he planned to rape me, he would have to kill me first. There was no way I was going out like that. I raised my leg and kicked him dead off in his nuts.

"Muthafuc..." He screamed, falling on top of me. I swung my fist wildly, landing a few blows across his face. He regained his composure then wrapped both his hands around my neck.

"Stupid hoe!" He yelled, squeezing my neck. I attempted to pry his hands from my neck but he had the grip of a python.

"Stupid...stupid bitch!" He screamed.

I felt my air passage closing up. Tears trickled down the side of my cheeks as I gasped for air. Suddenly he released me. I grabbed my neck then rolled onto my side attempting to catch my breath. My throat was burning and I felt like I would pass out at any second.

"Get up!" He yelled, jerking me up by one arm. He threw me up against the counter. I pushed my hair out of my face then looked at him. He reached into another pocket and pulled out a mini Ziploc bag fill to the brim with heroin. He dipped his finger in and scooped out as much as his fingernail could hold. He snorted the substance up quickly. He dropped the bag on the counter then looked at me.

"You won't get away with this." I said, breathless. "No one will ever believe I overdosed."

"No one will ever believe I overdosed." He mimicked me. He slapped me again.

"Hoe, I know that!" He snapped. "That's why I brought this." He reached behind him, into the waist band of his pants and pulled out a gun. I got weak in the knees as I stared at the chrome object.

"You think I'm stupid?" He asked, pointing the gun at me.

"Give me a little credit."

I looked past him and saw Damon was gone.

"What you lookin' at?" Beau asked. "Your man?"

"He can't save you, ma." Beau turned with his gun still aimed at me.

"What the fuck?" He said, seeing Damon was no longer lying on the deck.

"Come on, bitch." He grabbed me by the throat then pushed me towards the doors. "Let's go find this nigga."

"Wait..." I said, turning to face him. "This isn't about Damon..."

"I'm the one you want and I'm here. Please let Damon go."

Beau stroked my face softly. I thought there was a glimmer of hope for a moment. I was wrong.

"That's sweet, Ma" He said. "But we both know that ain't happenin'" He grabbed me by the hair then jerked my head back. He pressed the gun against my throat.

"I'm going to let him watch me fuck you." He said. "Then I'm going to kill both ya'll asses."

"Now go!" He held his grip on me as I walked out onto the patio in front of him.

"Yo, D," he called." You got ten seconds before I put a hole in this bitch's head." There was no response.

"Nigga, I ain't playing." Beau yelled. My heart felt like it was going to jump in my throat.

"Fine..."

"Ten"

"Nine"

"Eight..."

"Alright...alright don't shoot." Damon appeared from the garage. He walked towards us with his hands out in front of him. Our eyes locked.

"Still the damn gentleman," Beau laughed. "Even when you see a hoe is about to get you killed." He pushed me then kicked me square in the middle of my ass.

"Go 'head," he said. "Run to that nigga." I looked from Damon to Beau back to Damon. I was scared shitless that Beau may shoot me in my back.

"If you don't go," he said, pointing the gun at me. "I'm going to shoot your black ass right now." I moved quickly in Damon's direction. The tears that had stopped earlier flowed again. Damon pulled me into his arms then rubbed my face.

"Everything is going to be alright," he said, lovingly. *How do you figure?* He was obviously a lot more optimistic about the situation than I was.

I wrapped my arms around his waist and felt something pressed against his back under his shirt. I looked up into his eyes.

"It's okay baby," he said, strongly.

"D, don't lie to that bitch." Beau said, walking towards us. "Tell that hoe the muthafuckin' truth."

"You 'bout to die bitch!" He said, looking at me. "It's sad... but it's true." "You 'bout to die!"

"Back in the house," Beau ordered, pointing the gun. I wrapped my arm around Damon's waist and the two of us slowly moved towards our home.

"Walk in front of me," Damon said, calmly. I looked at him briefly then did as he said.

"You wanna get one last look at that phat ass!" Beau laughed, loudly. "I feel you bro!"

"Matter fact…gone and shake it." Beau said, licking his lips. I looked at Damon; he nodded his head in approval. I pulled my shirt up around my waist and made my booty bounce. I imitated the girl's I had seen on the videos. I spread my feet shoulder length a part then dropped down to the ground.

"That's what I'm talking bout!" Beau cheered. "Drop it like it's hot!"

"D, that's the same shit she use to do on my dick." He snickered.

"Oh…that's right, that's right…you seen the video." Damon's eyes narrowed to small angry slits. I looked over my shoulder at Beau. He smiled a sick seductive smile as he watched me. I rotated my hips and clapped my ass like my life depended on it. Actually, it did! He never saw Damon removing the crowbar from his pants, nor did he see the blow that came to the side of his head. He stumbled sideways never mumbling a word. The same sick smile plastered on his face as his finger pulled the trigger. I was frozen in place, stuck between life and death. My life did not rush before me but the people I loved did. Mama. Daddy. Shontay. Damon. I hear glass shatter but I don't feel a thing. The bullet missed me. Damon moved to get the gun while I stood in place. I was stuck like glue.

"Baby…"

"Are you okay?" I looked down at my bruised body then nodded my head.

"Go call the police."

I moved slowly stepping across the broken glass from the door, into the kitchen to get my purse. My hands were shaking like I was having convulsions as I dug through the contents. I finally remembered; I left my phone in the car. We had yet to have a home phone installed so I had no other choice but to go out to my car.

"I left my phone in the car." I said, voice cracking. "I'll be right back." I ran as fast as my aching legs would allow out the house to my car. I retrieved my phone from the inside console, flipped it open and began dialing.

9…1…

Three shots rang out piercing the night air.

Chapter 45

I stared at my reflection in the floor length mirror. It's been six months today, since Beau wrecked havoc on my life. Physically, all the signs of his rampage are gone. My scars and bruises have all healed. The door has been replaced at my home and the deck that was stained with blood has been completely replaced. All that is left now is the memories. I had a few sleepless nights but Damon was right there comforting me. We no longer talk about the night he killed Beau or any of the events that led up to that day. We focus only on the present and our plans for the future.

"Are you ready?" Daddy asked, smiling at me.

"As ready as I'll ever be." I adjusted the straps of my Vera Wang gown one last time. "I can't believe I'm getting married!" Rubbing his hand over my belly, Daddy smiled.

"I can't believe I'm going to be a grandpa." His granddaughter kicked at the sound of his voice.

"Me either," I laughed. "This is not how I pictured this day."

"Me, wobbling down the isle," I said.

"You still look beautiful."

"Thanks Daddy."

I smiled proudly at the small group of family and friends looking on as my father walked me down the garden path of mine and Damon's home. There was nothing countrified about the one hundred roses that surrounded us or the six piece orchestra that played. Everything was perfect in every way. As the two of use approached Damon, I looked at him wondering how I could be so lucky to have such a good man. The Lord knows it was nothing I did to deserve him but yet here he was waiting to make me his wife. I said it before: life can take some unexpected turns. It looks like mine finally took the right one!

Epilogue

I slipped away from the small crowd, not wanting to draw attention to myself. I had official business to settle now that the ceremony was complete. I walked over to my partner who had watched the entire ceremony from the side of the house. He wore Ray Ban sunglasses to cover his eyes and a dark blue Armani suit.

"You got something for me?" He asked, extending his hand to me. I gave him a firm handshake, then reached into the inside pocket of my jacket. I removed the brown envelope then handed it to him. He took it then slipped it inside his jacket.

"Aren't you going to count it?" I asked.

"Naw, I know you're good for it."

"I threw in a little extra for your trouble."

"Appreciate that," he said, coolly. "After all, you did almost get me shot."

"Call us even," I said. "You almost killed her."

"How was I supposed to know she was absent the day they taught defensive driving in school?" He joked.

"That shit ain't funny," I snapped. "Nor is it funny that you tried to rape her." I looked around to make sure no one was watching us.

"I should kill you myself for that one."

"You told me to make it realistic," Lawrence said, removing his shades.

"I told you to scare her."

"That's what I did," he said, arrogantly. Lawrence has always been an arrogant motherfucker. He studied my expression.

"I'm sorry man," he said. "I wasn't going to go through with it."

"You almost blew your cover that day at the restaurant." I said, changing the subject. The more I thought about him trying to rape Octavia the more I wanted to kill him.

"I told you to wear a disguise."

"I wore glasses," he argued. "Damn!"

"What's the big deal?" He asked.

"You got what you wanted."

"Besides, what's so special about this broad?" He asked, shrugging his shoulders.

"Why go through so much trouble?"

"You seen her," I said, smiling. "She's beautiful."

"Come on man," Lawrence laughed. "You've had pretty of fine ass hoes."

"Hoes that you wouldn't have to go through *this* much trouble to get." He paused then rubbed the patch of hair on his chin.

"She must have some bomb ass pussy." He laughed. I was not amused at all by his disrespect.

"Watch your mouth," I said, angry. "That's my wife you're talking about."

"My bad man!" He laughed, putting his hands up. "It's just that, I never thought I'd see the ultimate playa fall in love."

"I just don't understand what it is about this girl."

"I chose her." I said. "I did my homework on her."

That's exactly how it went down. I first saw Octavia's picture in Black Woman's Monthly. She was featured for the outstanding job she had done with the Ambiance. I was infatuated from the very beginning. She was fine, educated, and single. Those three things are hard to find in any woman. I had been watching her for a while. It was no accident that I showed up at her mother's home that day. I was far from lost. I knew my way around Huntsville, like I know my own nuts. I also knew Octavia's every move. I knew where she ate. I knew where she stayed. I even knew where she went shopping. I knew about Beau too, way before he mailed me the copy of their sex tape. I knew about their little date that night at the Low Key. It was Lawrence watching her inside the club. I gave her the opportunity to break ties with Beau but she didn't. That's when I stepped in. I approached Beau about doing business together. I'm a firm believer in keeping your enemies closer. I knew all about his bad business, but that was none of my concern. My only concern was keeping him and Octavia apart. In the end I wish things could have worked out differently. I still would have killed him; that was always a part of the plan. I just didn't intend for Octavia to show up that night at the house. I thought my plan was fool proof.

First, I had Lawrence post Beau's bond. Then pretending to be Octavia, I sent him a text message, asking him to meet me at our home. The only problem was that Octavia showed up, and he ended up beating the shit out of her and damn near killing her. I could have let Beau live but I couldn't risk him exposing the truth. That's why as soon as Octavia left to call for help; I put three bullets in his chest. He begged me for his life. However, I had to do, what I had to do.

"Tell me one thing…"

"What's that?"

"Would you do it all again?"

I looked across the garden and saw Octavia standing with our parents; laughing and talking without a care in the world. Smiling, I watched Octavia as she rubbed her swollen belly.

"Of course I would…"

The Love, Lies & Lust Series continues with . . .

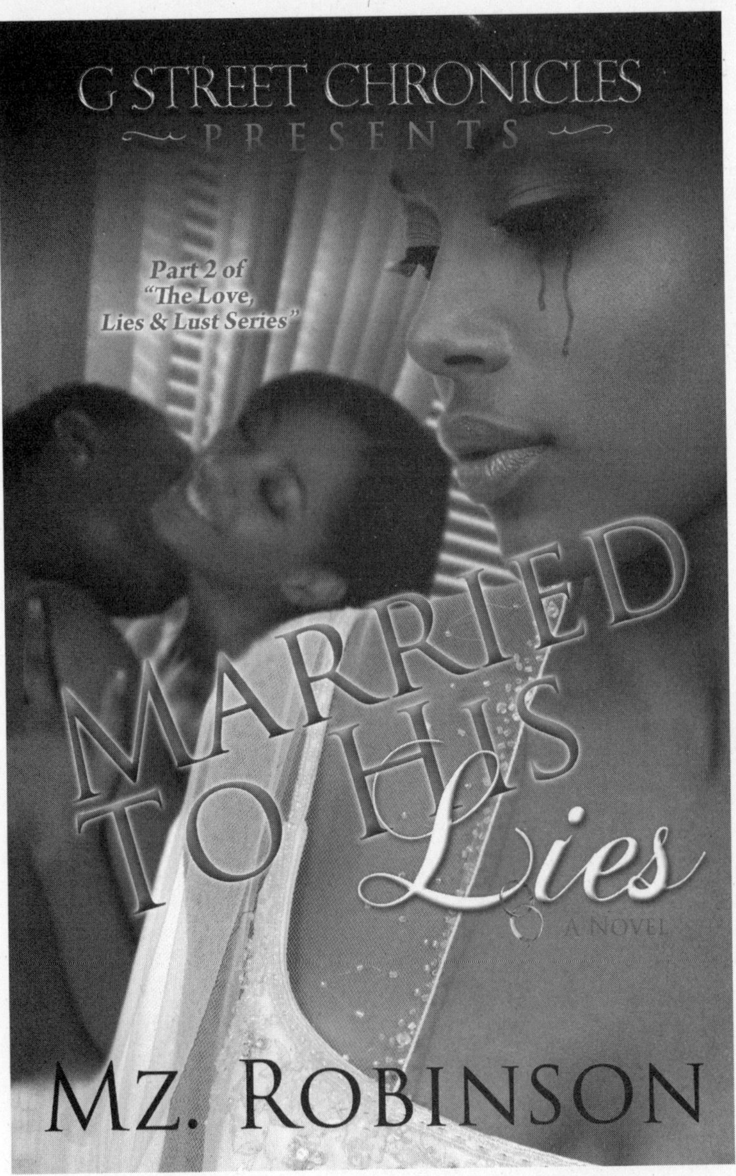

The Love, Lies & Lust Series Continues

CHAPTER 1

"I'm sorry, baby," Kenny said, kissing my forehead. "I promise it'll be just the two of us next weekend.

"You've been saying that for the last month," I said annoyed.

"What am I suppose to do, Shontay?"

Stepping back, I put some distance between the two of us. "Why don't you try telling Alicia that we've had Kiya for the last four weekends, and this weekend, we'd like to spend some time alone?"

Frowning, Kenny rubbed his hand back and forth across the stubble on his face. "Alicia is trying to get her cosmetology license," he said. "She works through the week, so that only leaves the weekends for her to go to classes."

I couldn't believe my ears. Not only was he canceling our plans for another Saturday alone, but he also wanted me to support his ghetto-tramp baby's mama in her educational endeavors. I had put my own education on hold to support him and our marriage, and not once did I get a thank you. Now he had the audacity to support Alicia's trifling ass.

"Maybe she should have thought about that before she decided to lay up with someone else's man," I snapped. "Besides, I thought you told me Kiya was going to be with her grandmother this weekend."

"She was, but Alicia's mom decided to go to Tunica," he said.

"She didn't tell Alicia until this morning."

Rolling my eyes, I threw my hands up in frustration. I was defeated, and arguing about the subject wasn't going to change a thing. Sitting down on the edge of the bed, I exhaled. "I'll think of something for the three of us to do together," I said.

"Thanks, baby," he said smiling.

***

Scanning over the selection of paperback and hardcover books, I searched for something to take home and read. I was spending a beautiful Saturday afternoon in Barnes and Nobles alone. After thirty minutes with Kenny and Kiya, I decided I needed a break. I pulled out a paperback titled G-Spot by Noire, and began to read the back cover.

"That's a hot piece," I heard someone say.

I looked up and found myself staring into a pair of gray cat-like eyes. The eyes complimented thick eyebrows and a pair of succulent-full lips. The man they belonged to had smooth, flawless skin, the color of pecans. I nonchalantly lowered my eyes, and glanced over his wide built frame. Even in the dirt-covered overalls he was wearing, I could tell he had large biceps and an athletic physique. He was wearing a dingy black bandana that hid his hair, and cement covered leather steel toe boots. Sexy, even covered in dirt, I thought. I redirected my attention back to his eyes, and asked, "Excuse me?"

He smiled, revealing a set of straight white teeth. "G-Spot," he said. His voice was deep and sexy. He had the type of voice that was perfect for phone sex. "It's a hot piece," he said. His thick tongue rolled along the edge of his bottom lip, causing heat to surge through the seat of my panties.

I shifted my weight from one leg to the other, and asked, "You've read it?" His eyes traveled from my face down to my low cut tank top, then back up again. "Yes," he said, "it's one of my favorites."

"Thanks." I said, giving him a small smile. As I turned around to walk away, I could feel his eyes burning a hole in my ass through my denim Capri pants.

"So, you're just going to take my suggestion and run?" he asked.

I turned around slowly, and my eyes locked with his. There was something so sexual about the way he looked at me. For a brief second I could have sworn I saw "Let's fuck", spelled out in his corneas.

"You could at least tell me your name," he said seductively.

Trying to control the flutters in my stomach, and keep my hardened nipples from poking a hole in my shirt, I crossed my arms across my breasts.

"Thanks again," I said, instead of telling him my name. "Have a nice day."

I quickly walked up the aisle to the checkout. I was practically running to get away from him, not because I thought he was a psycho or a rapist. But because, in less than five minutes, he had accomplished what my husband hadn't been able to do in weeks; he managed to make my pussy wet.

After making my purchase, I sat in my car watching the front doors of the store. After five minutes, he walked out carrying a large bag. He walked with his head held high, and this air of confidence. The brother was fine. I'm talking fine with a capital F, as in "fuck me fine". I stalked him until he climbed into a white Ford F150 with SB Building & Construction painted in bright red letters on the door, started the engine, and pulled out of the parking lot.

I reclined the driver's seat of my Honda Accord and unbuttoned the top of my pants. The dark tint on my windows prevented anyone from seeing inside. That was a good thing, because I sat there in broad daylight with my AC blowing and my fingers inside my panties, stroking my throbbing clit. I closed my eyes, and a vivid picture of the stranger filled my head. I massaged and played with my clit until I came. The entire time I had been daydreaming that he was down on his knees with his face in between my legs.

***

I walked through the doorway of my home and cursed. My living room was a mess. "Damnit," I muttered under my breath.

I tripped over a bikini clad black Barbie, and kicked the doll across the floor. I looked around the room. There were dolls and building blocks everywhere. The room looked like a toy factory.

Why can't he make her pick-up after herself?

Kicking my way through the toys to the kitchen, I contemplated on cleaning up my stepdaughter's mess, but then decided against it. I had been playing Kenny's maid for the last eight years, I was not about to do the same for his daughter.

Before Kenny and I got married two years ago, we had dated for six years. He was the first man I ever trusted; that's where I made my mistake. I thought he could do no wrong. I put his ass on a pedestal, and damn near kissed the ground he walked on. In return, he made a fool of me by running from motel to motel with woman after woman after woman. It's not that Kenny isn't a good man; he just has a big problem keeping his dick to himself.

He cheated more times than I can count, and probably more than I care to know. Before we got married, there were several occasions my best friend and I busted him with other women. It was never a difficult task to catch Kenny, because he was never good at covering his tracks.

Whenever there was a new female in his life, he would start acting real shady. He'd come in at the wee hours in the morning, stumbling over his explanation of where he was and what he had been doing. He even walked around the house with his cell phone, like it was glued to his hip. If he went into the kitchen to get a glass of water, he carried his cell. When he got up to change the TV, he had his cell. Even when he went into the bathroom to take a piss, he had that damn phone. Kenny carried his phone around like it was his second dick. So, it was quite obvious when he was cheating on me.

I have to give him some credit; he managed to keep his daughter a secret for the two years of our marriage. I found out about Kiya, courtesy of three-way calling. To make a long story short, I checked his cell phone call history online, and discovered he had been calling this one particular number several times a day. I had my girl, Octavia, call the number on three-way, and the two of us were greeted by the sweet voice of a little girl. When her father took the phone from her, his voice sent my heart straight to my toes. The little girl was Kiya Janai Green, and her father was my husband.

I kicked Kenny out of our home that day. I was hurt beyond words. Looking back now, I don't know if my heart felt more pain from his keeping his daughter a secret from me, or more so because another woman had given him the one thing I couldn't. My right to conceive and bare children was stolen from me at an early age.

Anyway, after two weeks of Kenny begging to come home, and my suffering through unbearable loneliness, I let him move back in. I swallowed what little pride I had left, and agreed to try and make our extended family work.

The sound of the door unlocking caught my attention. I sighed loudly, preparing myself for Kiya to come running into the room.

"Hey baby," Kenny said, walking through the doorway alone. He pulled out the chair next to me and sat down.

"Where's Kiya?" I asked.

"I took her to my mom's crib," Kenny said.

"How is Etta?"

"Good," he said smiling. "She asked about you."

I gave him my "yeah right" look, and rolled my eyes. Kenny's mother had no love for me whatsoever. I overheard her telling him once that I was holding him back. Imagine that. I have my Bachelor's in Elementary Education, a decent job as Assistant Director at a daycare, and good credit. Kenny worked for the City of Huntsville cutting grass, only had his GED because I helped him study for the exam, and he couldn't get a glass of water on credit without me co-signing. He wasn't even providing a roof over my head. The house we lived in also belonged to me.

My grandmother, Martha, God rest her beautiful soul, bought the three bedroom house for me before she died. To top it off, the 2000 Mitsubishi Eclipse he drove was in my name. Etta either had too much faith in her son, or she was plain delusional. I was not holding her son back, I was carrying his ass.

"I'm serious, she asked about you," he said unconvincingly.

I studied his facial features, while pretending to listen to him ramble on and on about Etta's garden. I loved Kenny, but he had nothing on the brother from the bookstore. Kenny is dark skinned, with high cheekbones and wide dark eyes. He isn't what most women would consider handsome, but he oozes with self-confidence.

His self-confidence gave him a certain sex appeal.

I stood up, leaned over and kissed his lips. I parted his lips with my tongue, while running my fingers through the low-cut waves in his hair. Standing up, he placed both of his hands on my ass. "How you feeling?"

he asked, in between kisses. That was his way of asking if I wanted to make love. I grabbed the hardness in his pants, and gave it a gentle squeeze. "Give me five minutes to start the shower." I said seductively. "I'll be waiting," he said, rubbing his hands up and down my backside.

***

Ten minutes later, I stood wrapped in a thick terry cloth bath towel. I was dripping wet from my warm shower, the shower I had anticipated on sharing with my husband. I walked into the bedroom and looked at him, as disappointment ran through my body. Kenny was stretched out across the bed, sleeping like a newborn baby.

He slept for the rest of the night, so I crawled up with my new book, and ended up reading it from beginning to end. The brother from the store was right, it was a hot piece. In fact, it was so hot that my fingers were deep inside my pussy, while Kenny lay beside me snoring.

The Lies We Tell For Love

"What would you do for love?"
"How would you handle the discovery that your marriage was built on lies?"

Damon Whitmore is a true go-getter who will stop at nothing to get what he desires. His wife Octavia was no exception. When Damon first saw Octavia he knew he had to have her. He went through great lengths until his mission was accomplished. Now, two years later, he and Octavia share a wonderful and lavish life together. Damon exceeded all of Octavia's expectations while managing to keep his secrets of deceit and manipulation hidden but what's done in the dark eventually comes to light and Damon's lies are slowly beginning to unravel.

When a face from Damon's past re-surfaces, Damon finds himself facing a life alerting dilemma that could cause him to lose the very thing he fought so hard to build—his family with Octavia. Damon refuses to lose and he'll stop at nothing, including murder, to keep his family in tact.

Octavia Ellis-Whitmore never thought she would be a one man woman. Living by a no strings attached policy, she kept her encounters with men strictly sexual. When she met Damon everything in her world changed. Octavia opened her heart and fell hard for Damon. Octavia is now living and loving her life to the fullest. However, history has a way of repeating itself and temptation has a way of finding Octavia. When things at home begin to get rocky, Octavia finds herself struggling between remaining true to the vows she pledged to Damon and exploring her feelings for a new and mysterious stranger—a stranger who has a startling connection to Damon and his past.

As the drama unfolds, lies and secrets will be exposed and lines will be crossed on both ends. How far will Damon and Octavia go to protect each other from the other's transgressions and how many will fall victim to the lies that have been spun in the name of love?

www.gstreetchronicles.com

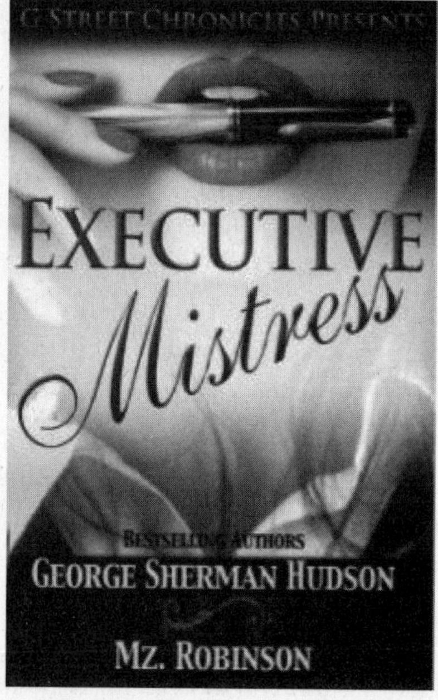

G&L Enterprises is the biggest marketing firm in the country. Each year thousands of intern applicants apply with the hope of securing a position with the illustrious firm. Out of a sea of applicants, Asia is bestowed the honor of receiving an internship with G&L. Asia is beautiful, ambitious, and determined to climb her way up the corporate ladder by any means necessary. From crossing out all in her path, to seducing Parker Bryant the CEO of G&L, Asia secures a permanent position with the marketing giant. However, her passion for success will not allow her to settle for second best. Asia wants the number one spot, and she'll stop at nothing, including betraying the man responsible for her success to get it. Asia, is taking corporate takeover to a whole new level!

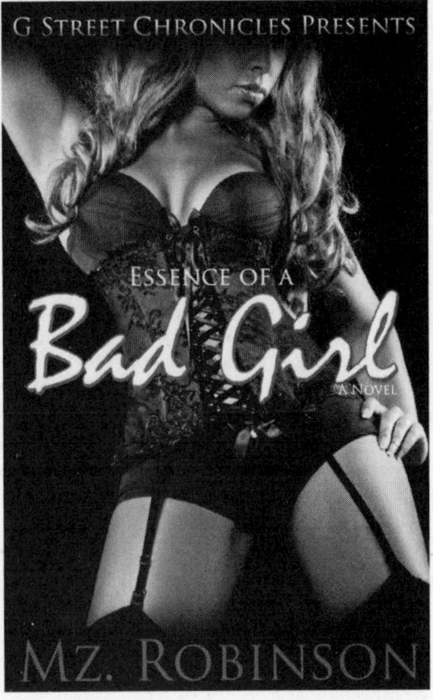

Lies, deceit and murder ran rampant throughout the city of Atlanta. Real and his lady, Constance, were living in the lap of luxury, with fancy cars, expensive clothes and a million dollar home until someone close to them alerted the feds to their illegal activity.

At the blink of an eye their perfect life was turned upside down. Just as Real was sorting things out on the home front, the head of Miami's most powerful Cartel gave him an ultimatum that would eventually force him back into the life he had swore off forever. Knowing this lifestyle would surely put Constance in danger, he made plans to send her away until the score was settled but things spiraled out of control. Now Real and Constance are in a fight for survival where friends become enemies and murder is essential. Atlanta's underworld to Miami's most affluent community—no stone was left unturned as Real fought to keep Constance safe while attempting to regain control of the lifestyle he once would kill for.

From the city of Atlanta to the cell block of Georgia's most dangerous prison, life under the City Lights would never be the same.

PRESENTS

Visit www.gstreetchronicles.com
to view all our titles

Join us on Facebook
G Street Chronicles Fan Page

City Lights
Beastmode
A-Town Veteran
Executive Mistress
Essence of a Bad Girl
Two Face
Dealt the Wrong Hand
Dope, Death & Deception
Family Ties
Blocked In
Drama

The Love, Lust & Lies Series by Mz. Robinson

Married to His Lies
What We Won't Do for Love

"Coming Soon"

The Lies We Tell for Love
(part 3 of Mz. Robinson's Love, Lust & Lies Series)

Still Deceiving
(part 2 of India's Dope, Death & Deception)

"Coming 2012"

Trap House
Drama II

Name: ____________________

Address: ____________________

City/State: ____________________

Zip: ____________________

ALL BOOKS ARE $10 EACH

QTY	TITLE	PRICE
	What We Won't Do for Love	
	Married to His Lies	
	City Lights	
	A-Town Veteran	
	Beastmode	
	Essence of a Bad Girl	
	Executive Mistress	
	Family Ties	
	Blocked In	
	Drama	
	Two Face	
	Dope, Death and Deception	
	Dealt the Wrong Hand	
	Shipping & Handling ($4 per book)	

TOTAL $ __________

To order online visit

www.gstreetchronicles.com

Send cashiers check or money order to:

G Street Chronicles

P.O. Box 490082 College Park, GA 30349